a garden of aloes

G. Davies Jandrey

THE PERMANENT PRESS
Sag Harbor, New York 11963

For information, address:
  The Permanent Press
  4170 Noyac Road
  Sag Harbor, NY 11963
  www.thepermanentpress.com

Library of Congress Cataloging-in-Publication Data

  Jandrey, G. Davies
    A garden of aloes / G. Davies Jandrey.
      p.   cm.
    ISBN-13: 978-1-57962-158-2 (alk. paper)
    ISBN-10: 1-57962-158-9 (alk. paper)
      1. Abused wives—Fiction. 2. Runaway wives—Fiction.
  3. Children of abused wives—Fiction. 4. Teenage girls—Fiction.
  5. Mothers and daughters—Fiction. 6. Tucson (Ariz.)—Fiction.
  I. Title.

  PS3610.A568G37 2008
  813'.6—dc22   2007039938

Printed in the United States of America.

In memory of Mary Ann Campau
who argued with me over every page.

G.L.F.M.

ACKNOWLEDGMENTS

My first reader is always my husband, Fritz. I thank him for his willingness and gentle criticism. Mary Goethals has waded through just about ever line I've ever written. For her indulgence, I thank her. I am ever grateful to Diane Cheshire, Annina Lavee, Ronnie Robinson, Heidi Vanderbilt, Jenny Vemich, and the Circuit Writers of Portal, Arizona for their thoughtful observations and support. For her professional input, I owe thanks to psychiatric therapist Virginia Zeeb. I thank Junardi Armstrong and Deb Twing for their insights. For her faith in my writing, I am grateful to Susan Zeckendorf. Without her suggestions and efforts on my behalf, this novel probably would have found a home in the bottom drawer of my desk, rather than in the fine, guiding hands of The Permanent Press.

Although all my characters exist only in my mind and on the pages that follow, I gave the character Sam my childhood fear of vampires. On nights when I awoke too full of dread to go back to sleep, it was my very own sister who'd let me crawl into the safest part of her twin bed, no small sacrifice since I was a rather chunky ten-year-old at the time. For this I owe Sandy Hopkins my gratitude and forever-love.

SAM

Last June, which was exactly one month after my eleventh-and-a-half birthday, Mom moved us to Tucson, Arizona. This was the beginning of the end of my childhood. I was disappointed to discover the end of childhood didn't mean the beginning of adulthood. If I'd known all this before everything happened, I would have tried to enjoy myself more when I was younger.

The day the taxi dropped my mom, Audrey, that's my sister, and me in front of the Oasis Apartments, the asphalt on the drive was spongy and so hot I thought my Jellies would melt. I looked around for the swimming pool promised by a big sign above the office on which a woman in a faded red bathing suit is diving into blue neon. The glare of white, peeling paint made my eyes water.

"Where's the pool?" I asked. Audrey picked up on the whine in my voice and kicked me in the leg. She was wearing the yellow flip-flops that matched her toenail polish, so it didn't hurt my leg as much as it hurt my feelings.

Mom didn't say anything, didn't defend me, scold or try to make a joke out of it. Just lugged the single suitcase stuffed with everything we'd brought from home through the door of our unit.

"But there is supposed to be a swimming pool," I whispered.

Audrey pinched me on the arm. "Just deal with it," she said, giving me the look, head tilted to one side, eyes bulging, that was supposed to make me consider Mom's feelings. But back then I had no clue how Mom might be feeling and only a vague idea of why we'd left my father and our perfectly nice home in Santa Rosa.

In the dim light coming through the dusty windows, I saw the ratty furniture, chipped Formica dinette, broken-down couch, balding overstuffed armchair, all of it smelling like accumulated old crud, and I was painfully aware of how far down we'd fallen. I was also aware that it had been my mother's choice to leave, not mine, that it wasn't my fault, but I was being punished for it anyway, that I had feelings too, but nobody was being particularly considerate of me, and that I had just been pinched for no reason. I started to cry.

Mom has a little scar just under her lip where she sliced it on a chipped glass. It's about the size and shape of a fingernail cutting and it turns from white to pink when she's hot or happy or sad or about to explode. It was turning pink right then.

"I'm sorry, Sammy," she said. "This is the very best we can do. It's just temporary." But she didn't sound sorry, didn't hug me, or hold my face between her hands like she sometimes does. Audrey glared at me and flopped down on the couch, dust poofing all around her. She pretended not to notice.

That very day I began keeping lists in a notebook I'd tucked in my backpack along with a half-dozen paperbacks I'd already read, but could reread in case of an emergency, which this clearly was. At the top of the page I wrote Santa Rosa. On one side I wrote advantages and on the other disadvantages. On the advantage side, I wrote Dad. Other things on that side included my kittens, Willy and Nilly, Tammy Gardener and her swimming pool, and my stuffed animal collection, which was resting on my four-poster bed back in Santa Rosa. On the list I put my bedroom filled with early American-style maple furniture, my desk with a lamp shaped like a spinning wheel that really spun when you turned the handle. The desk had a matching chair upholstered in pale blue velveteen to match my eyes. The walls were lavender, my favorite color, and the dresser was covered with a crochet scarf made specially for me by my grandmother. My closet was full of clothes, lots with cool labels. Most of these are still hanging there because we left in such a hurry, taking with us only the one big old suitcase. Mom promised we'd get new clothes when we got to where we were going. That was a big fat lie.

On the top of the disadvantage list, I also wrote Dad. From time to time that summer, I would add and subtract and rearrange the items on this list.

In the motor court apartment there's only one bedroom. Audrey and I sleep in the twin beds there and Mom sleeps on the Hide-a-Bed in the living room. For awhile, this sleeping arrangement, me in the same room with Audrey and Mom so close by, was the only item on the advantage side of the Tucson list that I also started keeping that day.

In back of the apartment, which Mom calls our bungalow to make it sound all cozy, there's a little yard, just blank dirt, not even fenced in. In front of the court there's a kidney-shaped island, the missing swimming pool, covered with white quartz rock and cactuses and scraggly bushes covered with gray fuzzy balls the exact size and shape of belly button lint. Eventually I learned the names for all of these plants, but that first day, all I knew was I could not touch them or climb them or smell them the way I could the trees in Santa Rosa. I also learned that between the hours of ten and four, it hurts to look at that white quartz rock, and plants you don't have to water provide very little shade and no comfort.

* * *

The first night in the apartment we slept on top of our coats because we didn't have any room in the suitcase for extras like sheets and towels. All night long I could feel the cooties crawling over me. Next morning, you could tell nobody had slept that good. Though I didn't mention the cooties, I'm pretty sure I wasn't the only one bothered by them.

After breakfast Mom announced that we'd have to buy sheets and towels right away, and I remember thinking Mervyns or Penneys or at least Target, right? Wrong!

"The manager says there's a thrift shop just around the corner," Mom informed us. Of course Audrey got all excited, thinking vintage, and I was wondering if there'd be used books, but believe me, New 2 U Bargain Center was not what either of us had in mind.

Now I'm a thrift store expert, but back then, it was a shock when we first walked into New 2 U—the yellow walls, not a bright, cheery yellow, but the dingy-yellow newspapers get after they've been sitting in the driveway for a week while you're on vacation. And there was a certain smell, like moldy bread, that was hard to take when you're not used to it.

So the three of us are just standing there, surrounded by things you can't imagine anyone actually buying: red leather cowboy boots with cracked, turned up toes—$3.50, assorted straw and cloth hats—$.75, racks of used clothes, but nothing old or cool enough to be called vintage.

"Good morning," Mother says to a woman behind the counter who's doing a crossword puzzle.

The woman, eyes magnified behind humongous rhinestone studded glasses, looks up, surprised. "Oh! Dear me. I didn't hear you come in. Can I help you find anything special?"

She stands up and Audrey whispers, "Looks like she's her own best customer."

Mother glares at us, the little scar under her lip turning pink, and we pretend to examine a pair of crusty Nikes, tongues handing out like a couple of tired old dogs—$2.

"No thanks," Mom says. "We're just looking."

"Take your time," the woman says, all smiles. "Have a good look around. Sometimes you don't know what you need until you see it."

Mom wanders towards the back of the store and I poke Audrey in the arm, whisper, "What kind of people buy this junk?"

"Shut up." she says.

"I was just. . . ."

"Shut up." This time she gives me a pinch and I see what she sees—Mom examining a plastic bucket.

"Only $.25," she calls out. Then it hits me. People who buy this junk are people like us. And for the first time I realize we're poor now. A hollow spot in my chest opens up wide, and all I want to do is run out of the store, away from the smell of mildew and the ugly yellow light, but Mom is pointing to a stack of sheets.

"Pick out the ones you want," she says, placing the bucket on the counter.

We start to go through the stack and I can tell Audrey is feeling just as weird as I am. "I'd rather sleep on my coat," I say.

"Just pick out some sheets and shut your mouth."

"But look!" I point out some kind of dribble on one of the sheets. "What do you think that is?"

"Rat piss, I hope."

"You hope?"

"Could be worse," she says, but I don't know how.

Mom comes over then, holding up a T-shirt. "What do you think, Sammy? It's your size."

And I can't help myself. I start to cry.

* * *

For the entire month of June, most of July, and a good part of August, we ate beans and rice, a complete protein, Mom informed us. We ate other things too, I guess, but it was the rice and chalky canned beans, Rosarita refried to be exact, that stuck in my mind, not to mention my throat.

Our kitchen is tiny, like a kitchen in a doll's house. The stove has only two burners and one little oven. In Santa Rosa, we had a range with four burners and a grill, two ovens, a microwave, a dishwasher, garbage disposal, built-in small appliance garage with a Cuisinart, blender, and a juicer.

Mom didn't miss her kitchen one bit. She said, "No time to cook, anyway." She had gotten a job as a telemarketer almost the first day in town and was working eight to five with overtime when she could get it. But I missed the food she cooked in that great big kitchen in Santa Rosa. Missed the steak, chops, meat loaf, potatoes, salads, and at least one vegetable every night, unless Dad, who sold real estate, was working late. Then we ate Weight Watchers lasagna, take-out Chinese, raviolis from the deli, but never Rosarita refried beans. And I missed my mom, who was no longer a full-time mom. Even when she got home from work, she seemed only part-time.

There are five other apartments in the court, each a separate little brick unit, with a red tile roof overhang and cement stoop. One by one, I got to know which people actually lived there and which were just passing through the court to get to Miracle Mile.

Besides Audrey and me, the only other kid is Chablee LeJardin. Her mom, whose name is Eden, is a little younger than my mom and pretty in a way that mine is not—my mom's a natural beauty, which means no eye shadow and her fingernails are her own. Eden's white, like us, but Chablee's what Mom calls *café au lait.*

After they became friends, Eden would bring a six-pack of beer over on her nights off, then Mom and she would pull two kitchen chairs out back and sit in the dark talking until the six-pack was long gone and Audrey, Chablee, and I had been sent to bed. On those hot, summer nights, I'd sit by the bedroom window, cheek pressed against the rusty screen, and listen to their whispers, soft and fluttery like the pages of an open book turning in the breeze.

Chablee is just about halfway between Audrey and me in age, but when we started school last fall we ended up in the same seventh-grade class. Although she was held back a year, it wasn't because she's dumb. In many ways, Chablee is smarter than me, smarter than Audrey, and even last June she already had breasts.

After all the trouble, I moved Chablee over to the Advantages of Tucson side of my list, but that didn't happen for a long time. No, for a long time, she was on the opposite side. That's because she and Audrey were all buddy-buddy and didn't want me around. They did take me on their so-called picnics in the cemetery, but only so I'd keep my mouth shut about it.

The cemetery is just down the street and big enough that we could spend an afternoon there without being noticed. Most people would be creeped out by the thought of a picnic in a cemetery. I was at first, but it's the only place nearby with real grass and trees. We didn't tell Mom about the cemetery because last summer, we were not supposed to leave the court while she was at work. We didn't tell Mom lots of things last summer. Audrey said, "Don't bother her unless we absolutely have to. She's got a lot on her mind."

Even though I had a lot on my mind too, it had seemed like a good idea at the time. And really, there was nothing wrong with going to the cemetery. When you think about it, a cemetery is a pretty safe place to be—safer than the Oasis Apartments, safer than Santa Rosa.

Mom had sold our car so we could leave Santa Rosa so we never went anywhere unless we walked or took the bus. I had no idea how big Tucson is, or that there's a zoo and a botanical garden and a university or that there are pine forests, cool and green, on top of the mountains rising up in every direction. For months, my world was just the court, the cemetery, and the street we walked every Saturday to get to the grocery store. The street is called The Miracle Mile. It's a miracle all right—a miracle that we weren't robbed or worse.

Last summer, I hated Saturday mornings. I remember the very first one. We had gotten up early so we could be back with our groceries before the real heat set in. But in Tucson, in summer, the real heat sets in the minute the sun comes up.

By the time we're on the return trip, each of us carrying two plastic bags of groceries, the sun is burning the east sides of our bodies. Because I'm small for my age I get the lightest bags. Even so, when the sweat drips and stings my eyes, I just have to let them sting. As cars swish by, they work up little whirlwinds of dust that stick to my sweaty legs and settle in my sweat-soaked hair. We are walking, heads down, past the Tropicana Adult Hotel and Bookstore. A man, bundled up in a hooded sweatshirt despite the heat, is curled in the doorway.

"That's a crackhead," Audrey whispers out of the side of her mouth.

"How do you know?" I whisper back.

"I've seen pictures," she says, so I know she doesn't know squat about any crackheads.

A woman in a pink velvet halter top and vinyl shorts is standing in the very last slice of shade alongside a building with a big sign in the window: Freddy's Fast Cash * Paychecks Cashed Here. She stares at us like we just climbed out of a spaceship.

"Good morning," Mom says, and I want to crawl under the sidewalk. This is Miracle Mile. This is why I hate Saturday mornings.

When we get back to the court, nearly dead from sunstroke, I see Chablee for the first time. She's sitting on the stoop in front of her apartment eating a handful of Kellogg's Mini Frosted Wheats right out of the box and drinking a Diet Coke. Her face looks like it's carved out of a big chunk of solid milk chocolate, perfect and smooth, but her hair's a mess, sticking out all over her head like clumps of broccoli. She's still in her nightgown, which is the silky type I've always wanted, but am not allowed to own. She's got boobs. I can see their outline under the thin nightie and I'm wondering how old she is.

I guess Mom and Audrey don't notice her sitting there because they go right inside. But I hold back, hoping she might say hi, invite me to share her box of Mini Frosted Wheats, not that I'm hungry.

"Hey girl, what you looking at?" she says in a snotty voice.

"Nothing much," I say just as snotty and start to go inside.

"Wait a minute." She sets the cereal box aside and gets up from the stoop. "Where are you going? Did I say you should go someplace?"

I consider running, then set my grocery bags down to free my hands just in case, though I have no idea how that can possibly help my situation, given that Chablee is twice my size. I give her a look that's supposed to say, *you're nothing more than a bug, or a speck of dust*, a look I've practiced, but never delivered until that moment.

"What's your name, girl?"

My mom had told us not to talk to strangers and under no circumstances were we to tell anyone our names, but she'd failed to prepare me for this situation.

"I asked your name. Can't you talk, girl?"

The sun's beating down hard on the bare skin where my hair parts, and I know the way I handle this situation will determine the course of my life on earth for a very long time. At this point, a fruity voice drifts from inside the chocolate girl's apartment.

"Chablee? Chablee, baby, bring your mama a glass of water would you sweetie-pie?"

As if by magic, this big bully, this uncombed girl with breasts, who is allowed to eat Kellogg's Frosted Mini-Wheats and Diet Coke for breakfast—no way a complete protein—drills me with a last hateful glare and runs into the dark entry, drawn there by a voice so sweet, so loving, that it could only belong to the mother of a beloved princess.

Then I hear my own mother yell. "Get in here Sammy! You've got the milk and it's going to spoil." I pick up my grocery bags. My mother didn't used to sound so cranky.

* * *

That same week, I also meet Dee, who is humongously fat. She's the one who rakes the trash out of the cactus garden and collects the rent. I guess that makes her the manager. The first time we meet, she's hanging on to her dog who's yapping like crazy at a mangy black chow peeing on the telephone pole in front of the court. She's dropped her mail and is red and wheezy from heat and effort.

I pick up the mail for her. "What kind of a dog is that?" I ask, suddenly missing Willy and Nilly more than ever.

"God bless you, Honey," she wheezes and takes the mail. "This here's a pure bred miniature greyhound. Only problem LeRoy—his name is LeRoy, accent on the Roy because it means king in the French language—he's blind. Bless his sweet soul. Cataracts is what it is, and mostly deaf too."

Now I notice his eyes look like two little satellite pictures of the earth. LeRoy is about the size of one of my cats, but with long skinny legs. Dee? All I know is that she's wearing a flowered print tent. The tent is sleeveless and I am treated to the sight of her upper arms, each the size and color of an Easter ham. Wide bands of bright copper circle each wrist, making her look a little like a pro wrestler but without the muscle.

"What's your name?" she asks.

"Samantha," I am able to answer because after the Chablee incident, Mom has instructed us to give our first names when asked, and if pressed, lie about the last. "But people call me Sam." Actually, nobody calls me that, but it is what I want to be called.

"You're Ms. Wallace's daughter?"

I nod. Wallace is the only name Audrey and I can agree on and Mom doesn't give a hoot. "One good thing about the motor court," Mom says. "If you've got the week's rent, nobody cares what you call yourself." So now we call ourselves the Wallaces.

"Well, I'm Dee," she says.

Finally the chow finishes peeing and sniffing and trots across the street. Dee sets LeRoy down on his spindly legs and looks at her mail, which consists of a catalog from the Big and Tall Shoppe and a Have You Seen This Child? postcard. I glance at the card, wondering if my picture might be on it. I'm slightly disappointed when I see it isn't.

LeRoy is not only blind and deaf, but ancient, warty, and nearly as hairless and pink as the baby rats they feed to gopher snakes in The Pet Place back in Santa Rosa.

Dee looks up from her mail and smiles. "Drop by any time, Samantha. We love to have company."

At the time I hoped the "we" might be Dee and her daughter, but I soon discover she lives alone, unless you count LeRoy. After awhile I begin to understand who she really means by we, but by then it's too late because Dee and I have already spent about a thousand hours playing canasta and we're sort of like friends, even though she's an adult, which is not the same as having a friend your own age.

But at that moment, Dee's curls, which are the exact color of Lipton Ice Tea, are dripping and my bangs are sticking to my forehead, so I just nod, figuring I'll never visit—our family not being the drop-by type. Besides, LeRoy's yapping again and it's hard to carry on a conversation.

"Remember now," she says. "Jesus loves you."

I think maybe I should say Jesus loves you too, but our family isn't the Jesus-loves-you type either, so I just nod my head again and wave good-bye.

Back in the apartment it's only slightly less boiling hot than standing directly under the midday sun, and Mom's sweeping dead cockroaches out of the oven. "Where've you been?" she asks, wiping sweat from her eyes with a paper towel.

I shrug.

"Oh," she says as if a shrug were some kind of answer, and sticks her head back in the oven. Part of me thinks it's none of her business anyway. Another part of me misses the mom who would have never let me get away with that.

Three of our neighbors I've never really gotten to know, since Audrey, who thinks she's master of the universe when Mom's at work, forbids me to go near them because they are just drunks or worse. Chablee, Audrey, and I used to call them names based on their most prominent features: Mr. Greaseball, who looks like the victim of an oil spill, She-Who-Knows-Too-Well-the-Tooth-Fairy, and The Sidewinder, a guy who kind of zigzags his way around the court. Audrey and Chablee used to call Dee Two-Ton-Fanny, but I never did.

The thought that these people might be someone's father, mother, sister, brother, or child didn't occur to me at the time. Looking back on it, I am disappointed by my lack of sympathy. I want to grow up to be a humanitarian, like Mother Teresa, whose biography I read last year in sixth grade, but last summer I was working hard on becoming an adult, which required me to narrow my focus.

* * *

One thing about Audrey is that she is not always a snot. Sometimes she can actually be pretty cool. When I'm having one of my phobia attacks she lets me sleep with her.

This phobia stuff started after I saw a movie called *Dracula's Daughter*, a classic Bela Legosi we rented one night Dad was at work. Since then, I've had this irrational fear of vampires. Some nights it's so bad I can hardly breathe. I lie in the dark, too scared to get out of bed because then my feet would be dangerously close to something under the bed—namely a vampire—which could grab my ankles and pull me under, plunge his/her fangs into my neck, and suck out all my blood. The worst part is from that moment on, I too would become the most unholy and disgusting creature on Earth: *One of the Living Dead*.

Audrey is the only one who knows about my vampire phobia. She says, "Learn to deal with it." I've tried. One time back home, I tried sleeping with the light on, but Dad came in and wanted to know why I was wasting electricity. Well, I couldn't tell him that it was vampires because that's an irrational fear and irrational fears weren't allowed in our household. So I just turned off the light because no way would Dad let somebody leave a light on just because.

It's not like I don't know my fear is irrational, but when I wake up in the middle of the night and everything is dark, vampires seem as real as the gun Dad keeps on the top shelf of his closet. At my age, being afraid of stuff like that is like so not cool.

Anyway, back in Santa Rosa, when I got scared in the middle of the night, I'd walk all the way down the hall in the dark to Audrey's room. She was really cool about it, never complained, and never told Dad on me.

When we got to Tucson, I thought things would be different, with her only a few feet away, and Mom so close by. But about a week after we moved here, I wake up and for no reason that I can think of, I'm scared. For a long time, I just lay in the solid dark, listening for suspicious noises, like the tell-tale sucking sound a vampire makes when he/she is attacking your mother or your sister, but the cooler makes such a racket I wouldn't hear an elephant walk across the floor, much less a vampire, vampires being notoriously light on their feet.

"Audrey," I hiss. "Are you awake?" She's making this humming noise which is like snoring, but more musical. "Audrey." This time a little louder. Still no answer.

I lie there, heart pounding, eyes bulging in the dark, and I am trying to decide which is the better strategy: stay in bed and wait for the vampire to attack, or risk an attack by getting out of bed. It's now or never, I think, so I stand up on my bed and leap into the air so that I land with my feet as far away as possible from anything lurking under the bed.

Audrey's still humming away. "Wake up," I say, touching her shoulder.

"Huh? What is it?"

"Can I sleep with you?"

Then, like always, she rolls over to make room for me.

"Can I sleep next to the wall?" Next to the wall is the safest part of the bed. Audrey rolls back towards the edge and I climb over her and scrunch down between my sister and the wall, pulling the sheet over me. Even though I'm burning up, I'm shaking.

"It's all right, Sammy," she says and curves her body around mine so I can sleep.

I take a deep breath, close my eyes and begin a silent prayer. "Dear God, please bless Audrey, bless Mom and Dad and Willy and Nilly. If you will help me get over my vampire phobia, I promise to be a better sister and be a more considerate human being. I will not complain no matter what, and I will mind Audrey when Mom's not home."

But even with Audrey draped around me and me next to the wall, I can't sleep. There's a hot poker burning in my chest, though I'm no longer shaking, and I feel sort of hollow as if my blood's been sucked out without my even noticing. It's like pain, but nothing in particular hurts and I feel tears stinging, first hot, then icy as they roll into my ears. What's wrong with me, I think, and pretty soon I'm crying out loud because I know even Audrey is not enough to protect me from this scary thing.

Audrey sits up in bed, yells, "Mom, Sammy's crying."

Now Mother is at the door of the bedroom. "Sammy, Sammy," she sighs. Her voice is not exactly mad, but there is an edge to it that tells me she is not all thrilled and delighted. "What's wrong?"

"I don't know," I whisper. That answer seems to be okay. She doesn't scold, just puts her arm around my shoulder, sort of like she did when I was little and used to wet the bed, and I feel ashamed in exactly the same way.

I'd like to tell my mother what I'm afraid of, but I don't actually know. It can't be vampires. Vampires must be an excuse, because there are no such things. But Mom is settling me down in her bed, and I feel so relieved, it's like my bones go soft. I can sleep now because I know she will be lying beside me.

* * *

I hate to be bored. To me boredom is like fear, and painful in the same way, that is slightly less painful than being tied to a stake and having honey poured over your entire body so red ants can eat you alive, one small bite at a time. When we first moved to the court there was nothing, I mean not a thing, to do.

I had already reread all the Harry Potters and a boxed set of *The Chronicles of Narnia*, which Tammy Gardener had given me for my birthday last year. I'd outgrown them, of course, but I was that desperate. Out of the five dollars Mom started giving us weekly for cleaning the house and helping with dinner, I'd bought a moldy paperback mystery at New 2 U, but was already three-quarters of the way through, and it had to last until the next Saturday.

This particular afternoon, Audrey'd been watching the soaps on the big old clunky TV Mom had bought us after her third paycheck. Audrey spends hours watching soaps. *General Hospital* is not so bad, but there's one in particular that she drools over. It's in Spanish, which she says she needs to practice now that we're so close to Mexico and all. But you can't practice something you don't even know, and believe me, Audrey doesn't know squat about Spanish. The program's really got too much crying and kissing for my taste, plus all I understand is *adios*.

Audrey's sitting right in front of the set so she doesn't miss out on any hot kissing tips. I could go outside, but when I look out the window I can see the heat waving off the asphalt—so hot it could seriously fry my feet right through my jellies. My head is actually aching, I'm so bored.

"Let's make some cinnamon pie tails," I suggest.

"Too hot."

"Oh come on. I'll clean up," I promise, cleaning being just about my only recreational activity these days.

Audrey, eyes glued to the TV, doesn't bother to reply and I know it's a lost cause.

I think of Dee—her invitation to drop by. On our way to the store last Saturday, Dee pulled up in this great big station wagon the color of New 2 U dentures and says, "You folks like a ride to the ABCO?"

Even though Audrey and I were just about dancing up and down with the possibility, Mom said, "No thanks, we need the exercise." Mom can be like that sometimes—namely a snot.

So anyway, I think of Dee and her invitation. Mom probably wouldn't mind if I just drop over—maybe LeRoy could use a walk in the boiling sun or something. I figure the palm tree at the side of the court would provide just enough shade for me and one skinny little dog. Anyway, death by heatstroke seems less painful than death by soap opera, so I kind of slip out the door, thinking Audrey's glued to the TV and won't know I'm gone for about ten hours, and I'll be home before that.

Remembering my promise to God that I'd mind Audrey, I almost go back inside to tell her where I'm going. But I figure, since I still have my vampire phobia, God has not kept his part of the bargain. Why should I?

Dee's apartment is on the other side of the court and I am careful not to look at the white quartz in the cactus garden as I pass because it would probably do permanent damage to my retinas, which I know for a fact can happen. Mr. Danner, my sixth-grade teacher back in Santa Rosa, made us write a report on body parts. I chose the eye. My report was an A+, so I'm just about an eyeball expert.

Before I even knock, LeRoy's yapping and scratching at the door. How he knows I'm there, I never do get. It takes Dee quite some time to open up, and she's huffing and puffing when she does, but she's smiling like she's happy to see me. I'm smiling too because it's nice to know somebody is happy to see me.

"It's Samantha. Well God bless your little heart, come on in," she says, adjusting her copper bands, which have turned the skin on her wrists the exact green of modeling clay, the kind kindergartners play with.

Dee's apartment is bigger than ours, or maybe it just looks bigger because it is so orderly. It smells better too, cleaner, like she just scoured out the sinks and the toilet with Pine-Sol. There's a small vase on her table, which is covered with a tablecloth of red and white checkered plastic.

"Pretty flowers."

"Zinnias. I just love them," she says, fanning her damp face with her hand.

A deck of cards lies on the table next to a big square canister, the kind that's filled with dozens of assorted butter cookies stacked in fancy paper cups, and there's a picture of Jesus on the wall. He's looking down at everything with very kind, very sad eyes. "We used to have zinnias in our backyard in Santa Rosa," I say. "You grow them?"

"Got a little garden out back. Can I get you something? A glass of ice water? A little snack?"

I shrug, following her into the kitchen which is the same as ours, but brighter, with clean, white walls. Matching flowered dishtowels are hanging on little brass hooks shaped like duck heads. On the refrigerator are hundreds of those magnetized words and letters you can use to write a message or a poem. *Let go. Let God, Smile, One Day at a Time*, I read.

I glance out the kitchen window and I'm amazed by what I see, not a hot little rectangle of dirt like ours, but a garden. I've read *The Secret Garden*, and of course it's not like that garden, but it's almost as surprising to find any kind of garden at The Oasis. There are pots and pots full of green and yellow, purple and red. "You've got a nice backyard."

She smiles. "Want to take a look?"

I follow her out the back door. "What kind of flowers are you growing?"

"Well the ones in pots—gotta grow most of these in pots because the ground's so hard. Let's see. These are verbena," she says, bending over a pot of violet-blue. "You know the zinnias. Those are my vinca and marigolds. I love the smell of marigolds, though most folks don't."

"Mom grew roses back home. Do you have any roses?"

"Just these rock roses, I'm afraid, which aren't really roses at all." She pinches off a few dead flowers and dried up leaves. "There, that's better."

"What kind of cactus are those?" I ask, pointing to a row of thorny octopuses. Each is topped with a red plume, which waves in the breeze, softening the line of the Cyclone fence that encloses Dee's yard.

"Cactus? No, those are aloes. Native to South Africa, those are." She tugs a paper towel from between her humongous boobs and pats the sweat from her upper lip. "I've got five different kinds."

"They look like cactus."

"They take the heat like cactus. Plus they don't mind the hard ground; spread like weeds if you give them a little water. That's why I love my aloes. They're tough, but they don't hurt you. See?" She says, touching the thorns. "Can't do that with cactus. Try it. Go on."

I reach out and touch the thorns lightly with one finger. They feel like kitten claws. I run my hand down the spongy pale green between the thorns. It's surprisingly smooth, like skin, and cool even in the hot, dry breeze.

"The hummingbirds love the blooms."

It's hard to imagine something so small and delicate as a hummingbird buzzing around in this heat. "Hummingbirds?"

"Oh my, yes, praise the Lord. Every morning they come to my garden. The red aloes are their favorite. Look here, an aloe baby." She points to a chubby little plant poking out of the ground like a fat green finger. "Real sweet, isn't it?"

As she leads the way back inside, I'm wondering about those hummingbirds. How can there be hummingbirds when I haven't seen a single wild animal, not a squirrel or a robin even, unless of course you want to count the cockroaches in our oven, which I don't.

But Dee is smiling and nodding. "Aloes," she says, winking as if aloes are her own secret invention. She takes a Tupperware container from the cupboard and holds it out so I can see.

"What's that?" I know it's a rude question, but I am a naturally curious person and I think it is a good idea to know what's in anything you might put in your mouth.

"One of my own special recipes. Call them Chocolate Fruit Beauties. What it is, is you take one tube of Pillsbury frozen biscuits. You just spread that out on a cookie sheet, pour one small can of Hershey's chocolate sauce over the top, spoon a can of fruit cocktail evenly over that, then bake as directed. Won a contest with that recipe. Well, it was actually just an honorable mention, but they sent all the honorables a coupon for one dozen cans of Hershey's chocolate sauce. You want some Dream Whip on that?"

"Yes, please." I figure it couldn't hurt. Dee puts a big glop on my plate. I am surprised when she doesn't cut a slice for herself.

As if she can read my mind, she says, "I'm watching my weight."

Watching it do what, I think, while old Leroy's nails are nearly tapping out the Morse code for *Don't forget about meeeee!* on the linoleum. He's whining and prancing as well as he can, given his decrepit state, so Dee takes a dab of Dream Whip on her finger and offers it to LeRoy who sniffs, then licks it off, all dainty. "There's my little gentleman," she says, and I'm smiling hard as if this is the cutest event I have ever witnessed in my entire life.

I take my own dainty bite, wipe the corners of my mouth even though I know there's not a single crumb there, and look around for something to talk about. Dee's still wearing the copper bands. They'd wrap all the way around a normal woman's wrist, but on Dee they only go a little more than halfway and they're on funny, with the open part on top of her wrists instead of the bottom. "Those are nice bracelets."

"Well, bless your heart."

"I've seen bracelets like that made out of silver, but never copper. Did you buy them around here?" I ask, just to make the kind of stupid small talk grown-ups are so in love with.

"Bought them in Bisbee. You probably never heard of the place."

"Bisbee? I think I read about it once in school." This is a lie I make up right on the spot just for practice. "How come you wear your bracelets like that?"

Holding out her wrist, Dee examines a bracelet like she's just now noticed that it's on funny, makes a quarter-turn adjustment until the opening is centered on the back of her wrists. "Some people swear that copper cures arthritis," she says.

I ignore the fact that this is an answer to a totally different question, and focus on this new piece of information. "It that true?"

Dee shrugs. "Could be. I sure don't have any arthritis in my wrists. Do you know any card games, Samantha?"

"Just Go Fish," I say, thinking I'd missed something, which is what makes the way adults talk so stupid—people just bounce over to card games without first finishing copper bracelets.

"Would you like to learn a new game?"

I should be getting home before Audrey notices I'm gone, but I haven't finished my Pillsbury thing yet. I look at the picture of Jesus and figure, under the circumstances, he would stay and keep Dee company. Besides, no vampire would come anywhere near a picture of Jesus.

"What are the rules?"

"First you deal out thirteen cards each," Dee says, already pulling the big chair up to the table. In seconds, she's got the cards out and is shuffling the two decks together like she's in fast forward.

* * *

When I get back to our apartment, Audrey's in the bathroom staring in the mirror. Her hair, which is just the opposite of mine, in other words long, thick, brown, and naturally wavy, is piled on top of her head and she looks sixteen in spite of her chest which is still almost as flat as mine. Audrey spent her money on a tube of lipstick—midnight red, which is actually more black than red, and an eyeliner—midnight blue, and it looks like she's spent the last hour layering it on. In a creepy, vampire kind of way, she looks pretty.

I've noticed that vampires are always really good looking, which seems weird. You'd think a steady diet of nothing but blood, even though it's probably a complete protein, would give you scurvy which makes your teeth fall out and causes oozing pimples all over your entire body. But every vampire I've ever seen has excellent teeth and a clear complexion.

"You look cool," I tell her because I'm still feeling good about being nice to Dee, and I don't want to break my record for humanitarian acts. Besides, Audrey really is pretty. She takes after our dad who is handsome for an older guy. I don't know who I take after.

"Where have you been? I was about to call the police." She's still gazing lovingly into the mirror, and I can see she is not all that concerned about my being missing all afternoon.

"I ran into Dee by the mailbox and she invited me over to her place." This is not a lie because it did occur, just not today. "She's teaching me to play canasta. It's a really awesome card game." This is a total exaggeration, but I want Audrey to think that I've had a less boring afternoon than she's had.

"Well, you're not supposed to leave the apartment, especially without telling me."

"I told you I was going to see if we had any mail," I lie. "I guess you just didn't hear me."

"Why bother? Nobody knows where we are, so how can we get any mail? How can you stand that Dee woman anyway? She's so gross."

"Shut up! At least she doesn't watch soap operas all day long and play kissy kissy in the mirror."

"You shut up, you little piss!"

"You're the little piss."

At this point, Mom's at the door. "Whiny baby," Audrey hisses just like a snake and pinches my cheek hard. I'll say this for Audrey, her timing is always better than mine, and it is only my return pinch on her arm that Mom sees. Of course, Audrey howls even though my pinches are never as hard as hers.

"Stop this immediately," Mom says, her voice red-hot mad. "I'm too tired to play referee. Audrey, you need to get dinner started. And you, Sammy. Go to your room until I call you."

I try to explain how it was, how Audrey called me a piss and pinched my cheek first so why is it me who has to go to my room, but it doesn't seem to matter. The scar under Mom's lip has gone pink and I know there's no use arguing.

There's nothing to do in my room but stare at the four gray walls that were probably white about a hundred years ago when this place was new. I lie on my bed, thinking about how far down we've come, while Audrey gets to help Mom with dinner. Mom didn't even bother to say hello. No kiss, no how was your day, no apology for leaving me to sit around this ugly apartment all day watching soaps with someone who totally hates my guts. Just *Sammy, go to your room.* This is not my Santa Rosa mother. That mother used to take a little time to get to the bottom of things.

I reach for my paperback, but I can't see the words too clearly because I am about to cry. Again! I put the book aside and take out my notebook, which is my only friend these days, unless I count Dee, which I don't because she's a grown-up. I cross out Audrey's name from the Advantages of Tucson side of my list and move her to the top of the Disadvantages side, bumping Chablee to second place.

I turn to a fresh page and begin to write:

Dear Dad,

How are you? I am fine, more or less. How are Willy and Nilly??? Well, here we are in hell. I don't like it very much but Mom says it's the best we can do under the circumstances which I find hard to believe. It's really hot here in hell. I met a girl named Chablee who is very snotty. She is the only other girl around besides Audrey.

Too bad she's so snotty. Mom's got a job now. She put Audrey in charge while she's at work. Knowing Audrey, you can only imagine what that is like. It's like hell, that's what it's like. (ha ha)

I also met this woman named Dee who's got a decrepit old greyhound that looks like a long-legged rat. He is kind of gross, but sweet. Dee is fat, but I feel that you should not judge people by their appearance, which is what Audrey does. Dee has been kind enough to teach me a new card game. It's called canasta. Have you ever heard of it? It's this very complex game you play with two decks. Dee is teaching me how to shuffle which is also very kind of her.

Mom doesn't understand how hard my life has become since we moved to hell. She is busy with work and doesn't seem to have much interest in me any more. I think she misses you. I KNOW I do. Maybe someday we'll be able to come home if you and Mom can make up. Maybe if you would promise not to be so mad all the time, we'd come home.

Do you miss us? Say hello to Tammy Gardener if you see her and kiss Will and Nilly for me (ha, ha)!!!

Love XOXOXOXOX
Your daughter Sam

Even if his life depended on it, Dad would never kiss Willy and Nilly, and he'd probably smack me if I used *hell* in front of him, even though he says that word and a lot worse. I leave the letter in my notebook. It's an unsent letter. Mr. Danner says, the purpose of the unsent letter is to examine your feelings. Besides, Mom says we are to have no contact whatsoever with our father. Part of me understands why. The other part wishes Mom would just get over it and take us home. Audrey says I don't know a thing about it, which is so not true.

I hear Audrey and Mom talking in the kitchen, all buddy-buddy. That's just fine with me. Dee has given me a pack of old playing cards so I can practice my shuffle. I take these out now and begin. My plan is to do one hundred shuffles a day until I get it right. Mom and Audrey have probably forgotten all about me anyway, so at least I can do something productive with my time, except I'm beginning to have that feeling again, kind of hollow and hot and shaky inside. Even though I didn't do anything wrong, part of me wants to apologize so I can go sit in the kitchen with Audrey and Mom. The other part of me wants to shuffle these cards until the spots wear off. If a vampire comes and gets me, so be it. It would serve Mom right.

* * *

After a dinner of guess what—crusty old beans and rice, that's what, which I couldn't eat because my stomach was still nervous and shaky from my phobia, not that anyone seemed to notice—I'm lying on my bed reading my book up too fast since there's nothing on TV but game shows and reruns because, of course, we don't have cable.

Mom must have spotted Chablee and her mom out there sitting on the stoop, because I hear her say in this chirpy voice she uses when she thinks she's got a hot idea, "Audrey, that girl looks about your age. Why don't you and Sammy go out and introduce yourselves?"

That is so like what a mother would suggest and so not like what any kid would actually do unless forced, especially me, given what I know about the girl in question, so I say no thanks, I have to finish my book. But Mom has made up her mind and Audrey is not protesting. So the two of them start to go on over there as if this were our neighborhood in Santa Rosa instead of a nasty motor court filled with winos and other weirdos. Of course, the last place I want to be is alone, so what choice do I have? None, as usual.

Chablee is sitting on the bottom step, resting her back against her mother's knees, a pick and a pile of colored rubber bands nearby. Mom just walks right over and says something about the sunset, which at the moment is turning the mountains the color of dried blood, which is very appealing if you are a vampire.

"Yes, this is absolutely the sweetest part of the day," the woman says in that fruity voice of hers. "My name is Eden LeJardin, and this is my Chablee." Chablee, who is wearing matching pink shorts and top, all trimmed in lace, sits up and smiles like she is just the nicest kid in the universe. Her hair is tied up in a hundred little broccoli bundles, each caught up with its own bright pink rubber band that matches her outfit perfectly, and I am thinking it probably took her mom hours to do it that way, hours of them sitting together on the stoop, her mom's hands gently parting and gathering each bundle, trying hard not to pull.

"Girls, come on and meet our neighbors," Mom says, as if we are not both standing right there and Chablee sneaks me a rolled-eye look, which is her way of telling me to drop dead. "This is Audrey, my eldest," Mother is saying, "This is my baby, Sammy." She shoves me forward. "And my name's Leslie." After a long pause, she adds Wallace.

"Well hey. It's nice to meet you all," Eden says. "Chablee's told me you all had moved in, and believe me, she's thrilled to have some girls her own age around. Aren't you, Sweetie Cakes. Chablee and I were just fixin' to have some ice tea. Would you all care for some?"

"Want me to go get the pitcher?" Chablee asks, using her mother's voice. Eden pats her arm and beams as if she has just named all fifty states and their capitals.

"No thanks," Mom says. "We don't want to put you to any trouble."

And of course it is not too much trouble and lala, lala, lala. To make a long story short, Mom and Eden decide since we are all about the same age, we can automatically be best friends—wouldn't that be nice? And my mother will just be all thrilled and delighted to keep an eye out for Chablee while her mom is at work, "and what is it that you do?" My mom asks.

To my surprise, she doesn't drop dead on the spot when Eden tells her flat out that she's an exotic dancer at JJ's on Miracle Mile, just like she is this normal working mom.

I think it's funny my mother can be all buddy buddy with an exotic dancer who's got phony fingernails, but would not even accept a ride to the grocery store from Dee because she is fat and wears designer clothes from Circus Tents Are Us. But people are like that. Of course, Mom has no idea what a snot Chablee is. But then I look at my mother and think maybe it's not just me who's desperate for a friend. This is not a good thought, my mom lonely and desperate. It makes me feel worse, sort of scared and mad and sad all mixed together like the refried beans and rice congealing, or whatever it is they do, in the pit of my stomach.

* * *

Like I said, that whole summer, Chablee was Audrey's friend, not mine, and that was just fine with me. I had Dee and LeRoy and my canasta. Every day, I went over to Dee's and my shuffle was coming right along. But because of the size of my hands, which are small like the rest of me, I could only do one deck at a time.

The reason I'm so small is because Mom tripped over a coffee table when she was pregnant with me, so I came six weeks early. She's always telling me I'll catch up, but so far that hasn't happened. I'm the smallest person in my class this year, just like all the other years.

Anyway, Dee thought I was some sort of canasta genius because most of the time I won. She had me keep score, which I could do in my head with my eyes closed. Old LeRoy also seemed to like me quite a bit. Even though he couldn't see, he knew it was me right off when I came to the door. Eventually, I got used to his warts and when I was there, he laid on my feet and snored while we played cards.

This one morning, Chablee was over our place. She and Audrey had big plans to polish their toenails—four coats, including base and top coat—they'd said, like this was going to be the event of the summer. But it was bring your own polish so guess who couldn't join the fun? Like I'd cared. Instead, I'd gone over to Dee's.

She lets me in as usual, but Old LeRoy is lying limp on the big chair and Dee, who's sittting on the floor, looks like she's been crying. I ask what's wrong, thinking LeRoy is dying, but she just sits there and sighs. I stroke LeRoy's pink hide and his tail wags, but you can see his heart isn't in it. "Is he sick?"

"No," Dee answers, kind of whispery and high.

"Maybe I should go home." I am trying to be helpful here, but Dee shakes her head no. I just stand there and wait, thinking she will come around, but she doesn't so I suggest we play a game of canasta.

"I don't know how," she says.

At first I think she is kidding, but the look on her face, which is sagging and somehow both old and young at the same time, tells me that she's not. I'm confused and getting scared, thinking maybe Dee's the one who's sick. Maybe she has fallen on her head and has amnesia and that's why she's sitting on the floor. I pick up LeRoy as if he might tell me what the problem is, but LeRoy is too depressed to talk about it. Not one yap.

Then Dee smiles a little. "I know how to play Go Fish." She pats the floor and I sit down, cross-legged while Dee smooshes the cards around like a five-year-old. I let Dee win on purpose and this must make her feel better, because after about five hundred games, she says, "Do you want something to eat?"

I don't, but it's the first Dee-like thing she's said all afternoon, so we go into the kitchen. When I go into Dee's kitchen, I always look at the refrigerator to see what the day's messages are. Today, there is only one: *HEP ME*

I am thinking HEP ME? HELP ME? I look at Dee who is busy opening a can of peaches. She divides the juice into two glasses and fills the rest with half-and-half. "Peach milk," she explains, handing me a glass. From the cupboard, she takes a canister like the one on the table, and we spend the next half-hour eating cookies and drinking our peach milk.

We're not talking, but Dee's face is no longer sagging and even LeRoy is tapping around the place, begging for his share. Again, I try to get to the bottom of her strange behavior, because that's the kind of person I am. I can't just ignore someone who seems upset, not like some people I know. No. If someone is sad, I'm the kind of person who wants to help. I figure Dee must want help or why else the message on her refrigerator?

"Are you feeling sick, Dee? Did you hurt your head or something today?"

"No, I'm just . . . I tried the alphabet, but it didn't work."

This sounds pretty stupid to me, but instead of saying so, I make my face look kind and encouraging, like Mother Teresa would. And Dee must feel encouraged, because she starts in with the alphabet, but she's saying it backwards; does this three or four times without stopping.

"Wow! That's really good, Dee." I'm still trying to sound encouraging, but I'm getting worried. Dee has said nothing all afternoon to indicate her brain is full of anything but Cup of Noodles.

"That's for when I'm scared," she says. "When I'm scared or when I can't sleep, Mommy told me to say the alphabet backwards so I won't have to think."

"Does it work?"

"Not today. Before you came, I just kept thinking and thinking."

"So what were you thinking about?"

Dee shrugs. "Scary things."

"Vampires?"

"Vampires? No," she says.

"I'm afraid of vampires," I say. "Especially when I wake up at night and everyone else is asleep. Sometimes it's all I can think of." Besides Audrey, who has sworn to God that she will never tell, Dee is the only person I have ever said this to, and I wait to see if she'll laugh.

"You should try the backwards alphabet."

"I don't think I can do it."

"It's easy. Just close your eyes and pretend you are looking at the alphabet, you know, the one over the chalkboard at school. Just look at that and read it from the back to the front instead of from the front to the back.

I close my eyes and try to see it. "ZYX," I start. "CBA," I finish.

Dee is laughing now. "You left out H."

* * *

Apparently Audrey and Chablee have finished applying all four coats of polish, because when I get home, their big feet are propped up on the coffee table, a cotton ball between every toe. Each has one ear plugged into Chablee's Walkman so they can listen to the same song at the same time, while they watch Oprah on TV. I observe this cozy scene for awhile, then move in front of the TV, waving my arms up and down so Audrey will know I'm home and not try to get me in trouble like she does just about every day. They ignore me.

I go to my room and close the door. I never did find out what was wrong with Dee. It just goes to show, we all have our moods, even if you're a grown-up. It reminds me of my dad. He had his moods too, mostly bad ones. Sometimes he'd come home from work and just sit in his chair, real quiet. Wouldn't even answer a question, like what are the major tributaries of the Mississippi River, or say goodnight. When I'd ask Mom if he was mad or something, she'd tell me not to worry. "He's just tired," she'd say. "Let him rest, Sammy." She was right. If we didn't let him rest, he'd get really mad and yell. Might even swat you hard on the bare leg, if you didn't watch it. Once in awhile he'd swat you even if you were watching it. I think that's why Mom left, but for me, a hard swat in Santa Rosa is no worse than being bossed around and ignored and friendless in Tucson.

And what about Dee? What's wrong with her? I lie on my bed so I can think better, but after a few minutes, I find I'm not thinking

about Dee at all. What I'm thinking about is breasts, or more spe-
cifically, how my life would improve if I had them. They're what
Audrey and Chablee have in common. As far as I can see, they're
the only thing they have that I don't, plus height. This is not what
I want to be thinking. It's simply what pops into my head. I try to
change the topic, so to speak, with compassionate thoughts about
LeRoy, who will surely die someday and maybe this is why Dee
is feeling sad and scared. But it doesn't do any good; breasts pop
right back up. It seems unfair that I'm supposed to act so grown-
up, without having anything about me that's grown-up.

Audrey's breasts are still small, but it looks like Chablee is
taking after her Mom, who has big breasts, even though the rest of
her is pretty skinny. I run my hands over my own chest. Nothing
has changed since this morning, of course, and I am afraid my life
will never change. Will I always be a helpless baby or will I wake
up some morning and find I am a different person, a person with
breasts who can laugh at vampires and be somebody's favorite?

After Chablee finally goes home, Audrey comes in and flops
down on her bed, feet in the air, so she can admire her toenails.

"You and Chablee sure are stuck together with Superglue."

"Shut up. You're just jealous."

"Jealous of you and Chablee? Ha, ha, ha."

"Shut up," she says, wiggling her toes.

"Shut up yourself," I say, because there is nothing to do around
here but get on Audrey's nerves. "You're always lying around
together, listening to the same Walkman and painting each other's
toenails like you're in love with each other, or something."

"Shut the fuck up!" she says.

This is the first time I've ever heard her use the F word. "You
shut up." I know I've really got on her old goat now. "You're just
mad, because you know it's true. The two of you act just like a
couple of lezzies."

"I said shut the fuck up!" She leaps off the bed and pinches me
hard on the thigh.

"Ouch! You didn't have to do that. You know what?"

"What, you little baby?"

"You're just like Dad. That's what!

"I am not."

"Yes you are. And when you grow up, you're going to treat your kids just like Dad treated us."

"No I won't."

"Yes you will."

"No I won't, because I'm not going to have any kids. They might turn out to be brats like you. Little whiny babies that never grow up and don't have a single friend!"

Why did she have to say that? I look at the spot where she pinched me and it's already turning reddish-blue and puffy. Without a word, I go to the kitchen for an ice cube to rub on it. I try not to cry, but by the time I pull out the ice tray, I am anyway, like usual. I am just a little baby, and that's what I hate about Audrey. She's always right.

Later she comes in and asks me if I want to make pie tails—her sorry way of making up, I suppose, but I don't feel like making up. I feel like telling her to stick her pie tails right up her you-know-where. I don't, of course. How can I? Audrey might not let me sleep with her later, if I don't make up with her now. Besides, making pie tails is better than doing nothing. Better than yelling at each other. Better than crying and feeling sorry for myself all afternoon.

DEE AND COMPANY

I see Brad's work on the refrigerator door: *Pizza gives strength to the weak and courage to the fearful.* I change *Pizza* back to *Prayer*. Though Brad can be an irritation and a slob, he is harmless enough. At least he knows how to have a little fun. We haven't been having much fun lately.

Even though I have come to accept my life as the will of God, I have always wondered why He continues to test me with one trial after another. I know God never places a burden upon us greater than we can carry. Still, I sometimes wonder, not question, because I would never question God's will, but I do wonder, why we need to carry any burdens at all, let alone such heavy ones. I pray about this.

And I'm not just talking about me. Take any one of the folks who live here in the Oasis. Take Gerralee, for one. Last week, she got an abscess and had to have another tooth pulled. Gerralee is an epileptic. Lost her front teeth during one seizure or another; lost the others, I don't know how. The drugs she takes to control the seizures don't always do the trick, and sometimes she just forgets to take them. Once in a while, I'll be talking to her and she'll get this kind of glassy look and, boom, down she goes like a sawed tree. So anyway, she has maybe a half dozen teeth left. When those go, they'll give her dentures, but I doubt she'll have the sense to wear them. After so many seizures, and so many falls, and so many drugs, Gerralee doesn't have much more sense than teeth.

Like me, she had a baby once. Girl, it was. Now Gerralee, she would tell you all about it. Don't even have to ask. Baby weighed 9 pounds 2 ounces, was 21 inches long, with a head covered in peach fuzz. Gave her the name of Jessica. But the baby got taken from her somewhere along the way. Gerralee can't recall anymore by who. But she sure remembers every detail about that baby right down to her little pink toes.

Oh well, Gerralee is a child of God and sweet in her own way. Once when she came up a little short on her rent, I made up the difference; wasn't much, just a few dollars is all. Next week she gave me four flowered saucers she'd picked up at some yard sale; wouldn't even take the dollar I offered. I know a dollar doesn't sound like much, but most people around here wouldn't turn up their noses. They're real pretty saucers too. Wish I had the cups to match.

The other day Gerralee knocks on my door.

"Dee," she says. "Do you got any spare change?"

Now Gerralee does not smoke or drink, but she does have a sweet tooth. It's a soda she wants, I figure, so I fork over a quarter. She looks at the coin, disappointed that she's still two quarters short of the soda.

"Every bit helps," I say.

Gerralee smiles that lopsided smile of hers. "That's what the old lady said when she spit in the crick and pushed her old man in after it." There's no malice in her voice. Just making an observation, I suppose. That Gerralee, she's a character.

Then there's my friend Jack, a veteran, though not of the bad one. The Vietnam War is not the only experience in the world that can turn a soldier's life sour. Jack is proof of that. He's an educated man, college graduate, but he can't hold a job. His place is full of books, but they don't make him a happy man.

"Bible's the only book can make you happy." I say this to Jack one time, and he agrees. Later when I bring him one, he won't take it. Isn't rude about it. Just smiles, Jack's got a sweet smile, and says, "Thanks for the trouble, Dee, but that book can't help me now." Course he's already been drinking. Probably should try again sometime when he hasn't been, but that time is hard to come by.

Now, I realize Jack brings a lot of burdens on himself and the truth is, I don't know everything that happened to him over there in the Gulf War. Wasn't even a real war hardly, but he came back with a ruined life just the same. He can't walk a straight line, drunk or sober, can't sleep, has pain in his every joint and muscle. It's a syndrome he's got. Got it over in Iran or Iraq; one of those two. I get them mixed up.

One time he says to me, "Might as well shoot myself in the head and put me out of my misery." Though he's smiling as he says this, the smile does not reach his eyes.

So I tell him, "Listen, Jack, I know something about pain and I know something about Jesus. Your life can be a blessing, pain or no, if you hold out your hand to Him."

"You're too good for this world," he says; pats my cheek. "I mean that, Dee, honey. Too good for this bad old world." Then he turns his back on me and the Lord and kind of weaves his way out of the court. Off to get more booze, I guess.

It seems like Jack's folding beneath the weight of his burdens. I suppose that's what separates those with grace from those without, the ability to carry the load and keep walking.

Compared to Gerralee and Jack, I'm blessed, is what. At least I am not alone. I've got my LeRoy, my garden, and my Jesus, so every day I have a reason to praise God. I also have my little friend Samantha. Talk about burdens, hers is a heavy one for someone so small, but I know from experience, He'll lighten her load if only she'll ask.

Don't tell me. I know what some of you are thinking: There she goes again. But if each and every one of us would just trust in the Lord, we'd learn to pull together and make this a better world, not just for ourselves either, but for every one whose lives we touch. Anyway, that's what I live for. You can laugh at me if you want.

From that very day out by the mailbox when Jesus first put Samantha into our path, I knew it was for a reason and it made my heart glad. That's what faith in the Lord does. I know not all of us have gladness in our hearts. That's a shame more than it is a sin, is how I look at it.

For awhile I was in a support group. But like our therapist, Doc Rayburn, says, you put two multiples in one room and you've got a crowd. Well, I'd have to agree with her. Let's just say I can't take crowds. Got plenty going on in my own head without hearing from those on the outside too. I just cannot take all the noise. It's like a conversation where nobody's listening and everybody's interrupting. It's not so bad when there's just two of us. Other times everybody wants to put in two cents worth, and I can't get a thought in edgewise. It's those times that make me tired.

Doc says, "Think of yourself as the president of a committee." Well, I've never been the president of a committee, so I don't have the least idea how to go about it. I just do the best I can, and with Jesus' help, Dee is getting stronger.

Don't worry about tomorrow, for tomorrow will worry about itself. Matthew 6:33-34.

I try not to worry, but sometimes, things get the better of me. That's why I gave the station wagon away. Now, don't put it all on me. Got nobody to blame but yourselves for that one. Anyway, was Big Dee who insisted, so don't complain to me about it. I did what I could; tried to make sure an adult—either Big Dee, Sister Sunshine or me—was in charge before we drove the car, but sometimes I got too tired and just could not stick it out. Had to take the bus home and leave the car behind—nobody seems to know where—too many times. Whose fault is that? At least, I don't have that worry anymore, though I know it was not a popular decision. You think I like taking the bus everywhere we go?

Just fat and stupid. That's all. What's the point?

Look it. I either got to take control or go somewhere dark and lie there, just melt away like a giant ice cube, like a glacier until there is nothing left. Is that what you want?

Nothing to give; nothing to receive. Why bother?

Now you've done it. I can't get my breath. It's like my lungs are filling with smoke.

Smoke from the fires of hell.

Just breathe. Close your eyes and stop thinking. Stop thinking and breathe. Have to stop thinking, stop feeling, stop listening. STOP THINKING!

So fucked up!

Fine, just FINE!

This is your life, Dee! Open up your eyes.

* * *

Well, sometimes I get a little overwhelmed with the way my life is unfolding. Impatient with myself and others, I might add. Tired of the pain. That's when I know I have to just turn it over.

Let go let God.

We do try to live by that. A perfect example is the day we get this postcard from my vet. Says LeRoy is due for his shots. Well, life is always interesting, isn't it? Since we gave away the station wagon, life is more interesting than ever.

Interesting meaning shitty?

Interesting meaning interesting. But I'm really not sure how we're going to cope, since dogs aren't allowed on busses unless they're helper dogs. Well, LeRoy's my sweetie, but he doesn't look like the kind of dog that could do more than help himself to dinner and a nap. Now don't say I told you so. What's done is done, so let it go.

Anyway, I get this bright idea. I put LeRoy's blanket inside a nice big grocery bag, one that's got handles. He hops right in.

I run into Gerralee on the way out of the court.

"Morning, Dee," she says, with her poor mouth kind of all collapsed because of her missing teeth.

"How you doing, Dear?"

Falling in step alongside me, she asks, "Where you off to?"

"LeRoy needs his shots." I open the bag up so she can take a peek.

"You going to sneak him on the bus?"

"That's the idea," I say.

"You're going to need some help with that. I can come with you, no problem."

"Thanks, Hon, but I guess I can manage," I say. She looks kind of down in the mouth, though it's hard to tell if she's disappointed or if that's just her mouth. The only thing Gerralee's got in her life is her yard sales. Oh, I know what it is; lonesome is what. And I do feel sorry for her, but I really don't want to complicate matters any more than they are already complicated. As usual, there's a lot of noise about it.

Jesus would not deny her.

Jesus doesn't have a dog in a shopping bag.

If she comes along everybody will stare.

With FAT ASS, people will stare anyway.

Oh well. What difference does it make, I am thinking. Sometimes the kindest thing you can do for others is accept their help. I read that somewhere and I believe it's true. So I say, "Come to think of it, I guess I could use a little help."

Gerralee takes one of the handles and right away I see it's lots easier on my hip this way. So we just stroll along to the bus stop. LeRoy, rocking like a baby in the bottom of the shopping bag, falls asleep, and Gerralee's all smiles, which is kind of unfortunate in a way.

All this goes to show if you just do what the Lord puts before you to do, your burden will be eased.

Sister Sunshine strikes again.

Hush.

* * *

My doc says we all have our demons. Problem is that I'm supposed to love mine, not fight them like it tells us in the Bible. She says my demons are all part of me, good and bad, and I need to take care of them as I would little children if I want to bring us all together in harmony. "It's a two-way street," she says. "You take care of them and they take care of you."

I do try to take care of all of us, but I can't trust any of them to return the favor. This has been true for as long as I can remember.

Back when I was in school . . . well, I was not a good student. Every day I intended to be, but there was always something. Brad ran with scissors, Little Girl could not get along with others, the twins wouldn't stop talking, and nobody but me paid attention. In junior high, they put me into a class for slow children. A learning disability is what they said was wrong with me. And maybe that was it. Certainly, I wasn't learning like the other kids. I just could not remember things is all, like the times tables. I still don't know my sevens or eights all that good. The nines I got. Mrs. Alden, was the teacher's name, taught me a trick. I still remember it: Add ten and subtract one.

Anyways, I spent three years in that class. Mrs. Alden, she had a way of looking us over, every one of us as we came into the room. She'd start at the top and end at the feet. Oh, she had a smile on her face, but you just knew she was trying to read what kind of day you were going to have like it was written in the way you walked in the door.

"What time did you go to bed last night?" she might ask or, "Did you eat any breakfast this morning?" Depending on the answer, a banana or a carton of milk might show up on your desk, or if you fell asleep in class, she'd let you be for a little while so you could catch up on your rest. If you smelled, you'd get a trip to the nurse and come back with a new pair of socks and tennis shoes. Sometimes she couldn't figure out what it was you needed, so all you got was a hug.

For some, it was kind of embarrassing when Mrs. Alden locked those eyes on them, and some went stiff if she tried to give them a hug. But for me, it was what I lived for, those soft arms around me, those eyes looking straight at me trying to figure out what it was I needed most. She finally figured it out, but by then it was too late.

I remember one day in particular. Brad is writing on top of the desk, well, he is carving actually because he's using the point of a compass. I've just moved over, and I'm kind of watching him out of the corner of my eye, too tired to pay much attention to what he's doing. Mrs. Alden comes by the desk. Without saying a word, she takes the compass out of his hand and goes back to the board where she is telling the class about circumference or something like that. Brad goes back to his writing, this time with a ballpoint pen, digging hard into the wood. Mrs. Alden strolls on by, takes the pen away, and goes back to the board.

When the bell rings for lunch, Mrs. Alden touches me on the shoulder. Says, "Dee, would you kindly stay. I need to have a few words with you." Of course, I'm not exactly sure what it is I've done, because Brad's moved over, just like always, the minute there is any trouble.

Mrs. Alden pushes my notebook aside and points to the words beneath, and it's like the first time I've ever seen them. "You'll need to clean that off." She goes to her desk where she keeps her cleaning supplies.

I look at the desk and am horrified. The words are ugly—*fuck* and *cunt*. And there is a small drawing carved into the top of the desk. At first, I think it's a man with glasses and a long nose, but then I realize with shame that it's a man's private parts.

"When you finish, you may go to lunch," she says, and hands me some sandpaper.

I am sanding away and pretty soon the tears are rolling down my face because no matter how hard I press, I can't rub out the words and the picture. I take the sandpaper and begin to rub it across the back of my hand. I rub until pinpoints of blood rise on my skin.

Mrs. Alden comes over, takes the sandpaper from me. Without a word she guides me by the hand to her desk, gets out the first aid kit; gently blots the back of my hand with Bactine.

"The janitor will get the rest of that off the desk," she says, searching my face as if there might be more ugly words written there, and I am so ashamed, I can't look at her. Then she takes me in her arms. Her hair is stiff against my cheek and smells like carnations, spicy.

"Can you tell me what it is, Dee?" she asks and hands me a Kleenex.

I want to tell her what it is; think I can, but the buzzing starts up.

"Don't you do it. Don't you do it. Don't you do it. Hurt you bad." Over and over it goes. Not like a conversation, not a voice in my head. This is Bones and that's just about the only message he ever has for me. It comes from some deep place, some cold and scary place, and the words fill my chest like smoke, making it hard to breathe. I can't argue with Bones.

* * *

Seems like time and again, just when you think you have come to the end of your rope, somebody hands you another few feet to hang onto. These extra feet of rope are God's little graces and they are meant to give us strength to carry on our journey.

Best example I can give was awhile back. It was on my birthday and I was hoping to get a card from somebody, maybe my sister

Lollie, or Frankie—he's my baby brother. Well, the mail is late, as usual, and I've checked the box two or three times already. Finally, in the late afternoon, the truck pulls up. There are two pieces of mail in my box. One is the electric bill. The other is a card, so I tear that open. On the front of the card is a picture of a pink, long stemmed rose. Inside it says: Does your driver's license expire on your birthday? Best Wishes, Ken, State Farm Insurance.

I don't know anybody named Ken. Don't even have a car anymore. I should laugh; it really is funny, you know, but somehow I just can't. It's my 40th birthday and nobody remembers but me and some Ken I've never heard of. I always send a card to my brother and sister on their birthdays; I even remember my Doc's birthday, May 8th.

Why do you expect any different?

Because I'm beginning a new decade. I'm changing.

Nothing has changed. Nobody remembers because you made it all up.

Made it all up? Reason nobody remembers is because it didn't happen to them and if it didn't happen to them, they think it couldn't have happened to me. But it did.

It didn't happen. You're a liar and that's why they didn't send you any birthday cards.

It happened. But sometimes I think . . . That's the worst of it, the real worst of it. Maybe they're right, and I'm just crazy, I sometimes think. It makes me feel lonely and angry, and scared! Nothing has changed; nothing is ever going to change.

This is your life Dee. Who gives a shit?

So I am standing by the mailbox and thinking nobody gives a shit and I guess there are tears running down my cheeks. Suddenly Jack is swaying by my side.

"Hey Dee," he says touching my arm. "Bad news?"

"Nope," I say, and take a couple of angry swipes at the tears. "No news at all."

Now anybody else would probably make some excuse and get the hell out of there, but Jack just smiles, gentle like he does. Cocks his head and takes a good long look at me—something most folks never do. "No news can be bad news too," he says.

"It's my birthday, Jack."

"And nobody remembered."

"Nobody but Ken."

"Who's Ken?"

"I don't know. Some insurance agent guy, I guess."

"Oh yeah, Ken the insurance agent guy," he says. Tells me how he got a card from him on his birthday too. We both get a laugh out of that since Jack hasn't owned a car in years.

"You have to laugh," I say, trying to keep up my smile.

But Jack says, "No you don't, Dee. Sometimes you have to cry." Then he invites me over to his place for a drink to celebrate my birthday. I remind him that I don't drink, but I'm beginning to feel better. Just the silly notion of joining Jack for a drink makes me smile.

"Buy you a soda, then," he says.

I consider it because the idea of being alone with me, and all the other me's who are as sad and angry as I am, is scary. And he is kind, in his way, and lonely. Anybody can tell just by looking, Jack's a lonely creature.

"Come on, Dee. I'll behave myself this time."

"What?

"I learned my lesson last time. I won't try anything; I promise."

Last time? I'm thinking. My stomach takes a loop and I'm trying to remember, but there is a hole where *last time* should be. Losing time, it terrifies me. Losing time means losing control. Nothing new, I tell myself. Stretch my neck. Try to hold on, relax, stay calm, though I feel them all crowding around, buzzing. Be present. Here. Now. Then I hear Miss Sunshine saying, "God bless you, Jack, but I really can't. LeRoy here wouldn't put up with it."

Still, I feel some better just because Jack reeled out just that little bit of rope. His sweetness is something to hang on to.

Back home, I feed LeRoy, put a Lean Cuisine out to thaw. All I can think of is forty years.

Forty years of sin. God's watching, but so is Satan.

God loves me.

Satan loves those God hates. God hates you when you sin.

The sin wasn't mine.

Whose then? God's?

God loves me. God loves me. God loves me. I will not listen. It's my birthday. I don't have to listen. WILL NOT LISTEN.

The light in the room is turning soft like it does just before sunset and the air shifts a little, a degree or two cooler is all, but I can feel it. I can see the mountains through the palm trees, just above the red tiled roofs. They're turning gold, then copper. I do love this time of day.

I'm so tired. All I want to do is lay my head down. I go to bed, imagine holding Michael, stroking his head, dark brown hair curling around my fingers. It's like grace to feel his presence, like a warmth upon my chest. Like grace, like walking on cool soft grass. Tears slip down my face, though I'm not sad or angry or scared, just emptied out. Everyone's quiet, not even a whisper. I close my eyes. I sleep.

* * *

Today's one of those days; feels like swimming through molasses. I'm so tired, I could cry. I do cry. I've been crying a lot lately. Doc says it's the stress of it all, finding my little Samantha in the shed like that, the police. And I'm terrified. It's not just the shit of my life that's scary. It's that when I think about it, remember things, it's my life, but it's not. It's like watching a TV in my head, but I can't turn it off or change the channel. It makes me tired and it makes me crazy.

Just put one foot in front of the other. Don't think, don't look ahead or behind. Left, right, left right, left right.

I close my eyes. The TV clicks on and there's a little girl waking from her nap. The little girl is me and she's not me.

The bed is wet and I start to cry because Auntie LeeAnn will be so mad. She stands at the door. I try to look around her for Uncle Birdie, but she fills the door with her apron and her big face and mouth full of teeth like the mean old giant from the Golden Book. I try to hide under the cover, but she sees me, knows I've wet the bed. Bad, dirty girl, she yells in the quiet voice. Yanks me out of bed by the arm. Yanks me all the way into the bathroom. From under the sink she pulls out the can with the little Dutch boy in the blue hat.

"You are a dirty little baby," she says, and pulls my panties down. "Lie down, now so I can clean you." But I am crying and I don't want her to clean me. She pulls on my legs and I fall. Hit my head on the tub.

"Got to learn not to wet, little girl," she says.

"Let me up; I won't wet anymore. I promise."

"You don't keep your promises. That's a dirty habit and we're going to break it right now." She spreads my knees. Powders me, like she does when she changes Frankie's diaper, but the powder is from the Dutch boy can. "You don't want to be a dirty little baby, do you?"

I shake my head. Don't want to be a dirty little baby.

"Well then, Auntie's going to clean you up. Every time you wet, Auntie LeeAnn's going to clean you up." She takes the scrub brush from the tub and rubs and rubs. It burns. I kick my legs, but she keeps rubbing. Pulls me to my feet; pulls up my panties.

"It burns," I scream.

"Nobody likes a dirty little baby. You got to learn not to pee the bed or nobody will like you ever." She picks me up and carries me into the bedroom. There is the potty- chair Daddy brought from home for Lollie and Frankie. "Sit in the chair."

That chair is for babies and I don't want to sit on it. "Sit" she says, but I won't do it because I'm not a baby. I'm crying. "I told you to sit," she yells. "You just don't want to be a good, clean little girl. Don't want to mind. Now I have to make you mind."

She holds me down in the potty-chair. She takes silver tape. Tapes my knees and my arms to the chair. "You just sit there, little girl, and think about your dirty habit." She closes the door.

I am burning down there like in hell because I am a dirty little baby. I cry but nobody comes and I am thinking and thinking like Auntie LeeAnn said. I am thinking I am in hell and my mommy is with Jesus. I want to be with my mama and Jesus. ZYX WVU TSR QP ONM LKJI HGFE DCBA, ZYX WUV TSR. . . .

It's dark. The door opens and Uncle Birdie comes in. "Shush," he says.

Uncle Birdie will help me. Uncle Birdie loves me more than anything. He cuts the tape from my arms and legs with his pocket knife. "Poor little girl," he whispers. "Did Auntie LeeAnn hurt my little girl? He carries me into the bathroom, undresses me while he fills the bathtub. I am in the tub and Uncle Birdie is washing away the burning powder. The water is warm, but I am shaking cold though I'm still burning. When all the powder is washed away, he lifts me out of the tub, wraps me in the big white towel; pats me dry. "Don't want to hurt this baby," he whispers.

"It still burns down there," I tell him.

Uncle Birdie puts the towel on the floor. "Don't cry, now. Lie down now and I'll put the medicine on you." He opens the big jar of cold cream. "Open up, little girl," he says. "Got to rub the medicine in good."

I spread my knees. He rubs, rubs, rubs, gentle. Uncle Birdie doesn't hurt me. Uncle Birdie loves me.

* * *

I open my eyes and am surprised to find that this scene, played so many times before, has lost the power to terrify and enrage me. When did that happen, I wonder. It's like something once upon a time or maybe it's more like the vicious junkyard dog, grown old and weak, who's lost its teeth. It's still mean and ugly, but it can't bite and tear anymore. Could be my life is changing after all, bit by bit, memory by memory turned old and toothless.

I think of my mama, as I often do these days. I was so little when she left, I don't remember much, but I remember this. At night, I'd be lying in front of the TV, Mama'd say, Baby Dee—this is what she always called me—it's time for bed. Well, I'd pretend to be asleep, wouldn't move a muscle, and she'd have to carry me to bed, my head against the soft of her neck. Smelled like talc, some sweet kind, she did. Her lips would brush against my ear, my cheek, my forehead, trying to tickle me awake, but I'd keep my eyes clamped shut until she tucked me in. Until I heard her sing-song, "Sleep tight, all night, love my baby with all my might." Then I'd open my eyes, so I could kiss her good night.

I close my eyes. Try to see my mama once more, but where her face should be, there is nothing but an empty hole.

Rise and shine!

I pull myself out of bed.

Get up lazy daisy. Let a smile and Lord Jesus be your umbrella.

Someone is knocking at the door. I sit at the edge of my bed and practice smiling.

I swing the door open wide. "Praise Jesus. It's Samantha. Come on in." The words come from my mouth, but they belong to Sister Sunshine of the Full Immersion Baptist Church. Some days, if it weren't for Sister Sunshine, I'd never even get out of bed.

CHABLEE

My full name is Chablee Aziza Muhammad-LeJardin. It was my
father who named me. Chablee is a fine French wine and goes
with LeJardin, which means the garden in French. Aziza is African.
It means perfect and goes with my father's last name Muhammad.
He was the one who caught me, right in his hands, when I came
out of my mother. When I was born, I just came spilling out like a
fine French wine, light and perfect. That's what he said. Said I was
made part light from my mama and part dark from him and my
name should be part of my mama and part of him.

Last year I wrote this poem about my name. I got an A on
it, and I think it pretty much said everything that was important
about me at the time I wrote it, which was when I was twelve.

I Am Me

Clever as a fox, I won't fail.
Happy as a monkey hanging by her tail.
Agile as an athlete and just as fine.
Bright as a light bulb, see me shine.
Like brown sugar but twice as sweet.
Elegant as a rose, so smell my feet.
Elusive as a butterfly, floating out of reach.
    I am C h a b l e e Aziza LeJardin,
    And I practice what I preach.

I would probably write a different poem about me now that I'm
thirteen and know what I know.

One thing that's cool about my mother and father is that they
chose their own names, first and last, names that they felt went

with who they wanted to be. This was even before they met, so that was just this weird coincidence, something they had in common, like they were meant for each other, like they were meant to have me, perfect daughter, perfect like their love. That's what Mama says my daddy said when I was born.

When he became a Muslim, Daddy chose the name Mukisa Abdul Muhammad which means Good Luck Son of the Prophet of God in African. Before that, he was Terrance Duwayne Edwards, which is a slave name.

Before he went away he gave me his ring. It's solid gold with TDE outlined in real diamonds.

"Don't forget who's your daddy," he said and put it on a chain for me to wear around my neck.

I never take it off, not even when I shower, not that I'd ever forget who's my daddy. Even if I didn't have a ring to remind me, I'd still think about him every day. Every night before I go to sleep, I have to say good night to my daddy. It's sort of like a tradition with me or maybe it's like a prayer.

When I was little—was when Mama and Daddy were still together—we lived in a real house, with a back yard and one of those little-kid swimming pools, and I remember there were rose bushes. Daddy would come in to kiss me good night and say, "Daddy loves his little lady." I'd put my arms around him and just hang onto his neck, breathing him in. Aramis cologne, that was his smell, that and cloves on his breath. Even if he came in late, he'd kiss me good night, wake me up to do it, so that I'd always know when my daddy was home and that he loved me. It made me feel safe.

Well, I keep a bottle of Daddy's cologne on my nightstand and every night I open it and take a whiff so I can feel that way again. Feel that any minute my daddy might walk through the door to kiss me good night. And I tell him out loud, "Good night, Daddy. I love you."

Mama was Nadine Crump, which she says is a white trash name and changed for obvious reasons. Crump rhymes with dump, rump, grump, frump and plump. Thank God, Mama changed it to LeJardin, which rhymes with nothing bad I can think of.

Anyways, I love my name. Chablee Aziza Muhammad-LeJardin is no way the name of anybody's damn slave. It's who I am and I'm never going to change it. Not for n o b o d y.

None of my friends have parents like mine. Oh sure, maybe some kid's dad went to jail once, or maybe somebody's mom worked her way through college at Hooters, but nobody has a dad in jail *and* a mom who's a topless dancer.

Mama says, "Tell the truth and it will set you free." That's because Mama's not in the seventh grade and thirteen years old instead of twelve like all the other seventh graders. So when people ask me questions, like where's your daddy, I lie. It's easier. I lie about a lot of things; sometimes it's a problem, but mostly not. I figure the truth is really nobody's business but mine.

Mama doesn't see it like that. She always says, "It's harder to hide a lie than tell the truth." Mama says a lot of things about a lot of things. Still, I can see her point about telling the truth. When you tell the truth, you don't have to remember so hard what you've said.

But there are some things I can't lie about, like the color of my skin. Last year, I was having lunch with two of my friends who just happened to be white. We're just minding our own business when this black chick I don't even know comes up to me and says, "Why you acting so white?"

"Same reason you're acting so black," I say. That shuts her up. I got some white friends, I got some black friends, but if you want to be a friend of mine you got to accept me for who I am, Chablee LeJardin, not vanilla or chocolate. I'm my own special flavor.

So Audrey and I are looking at a *Cosmo* this one time and trying to decide what our exact skin tone is. Audrey is definitely an ivory blush, but I can't find one that's just like mine, and she goes, "Your tone is *café au lait*." And I'm all like, café what? But then she explains that it means coffee with milk. I like that, except it should be coffee with cream, because I'm so smooth.

* * *

This last summer was weird because it was both the best and the worst. It was the best, because Audrey moved in practically next door. Audrey knows just about everything about me already, and that's cool. Plus, because we live in the same dump, I can have her sleep over. That's something new for me. My friends are always like, "Why don't you ever invite us over to your house?" I tell them my mother's got cancer and they never ask again. It makes me feel bad to lie about my mama, like by saying it, it might come true, but what am I supposed to do? No way am I going to tell them that Chablee LeJardin lives in a dump surrounded by hos, winos, drug addicts, and crazies, and that's why they can't come over to my home sweet home.

I tell Mama, "Why can't we move someplace where I can have my friends? Someplace cool with a rec room and a pool."

Her answer is always the same. "That's part of the five-year plan."

Mama has all these plans. She's got a two-year plan, a three-year plan, a four-year plan, a five-year plan and a ten-year plan. According to the five-year plan, we move to a condo my freshman year of high school. If it's not part of the plan, it doesn't happen, but if it is, it does. You can count on it.

My gold-trimmed, white French Provincial bedroom suite was part of the three-year plan. Until Audrey, nobody ever saw it but Mama and me. When she bought me that suite, she gave me her angel statue. It's creamy white with wings trimmed in gold, to match the vanity. When they first fell in love, my daddy gave her that angel to watch over and protect her when he wasn't around. It's special.

Sometimes Mama and I have our own sleepover parties on her nights off. Watch a video and eat popcorn like we're best girlfriends. We've done this for as long as I can remember. It used to be fun.

The other night I ask can Audrey sleep over. "What, again?" Mama says. "It's my night off. I thought we could have our own little sleepover party, just my baby and me."

Mama's so like, let's be girlfriends. She practically lives her life for me, so I say, "Cool," like I really mean it. If I were to tell the truth, which is that it gets boring spending the night with just her, she'd go into this pout and make me feel all guilty, and I'd end up spending the night with her anyways, just us two. So I pretend I'm like having the time of my life, which is the same thing as lying.

But lots of nights last summer, Audrey got to sleep over, which is why this was one of the best summers.

The worst thing about last summer was what happened to Sammy.

The first time I ever saw her was at the beginning of summer. She was coming home from the ABCO with Audrey and her mama. She was so little and shrimpy, I had no idea we'd be in the seventh grade together when school started up. Of course, I had no idea what was going to happen to her later on and that we'd get to be like friends because of it. Mostly this was because she needed one and I was there and all. It doesn't sound very nice, but if it wasn't for Audrey, Sammy and I wouldn't be friends, her not being the kind of girl I'd hang with under normal circumstances. But we're in the same grade and have the same lunch hour, so Audrey tells me, watch out for Sammy, and I tell her that's cool. So now I'm supposed to be like Sammy's bodyguard, or something.

But that first morning I saw her, I didn't even like her. I'm just sitting on the stoop eating my breakfast and minding my own business and she's like just standing there staring straight at me like she's never seen such a mess. I have to admit, it made me mad. I was all like, you think you're so hot in your little shorts—so what they're Tommy Hilfiger. And so what if my hair's all nappy, and I'm just wearing my raggedy old nightie? What makes you such hot shit? But what I thought back then doesn't matter, because now we're cool.

* * *

Awhile back, I'm watching Mama get ready for work. She has a snake tattoo that wraps around her hips. The snake's head is just below her belly button with its tongue pointing south. "I want to get me a tattoo," I tell her.

She's pulling on these high heel boots she always wears when she dances. They go up nearly to her crotch. "You're not getting a damn tattoo, least not as long as you are living under my roof and eating my food."

"You got one."

"That's because I was young and foolish."

"I want to be young and foolish."

"Not until you're old enough to know better," she says and smiles at me like she does. "Besides, lawyers don't have tattoos."

"You're the one wants to be a lawyer."

"I'm too old. You wait. When I quit dancing, I'm going to make a million dollars selling real estate while you go to law school."

Mama thinks I'm going to be a lawyer. Maybe I will someday. If that's what I want to be, that's what I'll be. I don't really want a tattoo anyway. Just want to hear what she has to say about it. "Why don't you just quit dancing now?"

"Because some little someone wants to move into a fancy condo."

"That's not why you dance. You dance because you want to dance."

"You don't have a clue, little missy," she says, her voice gone all hard.

She starts to rat her hair. Mama's normal hair is long and soft and wavy. When she dances, she wears her hair big and stiff. For awhile I just watch her pull the comb backwards through it until it's standing up like she just put her finger in a light socket.

I know I've pissed her off, but she's got no right to put it all on me. She danced before I ever was born. She was dancing when she met my daddy.

"I'm going to start waxing my bush, then," I say.

"You don't have enough hair down there to worry about," she says.

"Yes I do and it's gross."

"Waxing's a pain. When I quit dancing, I'm going to let my bush grow out down to my knees. And don't you worry," she says, smoothing her hair over the tangles. She's facing the mirror, but she's looking at me. "I'm going to quit. It's part of my ten-year plan.

When you go to college, I'll get my real-estate license. Or maybe I'll just become a paralegal and when you get all set up in your fancy office, I'll come to work for you. Wouldn't that be fun, us working together in the same fancy office?"

"Why do you always wear those long boots? They are like so totally tacky looking."

Mama turns away from the mirror and looks straight at me then. "These boots cost over a hundred bucks. What's wrong with you tonight? You got a bee up your butt or something?"

I shrug. "It's just I think those boots look skanky."

"Skanky? These boots are like . . . I don't know. When I dance, I've got to have some part of my body that's only mine, even if it's just the skin on my legs."

"That's just plain stupid," I say. Even though I feel sorry the minute the words leave my mouth, that doesn't stop me. I just can't seem to quit trying to rub it in. Whatever *it* is, I don't know my own self. "You show your titties to the world and every nasty old man in it, but you hide your legs inside those ugly boots."

Now I have her full attention. For a long time, she just sits and stares at me. I stare back my coldest, don't-give-a-shit, stare.

"What the hell is this all about? This isn't about tattoos, or waxing your bush, or my boots!"

She gets up then and sits beside me on the bed, puts her arm around me, pulls my chin up so I have to look into her face. That's when I start crying. Didn't even know I was going to. Without another word, Mama makes a phone call; tells the boss she can't come in to work. When I hear this, my bones are like melting, I feel such a rush of relief. Somehow Mama knows things about me I don't even know myself. Sometimes that's a good thing. Sometimes it's so not. "Sorry, Mama."

"It's okay, sugar," she says, kissing the top of my head.

"Just for tonight, Mama. I promise."

"It's okay, Baby. There is nothing in the world more important to me than you." When you get scared or worried, I'll always be here to drive that old boogeyman away.

I hate feeling like this, all scared and weak inside.

Mama hands me a Kleenex. "You want to talk about it?"

I don't. Just want to be here with my mama feeling safe. "I understand about the boots," I say, loving her with all my heart just then, for knowing what I need without my having to ask.

* * *

This may sound weird, but one of my favorite places is the cemetery. To me it's like a big green park, with trees and grass, not creepy at all, just quiet. No pimps or hos or crackheads allowed. And it's private. You can sit behind one of those big old headstones and nobody will mess with you.

The best spot is the grave of Lily Crabb because it's under the biggest, oldest pine trees in the cemetery. She died a long time ago, way before even my own mama was born. I like to rest my back against her headstone. Sometimes I pretend she's my grandma. I've never met either of my real grandmas. From what I hear, I don't want to, so it's nice to pretend that I have a grandma just down the street under the big pines. I can go there any time I want and be with her.

I've taken Audrey and Sam there lots of times. Last summer, we'd take our Cokes and chips and have us a little picnic right there with Grandma, though I've never told even Audrey about that part. Why should I? That stuff is just between Lily Crabb and me; nobody's else's business.

One afternoon, we're just walking around in the shade, reading the names and dates on the headstones. Some of them are over one hundred years old. Lots of the folks buried there are kids and babies. It makes you wonder what happened to them, to die so young. There's one girl my age exactly: Vicky Ann Perish, 1976–1989. "Look," I say, "That girl was just my age when she died."

"Wonder what happened to her," Audrey says, leaning over real close as if the answer were written on that stone.

Even though I've just been thinking the same thing, I say, "Don't know. Don't want to know," because I just can't stand to think about all the ways a thirteen-year-old girl might have died. How are her parents doing, I wonder. My mama would go crazy if anything happened to me. It's been years since Vicki Ann died. Do her parents still cry when they think of her? I bet they do. To make matters worse, there's a practically brand new teddy bear somebody left on the next headstone over. Sammy picks it up. "Who do you think left this here?"

"Might be her daddy left that," I say, without thinking, because suddenly I'm missing my own daddy bad.

Sammy is reading the headstone. "Susanne Lee Tibbs, June 16, 1957 to June 16, 1958. One year old exactly. I bet they called her Suzie."

"How totally sad," Audrey says. "What would it feel like to lose your baby on her first birthday. I wonder what happened?"

"Choked on a birthday candle," I say.

"How rude," Audrey says and starts to giggle.

And I can't help it, I start to giggle too. It's not funny, but something inside me is bubbling up. Then I realize that Susanne Lee Tibbs died more than forty years ago and somebody's still loving that little girl, bringing her a teddy bear on her birthday like she's still alive. I don't know why, but I snatch that bear right out of Sammy's hands and stuff it in my purse. Sammy and Audrey look all shocked and outraged, but I don't give a damn. At that moment, I just have to have it. Then I throw back my head back and laugh again, like stealing this teddy bear off a baby's grave is the funniest thing in the world I ever did. But the truth is I just can't leave that teddy bear all alone in the cemetery with no one to love it. Just a little old stuffed animal, but it hurts my heart.

Audrey pokes me in the side with her elbow. "You are like so evil," she goes.

"I know it," I say, swinging my purse around and around like I'm a drunk. And I am feeling silly and a little drunk too, because there's nothing better than being right there, with Audrey thinking I'm one crazy-assed wild dude, not afraid of anything in this world. I sling my arm over her shoulder and we stagger around, laughing our heads off. Sammy's standing there looking all bent and that just makes us laugh harder.

Later is when I tell the lie about my daddy. I don't even remember exactly what I said, except I said he was dead.

When I get home, I put that bear on my bed. Mama says, "Where'd you get that little guy?"

"Audrey gave it to me," I say. "Isn't he cute?"

But that night I have to get out of bed and put the teddy bear in a drawer. Next day I put it in a paper bag and stuff it, deep as I can, in the dumpster. Don't know why, just like I don't know why I took it in the first place. Every time I think of it, I still feel bad, like I committed some sort of mortal sin, or something.

* * *

Once a month I talk to my daddy on the phone. I hate to because I never know what to say and I'm like, "Hey, Daddy." And he's like, "How's my little lady. You minding your mama?" I tell him I am and then there's this big old silence until finally he asks can he speak to my mama.

I can't talk to my daddy on the phone. Can't say how much I love him and that I miss him, 'cause when I do, his voice gets all thin and watery and I can hear him breathing through his mouth, can hear him swallow even. Think maybe he's crying. How is that supposed to make me feel, anyway? It just gets too weird and I'm happy to hand the phone over to Mama and listen to her say "Uh huh, uh huh, uh huh," till I want to scream, JUST HANG UP THE DAMN PHONE! Why should we have to phone him every month anyway? It's his own damn fault he is where he's at instead of here with us.

When Mama gets off the phone she's all like, "Why do you do that?"

"Do what?" I say.

"You know perfectly well what," she says. "He's your daddy. Why can't you just talk to him? Tell him about what you've been up to."

"Haven't been up to anything, so there's nothing to tell him."

"At least you could tell him you love him. I know you do. And you miss him."

"He knows all that."

"Maybe he does, but once a month it might be nice to hear it from you."

I just stare straight through her; don't ask how nice she thinks it might be to hear your own daddy cry. Sometimes I want to ask, *Why you all doing this to me?* But then she'd just ask what the hell am I talking about and do I think I'm the center of the universe. So it's best I keep my mouth shut. Why should I have to explain every little detail of my life and why it sucks?

LESLIE

At age thirteen, my daughter Audrey is already a realist. She's always telling me to "deal with it." I'm never sure whether this is advice or back talk, but I do try to deal with whatever comes my way, though for years my method of dealing involved a lot of silence and denial. I've been trying to change that, make up to my daughters for those years, but I've failed completely to provide the one thing I've turned our lives upside down for. How do I deal with that?

We moved here, my daughters and I, from a town in Northern California; which one is not important. We left in a hurry with the intention of disappearing, leaving most of our worldly possessions behind: the three thousand square foot house, the kitchen with dishwasher, roomy pantry, three perfectly appointed bedrooms, each with a walk-in closet full of clothes with the right labels, and of course, a washer and dryer, things I never really appreciated until I had to do without. I could go on and on about what we left behind.

My husband, Frank, wasn't always mean and hurtful. But over the years, what with the kids and the pressures of his job, he changed. It was a gradual kind of thing. At first, he was simply cruel in small, consistent ways; or worse, he made a little game of kindness: trips planned, then cancelled, gifts given in a flourish of generosity, destroyed in a fit of anger. Somewhere along the line, things took a bad turn. I don't know why. Happy times, like birthdays and Christmas, might get shattered by a fist, or worse. Afterwards he'd say he was sorry, cry into my lap. This was not an act. He was truly sorry about the hurt he'd caused. I'd stroke his back, his fine, white-blond hair, just like I'd do the girls when they were hurt or sad. He was like my child. How could I not love him? We'd start over again then. He'd be his old loving self. I'd breathe out, tell myself we're over the hump now. How many times did I say just that? When the drugs started, of course things got worse. But for a long time, I just held on and waited to get over the next hump.

I'm trying to leave all that behind, but the girls will forever bear the marks of his abuse, some invisible, some bright as blossoms.

Did he love us? He'd say so. Certainly, he told me he loved me, loved the girls. But there is a difference between love and pride of ownership.

If Frank really wanted to, he could find us. My hope is that someday he'll meet someone enough like me, or rather like the person I was all those years, and he'll want to remarry. Then a lawyer, rather than my husband, will track us down and I'll be served with divorce papers. With luck, my girls will be too old by then to be used for leverage or revenge.

Maybe I didn't have to disappear, like some women who fear for their lives and the lives of their children. But it seems every other day the newspaper reports another case—another woman who's tried to leave an abusive relationship the legal way, a woman who has taken every precaution—restraining orders, new locks, bolts and burglar alarms—but somehow gets killed anyway. Sometimes her children get killed too. So I stole my own daughters to protect them and to save myself. Women have been put in jail for doing precisely what I have done.

I stole my girls and ran as fast and as far away from my husband as the cash I got from selling our car would take us. It took us all the way to the Oasis Apartments, Tucson, Arizona. The effort, the fear and responsibility of that act, left me exhausted. Still, I'm trying to follow Audrey's advice; trying to deal with the terrible consequences of that decision, day by day. Deal with it, Mom, she says. I must. There are no other options.

When we first moved into this apartment, an old converted motor court furnished with other people's castoffs and yard sale bargains, I promised the girls it would be temporary. A promise broken. I didn't know then about poverty. Didn't know that poverty begets poverty. That this is a physical law like the law of inertia, with which I am more familiar. I set myself in motion once and came to rest here. Further advancement seems impossible.

As bad as it is, I know it could still be worse. At least I've made a couple of friends here in the court. Eden, my closest friend, is a topless dancer at a club just a few blocks away—that's the kind of neighborhood we live in. Despite her profession, we have lots in common. Her daughter, Chablee, is only a year younger than than Audrey for one. Neither of us have families we can turn to for help—my mother and father were lost to me years ago, and my sister is the kind of self-satisfied woman whose assistance would cost more than I can afford.

Eden once told me her family lived out of state. "Which one is that?" I asked.

"The state of denial," she answered. We have that in common.

In common, Eden and I have broken-down coolers, noisy plumbing, lousy insulation, and a persistent fear edging along the lining of our stomachs for our daughters' safety. One thing we don't have in common is Eden's smart-assed answers to life's most prickly questions and the belief that the best is yet to come.

One evening, we're sitting out on the stoop as we often did last summer, and she's telling me all about her plans. Audrey and Chablee are watching a video and Sam's gone off to bed.

"When Chablee starts high school," she says, "I'm going to buy us a condo. It may be on the south side with the Mexicans, it may be small, but it will be some place nice my daughter can bring her friends to. And there will always be ice cream and sodas in the fridge and they can listen to whatever music. Anyone she wants to invite, brown, yellow, or green is welcome as long as they behave."

"Nice dream."

"It's going to come true too. I've almost got enough money for the down payment. What are you doing to do to make your dreams come true?" she asks, and I tell her I don't have any at the moment.

"Well you better get you some, girl," she says. Cause without a dream, there's no plan, and if you don't got a plan, you are NO WHERE."

"Okay," I say, willing to play the game. "I dream that down the line there will be a light at the end of the tunnel."

"You might kid about the light at the end of a tunnel, but I swear there is one. You just got to keep reaching. Keep reaching. It's there. I've had my hand on it more than once. You'll see, Honey," she says, patting my knee. "The best and brightest light there is."

That's Eden. The best days are yet to come.

Recently I've gotten to know another woman in the court. I guess Dee's chronically mentally ill, which is bureaucratese for crazy. But Dee is neither ill nor crazy. Just the opposite. Her peculiar ways are a creative defense against sickness, disorder, and craziness.

Dee's favorite subjects are her dog, LeRoy, and her personal savior. I know nothing about her family, nothing about her that happened before the Oasis Apartments. She is forty and I am thirty-four. She weighs over three hundred pounds, I'd guess. After a heavy meal, I might tip the scales at 105; that's up five pounds since California.

"Les, you got too much nervous energy," Frank used to say. Nervous energy? It's true, I guess. My energy made him nervous. But he was right that I suffer from too much of something. I'm not sure what that something is, but it has driven me from a rock to a hard place all my life. It's the part of me I wanted to leave behind in California, the needy part that made Frank think I would never leave him regardless of what he did.

"All is possible if you give your life over to Jesus." Dee explained to me shortly after Sammy was hurt. But I've got no plans to give my life over to Jesus, or any other man ever again. Not because I think all men are bad, but simply because I have no faith in my ability to tell the good ones from the bad.

Though Dee and I are really nothing alike, we do have one thing in common—my daughter Sammy, who is half of everything that is important in my life. Dee and Sammy are great friends and companions. Maybe that's because Sammy doesn't judge her the way she seems to judge me. Doesn't judge Dee for the protective layers of fat that cloak her body, or expect her to shed them so she can be more comfortable with the way Dee looks. Dee's devotion to Jesus and the yappy, lap-happy LeRoy does not seem to offend Sammy either.

I wish I could be so non-judgmental. I am trying. I owe it to Sammy and to Dee. As a matter of fact, I owe a lot to Dee. She was there for Sammy when I was not.

* * *

It's fall, or what passes for fall in Tucson. The weather is cooler, but there are no yellows or reds, just clear, hard blue sky and air so dry it makes my eyes water.

Sammy turned twelve last month. To celebrate, I invited Eden, Chablee, and Dee to join us for a surprise party in the park. Never mind that the grass was brittle and brown; there were real trees, pines and eucalyptus, and a place for the girls to kick the soccer ball around. We grilled hot dogs to eat along with potato salad. There were two cakes, lemon pudding and chocolate, Sammy's favorites. Two cakes to make up for everything else that was missing from that party: the bunch of giggling twelve-year-olds, a stack of presents in fancy wrapping, and a big backyard with soft grass and trees turning red and gold in the frosty mornings. Trying to make up for everything missing or just plain wrong in Sammy's life with those two cakes.

After we embarrass Sammy by singing "Happy Birthday" to her in a public place, and she's blown out the candles, I begin to serve the cake—Dee first, because she seems more like an honored guest to me. When I ask which kind she wants, she says, "We can't decide." So I give her one of each and try not to think about how big she is or her habit of using that papal "we." Try not to watch as she eats, reducing the distance from food to mouth as much as her girth will allow. Head lowered, she puts food away with the serious intent of a half-starved adolescent boy, stopping only long enough to let LeRoy lick icing from her fingers. Later Sammy explains that Dee is like that sometimes. Like what, I want to ask. Instead I make a mental note to be less critical. Who am I to criticize anyone?

When we finish the cake, Sammy opens her presents. There is one box of colored pencils, one box of crayons, and a tablet of stiff, white drawing paper from Dee. This is her second gift to Sammy. The first was a little aloe plant. It came with a promise that in time, it would multiply until the dusty little rectangle of dirt behind our unit is covered with pale green aloes topped with plumes of bright red. It seems like a tall order for so small and unpromising a plant, but Sammy planted it with hope, if not absolute faith, that it would achieve this destiny.

Other gifts include long coveted nylon cargo pants from Eden. From Chablee there is a diary, which is a surprise. I would have expected nail polish or make-up. There is a new backpack from the ever-practical Audrey. And from me? What could I possibly give my daughter to make up for what has been taken away? I settled on a soft, heathery-blue sweater to protect her from the cool morning air that is fall here in the desert. She holds it beneath her chin and the blue exactly matches her eyes. I have to turn away from those eyes.

When we're done with our cake, Dee, Eden, and I sit at the picnic table and watch the girls kick the soccer ball across the open grass, breeze whipping their hair, the edges of their baggy shorts. They run up and down, up and down trying to control the ball at high speeds, perfecting a tricky fake pass-off of Chablee's invention. They are tireless and without an apparent care between them. It's a pretty sight, these careless girls. Our daughters—Dee certainly has earned a right to claim a mother's share—we watch them in silence and admiration.

And that was her twelfth birthday. It would have seemed normal enough to anyone watching. And in so many ways our life looks normal from the outside. Get up. Get dressed. Get the girls off to school. Get to work. I'm a telemarketer. That's all this town was offering to a not-quite-college graduate. Oh, I guess I could move up to Phoenix and find something better. I really should, but they say Phoenix has only two seasons: summer and hell. Here, at least the rain comes, heat abates, the seasons advance; I need some sense of forward motion in my life. Most important, here we have friends.

* * *

If Dee is my model for Christian charity, Eden is my safety valve. With Eden, I can let off some of the steam that is forever rising up inside me and threatening to blow me out of the water. We share secrets like I once did with best girl friends before I met Frank. Once Frank was in my life, the kinds of secrets I had were not the kind that could be shared with anybody.

Sometime before Sammy was hurt—time is now divided between before and after Sammy was hurt—the girls are off someplace, I can't remember where, and Eden and I are sitting on the stoop. I'm feeling younger than I have in years, talking about times so long ago it seems they belong to someone else's life. Out of the blue, Eden leans forward and whispers, "Had an abortion once. Did you ever?"

"A miscarriage, never an abortion."

"It was after I moved out here from Arkansas. Was sixteen."

"Do you ever regret it?"

"Nah. The man was long gone by the time I realized I was knocked up, not that it would have made any difference. No way was I going to have a kid, any kid—not then, not ever, was my thinking. Wasn't doing all that great taking care of myself. Anyway, I never regretted it, but I sure didn't want to ever go through that again."

"Was it painful?"

"Sort of, but that wasn't it. Just never wanted to have to do that again, ever—put to an end some little bit of potential. The whole thing left me feeling I'd missed out on something important, and I'm the kind of person who doesn't want to miss a thing. Not one thing. After that, I was always real careful. Don't know how Chablee ever got started, I was so careful, but she did. She's always been so damned determined; I guess that was it. Anyways, never regretted that either."

"What about your miscarriage?" she asks.

"Frank and I had been going together a few months. He wasn't my first. To be honest, by the time I'd met Frank, I'd lost count. But he was the one who really got to me. He was older by nine years, for one thing, was already making a good living in real estate; not real handsome, but built, and so polite and attentive. What can I say? He just knew how to do things. He seemed so in control. You know?"

"I know exactly."

"Frank was always reaching for my hand, wrapping his arms around my waist, hugging me, didn't matter who was watching. I'd never even seen my parents kiss or hold hands. Frank was not anything like my father, so I was not going to turn out like my mother. That's what I thought. Then stupid got pregnant."

"Stupid?"

"Well, it was stupid."

"Okay. Go on. Just don't call yourself stupid in front of me."

"Wait until you hear the rest. So Frank and I are having this argument. It had nothing to do with my being pregnant. He was really happy about that. It was just that he wanted me to quit my waitress job. Mostly, he was in a rush to get married, but I wanted to finish my last semester of college. Needed that job so I could. It's a long story. Anyway, Frank was furious with me. We were standing on the outside landing to my apartment, yelling at each other, and one thing led to another. He grabbed my arm and I lost my balance. He didn't push me . . . I'm pretty sure of that."

"A real sweetheart, that boy."

"A few days later, I began to bleed. Frank was devastated when I miscarried. Really, he cried. Put his head in my lap and cried and cried. That really got to me. He went on and on until I actually began to feel sorry I'd caused him so much pain. So I told him it wasn't his fault. Over and over. Said it so many times, I guess I convinced us both. Right after that, he asked me to marry him. I should have run like hell, I know that now, but I loved him and he was so sorry, so tender. Three months later I was pregnant with Audrey."

"Let me guess. You never finished school."

"Right. One semester shy of graduation."

"What did your folks think of Frank?"

"Loved him like a son, especially my father. Thought he walked on water and was way too good for me."

"Your father said that?"

"Not in so many words, but I got the message. The first time Frank really beat me up, my father asked me what happened. Of course I lied, told him I tripped over Audrey's tricycle. He was more than willing to believe it. 'Well, you look like something the cat dragged in,' was all he had to say. My mother had nothing to say at all.

"That's mighty cold."

"Well, I hadn't been the perfect daughter; that would be my sister. Anyway, I made my choices. They were the wrong ones, of course, but they were all mine," I say, trying to smile. Eden doesn't smile, just nods her head like she knows exactly what I mean and it all sounds perfectly reasonable to her.

That someone might think that I'm a reasonable person, doesn't question my choices or second-guess the decisions that brought my daughters and me to these exact circumstances, momentarily lifts the tremendous weight I carry in my heart, and I feel so light I could almost levitate.

* * *

I have trouble sleeping, going to sleep and staying there. At least once, and sometimes two or three times a night, I get up and stand in the doorway to the girls' bedroom. Just listening to their breathing, assuring myself that they're safe soothes me.

As I stand there, I feel like I am the same person I was years ago, when the girls were babies and sharing one room. It's surreal, like one of those pictures that flips if you stare at it long enough— the old witch becomes the beautiful lady. My life flips like that and it seems the other life, the one I have left forever, is the real one, the beautiful one; the one I'm living here and now is only part of a disturbing dream that will end as soon as I wake up.

It's calming to imagine that we'll be transported back home where it's green and sometimes even chilly. Things will have miraculously changed in our absence. I imagine Frank without his demons, his drugs. See him the way he was at his best, holding the girls on his lap, reading them stories, not angry, jealous, or resentful. Frank will be whole and well—the person he never really was.

It was this fantasy of return that enabled me to leave him in the first place; this fantasy enables me to tolerate life the way it is now. When I can't sleep, sometimes I indulge in it. Is it so harmful?

Last summer, Sammy and I had a terrible fight, our first real fight. At its root was this fantasy of return. "Will we ever go back home?" She wanted to know.

Pulling her onto my lap, I want so badly to share my fantasy with her, reassure her, *"Of course we'll go home. This is only temporary,"* I want to say. She's crying against my neck and I know it's all I have to say to make the tears stop. Instead, I tell her I don't know, tell her she's too young to understand, but I don't say one word that will make her understand. To do that would spoil my fantasy. So I say, "I don't have any solutions." But she knows this too well already. A mother is supposed to have solutions. I have none, so I send her to her room. When she challenges me, I run out the door. I'm a coward. Can't face her rage and I can't face the truth. I stand in the courtyard, the heat from the asphalt washing over my legs in waves. No car, nowhere to go but the street or back inside. I choose the street; at that moment, it seems safer.

I'm walking along Miracle Mile, I don't know how long, through one pool of neon to the next. Cars drive by, some slow to a crawl, then speed away, leaving me walking through eddies of dust. What am I thinking about? About Sammy and how I've failed her? About my daughters whose lives I've brought to near ruin, first by indecision, then by bad decisions? Not at all. I'm thinking of Frank. How I miss him, long to have him take over my life again so I won't have to make any more decisions.

At some point, the thoughts that are slowly propelling me down the street are interrupted by a car pulling up alongside me. It's a big old yellow station wagon. LeRoy is yapping in the passenger seat. Dee leans over to the open window. "Good Lord, get in the car," she says, and I do. Don't even give it a thought.

"Ms. Wallace, honey. What are you doing out on the street at this hour?"

"Call me Leslie."

"Bless your heart, Leslie. You know what kind of folks are on this street at night? What they're looking for? And where are your shoes?"

I'm reluctant to trust my problems to this woman, whose own life seems raw and ugly to me, but I'm so lost. "Sammy and I had a big blowout. I just needed to get out and think things over."

"Should have come to my place. You're always welcome."

"Thanks," I say, thinking that would be the last place I'd go. Still, she's in control now and I should feel grateful. I don't. She's driving me home and I'm not ready to face my children.

"Say, would you like to grab a cup of coffee or something?" Dee asks.

I nod, tears smarting.

"Well, there's a Denny's just over on Oracle"

"I'm a mess."

"Won't matter, Hon." Dee says, wheeling the car slowly across three lanes of honking traffic. "It's just Denny's."

I'm surprised when Dee orders only black coffee. I expected, I don't know what, coconut cream pie, at the very least."

"So what was it all about?" she asks, stirring a packet of Sweet 'N Low into her cup.

"About going back to California, back to Sammy's father. She misses him. Misses everything."

"So what keeps you from going back?"

"Honestly?"

"Do you want to be honest? You can always make something up, if you don't. I won't know the difference."

"Sammy never talks about California, her father?"

"Not really. But I figured things weren't all that great back there. People who have a choice don't move into the Oasis."

"We ran away."

"Bless your heart."

Dee takes a sip of coffee, takes another. When she doesn't press me for details I find I'm disappointed, find I need to list the reasons we ran away so I can see them all clearly again myself. "A lot of times he seemed depressed," I offer. Dee doesn't even look up from her coffee. "But sometimes he'd just get in a rage," I add, then lower my voice to a whisper because I'm ashamed. "Then . . . well mostly he just beat on me. But sometimes he hit the girls too."

Brows furrowed, Dee nods, sips coffee.

"He keeps guns in the house and cocaine." Dee is still silent. It is this silence that compels me to say more so she'll finally react. I need her to understand.

"One night, it was late, long after the girls and I had gone to bed, I hear him come up the stairs. When he doesn't come to bed, I get up to see what he's doing. It's eerie; he's just standing on the landing. Moonlight from the window pouring over him. I'm about to tell him to come to bed when I see the gun in his hand. For a long time, he stands there, not knowing I'm watching. After awhile he goes back down stairs. I don't know what he was thinking standing there. Was he thinking of using that gun on himself, or me and the kids?"

"That's when you left him."

"Yes," I say, but this is a lie. I didn't think about leaving that night. What I did think about was the other gun Frank kept loaded on the top shelf on his closet. I knew exactly where, could imagine the matte gray handle just visible over the edge of the shelf for easy access in case of intruders, for easy access in case some night he couldn't get it up and felt like ramming it inside me.

That night, while Frank was standing on the landing, just a silhouette against a square of blue-white moonlight, it occurred to me that his death would be the perfect solution to all our problems. If I shot him right then, as he stood gun in hand, how could anyone say it wasn't self-defense? But I didn't have the courage to shoot him. At that moment there wasn't one thing I could do to stop him if he chose to use that gun on me.

Still, I did not take my daughters and run, not that night. I don't want Dee to know this; I don't want anyone to know.

"The Lord must have been sitting on your shoulder guiding your way," Dee says at last, and I suppose I've said enough.

I'm beginning to understand why my Sammy finds so much comfort in her company. For a moment I feel jealous of Dee, then ashamed of myself. I should be praising the Lord, as Dee certainly would, that my daughter has made such a good friend.

"So what are you going to do, divorce him?"

"If I did that, he'd know where we are and I don't want him to find us," I say. What I don't say is that part of me longs for just that.

SAM

Last summer, I have to admit, I was pretty ignorant when it came to sex. I knew the basics, of course, but none of the details. Maybe if I'd had a little more information about the details, I wouldn't have been so dying to know and things would have turned out different. Who knows? Well, it's too late now.

Anyway, this one evening, we were sitting on the curb in front of the court, Audrey, Chablee and I, when a truck drives by with three boys inside.

One of them shouts, "You bitches like to do it doggy-style?"

Chablee throws them the dirty finger. Then she and Audrey bust out laughing, bending over and slapping each other on the back. Of course, I'm just standing there feeling stupid because I can't see what's so damn funny. When they stop laughing, Chablee says to me, "I bet you don't even know what doing it doggy-style means."

"I do so," I lie and run into the house before she can test me on it.

Of course, I know "it" always means sex, but the doggy-style part—what does that mean? Doing it standing up or on three legs like a dog peeing? Or squatting? But none of that makes any sense and I wish I hadn't lied about knowing. I'll never learn anything if I always pretend I already know. But it's the way Chablee uses what I don't know to keep me out of their little club—The Girls with Breasts Who Know How to Do It Doggy-Style Club—that gets me, and my sister is just as bad. Two's company, three's a crowd. So I lie. Who cares about how dogs do it anyway?

That night, while Mom is taking her shower, I ask Audrey about it.

"I thought you already knew," she says.

"I think I do, but I want to make sure."

"You tell me what you think it means,' she says. "And I'll tell you if you're right.

To me this sounds like Audrey doesn't know squat about doggy-style, but I'm not going to miss the chance to talk about it by saying this. Instead I say, "Well, I think it means . . . " I pause, trying to make up something that sounds intelligent. "It means, at least this is what I heard, it means when a man and a woman are doing it, you know, like when they're having sex, well . . . they do it like dogs."

"Yeah, that's pretty much what it means."

"What I was wondering though, is if they're doing it like dogs, does that mean standing up or what?"

"Standing up, of course."

"So if they do it standing up, how does the man get his thing inside the woman's thing. I mean, a man's thing hangs down, so does he just shove it up there or what?"

There is a long pause and I can almost hear Audrey thinking. "It only works if the woman is shorter than the man," she says.

"Well duh, I know that, but how does he get it in there?" I have visions of a special kind of tool for putting a penis into a vagina, something on the order of a shoe horn, but I've never heard anyone mention such a thing and there isn't anything like that in the drug store. I know because I've looked.

"He just puts it in, that's all."

Audrey's voice is getting all irritated, so I guess we've come to the limit of her sexual knowledge. Still I want to make sure. "So what have you done?"

"Done? You mean with a boy? Like I'd tell you," she says and now I'm pretty sure she doesn't know any more about the subject than I do. Somehow, this is not good news.

* * *

As I've said, the cemetery was the closest thing to a park anywhere near Miracle Mile. With grass and real trees, it was about a hundred degrees cooler than the motor court, and big. Not too long after we'd met Chablee, she started inviting us to go on her so-called picnics, which meant chips and Coke at the cemetery.

The first time we went, this old dude with a comb-over that looks like it's growing out of his left ear tries to stop us. But Chablee just tells the guy we're visiting Grandma, even gives him the name. "Mrs. Lily Crab," she says and points in the general direction of the shadiest, best part of the cemetery. Funny thing, there really is a Lily Crabb, spelled with two b's, who died in 1932.

As soon as the guy turns his back, all three of us just start laughing and slapping each other on the arm, and I'm feeling pretty good because for once I'm included.

We're just wandering around, looking at headstones, as if walking on people's graves is the most natural thing in the world, like being at the mall or something. Some are over a hundred years old and lots of them are just kids and babies.

It's funny and kind of sad, what some people leave on the graves. Plenty of them have dusty plastic flowers and little American flags, but it's the balloons that get to me. And then we see it, a brand new little teddy bear leaning against a headstone.

"Susanne Lee Tibbs, June 16, 1957 to June 16, 1958," Audrey reads. "This little girl died on her first birthday. How totally sad."

"So long ago and her mother still brings her a present," I say, picking up the bear and straightening its red bow tie.

"Might be her daddy left that," Chablee says.

For a long time we just stand there all quiet and sad. Suddenly, Chablee grabs the bear from my hands and squeezes it like she's trying to determine its freshness, then stuffs it in her purse. "Won't know the difference anyway."

Audrey begins to giggle and pretty soon, the two of them are whooping it up as if this is the major comedy of the century, something I just don't get. How would they feel if that were their little girl and somebody stole her teddy bear? Audrey and Chablee are so warped. If I could, I'd just leave them there laughing like idiots, but then what would happen? They'd hate me even worse, that's what. So I pretend to be totally absorbed in the headstone of Yin Yick Lin. There is a picture of Yin, but the inscription is in Chinese so I can't tell a thing about him, not even when he died. Still it's more interesting than watching those two dance around like a couple of drunks.

Finally, we settle down, our backs against a humungous headstone. The branches are thick and close together overhead so it's dark and almost bearable below. Chablee pulls the Cokes out of her pink patent leather back pack. She's brought three of them in a Ziploc bag full of ice so they're still nice and cold.

"Where's y'all's daddy?" She asks this all of a sudden, like it's been a burning question for some time, and she can't wait one more second to discover the mysterious answer.

"My mom left him," Audrey says, straight out and I am amazed how cool she is, not embarrassed or angry. Just 'my mom left him'. The words make the Coke fizz in my stomach and I burp behind my hand.

"How come?" Chablee asks and I am anxious to hear the answer.

Audrey shrugs, like she's totally bored. "Didn't get along, I guess,"

I can see Chablee is no more satisfied with this answer than I am, but before she can say so, Audrey turns the table on her. "How about yours?"

"Dead. My daddy is the only man Mama ever loved and he's dead."

"How sad," Audrey says, like suddenly she's the most caring individual in the universe. "How did he die?"

"There was this fire in the middle of the night. I was just a baby. Daddy woke up but Mama was unconscious and half-dead from breathing all the smoke, so he carried her downstairs and outside. Then he came back to get me. Had to crawl on his hands and knees because the whole apartment was full of smoke. He felt around until he found my crib. Then he grabbed me and threw me out of the window to my mama. That's the last time she saw my daddy alive."

"Wow! Your dad died saving your life. That's like so totally heroic," Audrey says, but I'm wondering how her mother managed to catch a baby when she was practically dead from smoke inhalation. For obvious reasons, I don't ask.

"He was a hero for sure," Chablee's saying. "I wish I could remember him, but like I said, I was just a little baby. I've got a picture though. You want to see it?" Chablee digs out her wallet and pulls out the picture. "He was handsome too," she says offering the photo to Audrey.

I look over my sister's shoulder. A tall black man wearing dark glasses is leaning against a car. He smiles into the camera. The photo is too small for me to tell if he is handsome or not, but I tell her he's a fox, and for the first time ever, Chablee smiles at me.

"He was the love of my mama's life. Since him, she's been a celibate."

I figure I must have missed something so I ask, "What does your Mom celebrate if the only man she's ever loved is dead?"

Chablee shakes her head as if I am too stupid to continue breathing out of water. "Celibate, not celebrate. Don't you know what a celibate is?"

This sounds like it might have something to do with sex and I have no intention of missing another opportunity. "No," I say, even though admitting it makes my face hot.

Chablee gives Audrey a poke. "Why don't you educate your little sister?"

"I've tried but it's impossible." Audrey says, flinging the hair back from her face in this really dramatic way she has recently developed. She thinks she's so hot. No way am I going to let Audrey get away with that, so I say, "I want to know now, Chablee, please. You tell me," I say glancing at Audrey, who's biting at the skin around her cuticles and probably doesn't know squat about celibates.

"Well," she says, settling back on one elbow as if she is bored to tears, "A celibate is a person who makes a vow never to have sex. My mama was so in love with my daddy that when he died, she vowed never to have sex again."

I am thinking, is that all there is to it? The grass is dry and scratchy. It's making my butt itch and the elastic on my underpants is all worn out so I've got a serious wedgy, but there must be more, so I try to look fascinated.

"I'm a celibate too, at least for now," Chablee adds.

Well, of course, I'm thinking. What else could a thirteen-year-old be? That's how ignorant about sex I was at the beginning of that summer.

Still, Chablee smiles at me and I am encouraged. "So your mom dances topless?"

Chablee nods. Her eyes dare me to say one word about it, but I can't help myself.

"What's it like, having a mother who dances topless?"

"Like normal, what do you think?"

"Yeah, but what's it like?"

"Do you think my mama lets me go where she dances? I'm not even allowed to walk down that street, much less go into the club. Hell."

"Don't get mad," I say, plucking at the grass. "I was just wondering."

"Well, you can stop wondering. To my mama, it's just a job. Pays the bills. That's all. Nothing wrong with that. Beside, she only shows her titties. There's people in France, men and women both, that show more than that for free on the beach."

"That's gross, walking around naked on the beach," says Audrey. "Man's thing just dangling."

"Like a wet breadstick," says Chablee.

"Like a wet noodle," says Audrey.

"Like an old turkey neck," says Chablee.

"Like a bagel," I say.

"A bagel! What the hell are you talking about?" says Chablee. "A man's thing no way looks like a bagel.

"I saw a man's thing once that looked like a bagel," I say.

"You are such a little liar," Audrey says. "You have never even seen a man's thing."

"You don't know everything," I say.

"I know you have never seen a man's thing if you say it looks like a bagel."

I shrug like I don't give a damn.

"What a minute," Chablee says. "You mean beagle? One of those wiener dogs?"

"Oh yeah." I say, laughing my head off. "Beagle not bagel."

"That's a dachshund, not a beagle, stupid," Audrey says to me, even though it was Chablee who said beagle first.

* * *

Audrey got to sleep over Chablee's lots of times last summer. I didn't. As usual there was no room for a third person. This one night, she was over Chablee's and they were watching some dumb scary movie on the VCR, which I wasn't allowed to see because "You know how you are, Sammy" and lala lala lala.

It was Eden's night off, so after dinner she comes over with a six-pack of beer. We drag the kitchen chairs outside. The air is warm and smells of hamburger grease from the Burger King down the street, which is not a bad smell if you have just eaten another plate of refried beans and rice.

So Eden and Mom are sipping on their beers and talking about nothing in particular. Eden is telling us that she was born and reared in Someplace, Looisiana. A person doesn't ever want to find himself run out of gas in Someplace, Looisiana, she is saying, except instead of doesn't she says duddn't, which sounds kind of ignorant, I guess, if you're not from Looisiana.

"It's the end of the earth and hell combined. Wudn't a thing there but four churches, a Dairy Queen, and Gonzo's Towing Service and Garage. That's it."

Mom picks up my bare foot and begins to rub it between her hands like she used to do all the time in Santa Rosa, and I'm feeling safe and just happy to be there. "Your family still there?" she asks.

"Just Mama and my step-daddy, he's a deacon in one of those four churches I mentioned. Everyone else is long gone."

It's already dark, or at least, as dark as it gets around here, which is not that dark what with all of the traffic lights and neon, but I'm beginning to feel sleepy anyway because of the foot rub. Then my Mom says, "And your husband? The girls tell me, he passed away."

And I am soon wide-awake again because Eden says to me, "Is that what Chablee told you? Well that's a new one. No. Muki,

Chablee's daddy, is doing time at Fort Grant. She talks to him once a month on the phone."

"Chablee told us he died in a fire while saving her life," I say.

"Well, Chablee says a lot of things when it comes to her daddy. A lesson I learned long ago is to hold my head up and tell things like they really are, because sooner or later the truth is going to come out. It's a lesson Chablee hasn't learned yet, evidently. But ya'll don't be too hard on her. It isn't easy to be Chablee."

It's not easy to be Sam either, I am thinking, but at least my dad's not a jailbird. And I'm wondering if her father is a robber or a murderer, but I have better sense than to ask. Instead, I ask, "Do you still love him?"

Mom shoots me a mind-your-own-business look, but it's too late. Eden's already answering. "Good question," she says. "The only man I ever truly loved, I think, was Chablee's daddy. Thought he was the love of my life, but after awhile, I realized I couldn't love him the way he wanted and love my baby the way she needed. I had to make a choice. I chose Chablee, so I guess you could say Chablee's the love of my life now."

No way am I the love of my mother's life; that would be Audrey. Still, it's my foot she's rubbing for once, not Audrey's.

"Do you and Chablee visit your husband in prison?" Mom asks.

Eden shoots her a look I'm not supposed to see. By this time, Mom has finished her second beer. I can hear it in her voice, which is all soft around the edges when she tells me I have to go to bed. I don't protest. Their chairs are right outside my bedroom window.

As I'm putting my pajamas on, I hear Eden say, "It's not that I want to punish him, but I just don't want to take my little girl inside that place. I visit once in awhile by myself; I can't help it, but I won't take my daughter. If Chablee ever found out I was going without her, she'd have a shit fit, because she's always begging to go. But sometimes you just got to protect kids, seems like, from the very thing they want most in the world."

As I brush my teeth in the bathroom, I am thinking it's bad enough Eden won't let Chablee see her dad, but then to visit him behind her back seems really sneaky. And I'm thinking parents do all sorts of sneaky, secret things behind their kids' backs and excuse it by saying they're doing it to protect them. Protect them from what, I want to know. Their own fathers?

Back in the bedroom, I kneel at the open window, my nose against the screen which smells hot in the exact way Audrey's hair dryer smells when she runs it too long. That smell makes me feel funny so I put my hand over my nose so I won't have to smell it.

They're almost whispering now, but I can hear Eden saying, "I was raised in it, but I don't go anymore. You know what religion is to me?" She pauses to take a swallow of beer. "To me, religion is a man with a Bible in one hand and his stiff dick in the other, excuse me for saying so. That, I learned at my step-daddy's knee."

Well, my ears perk up at the word "dick" and even though my knees feel like they have nails in them, I don't move.

"What do you mean? What did your stepfather do?"

"Daddy-Elder? That's what everybody called him—even my mama, him being a deacon of the church and all. Anyways, one day after church, I guess he was all fired up with the Holy Spirit or something, he just pinned me up against the wall. Man's hand could move faster than a lizard up a tree and before I could spit in his eye, it was in my panties."

"I know people think this kind of thing only happens to trashy folks," Eden is saying, her voice rising. "Well, we weren't trash, least not on the outside. The first time it happened, I told my mama. The second time, too. Third time, I just got the hell out."

"You mean your mother didn't do anything?"

"Sure she did. First time, she smacked me and called me a liar. Second time, she smacked me and called me a liar and a whore. Figure that one out. Not only was I a whore because I tempted him to put his hand up my nice Sunday dress and into my clean, white panties, but I was a liar to boot, because nothing of the sort ever did happen. Well, I wasn't going to stick around waiting on my mother to kick that dirty old man out. She was too busy running around playing church wife. You know some folks wear clean clothes over dirty underwear."

"How old were you?"

"Not quite fifteen. I know you're thinking, well, that explains it: molested by her step-daddy, run away from home at the tender age of 15, husband in prison, no wonder this woman does what she does, but you'd be thinking wrong. My work has nothing to do with any of that."

"I wasn't thinking that," Mom says.

"Well, people make a lot of assumptions about topless dancers. Think we're junkies or whores. And it's a fact, on Miracle Mile, you can't swing a cat without hitting a junkie or a whore, but I'm not either one of them."

"I wasn't thinking that either, but I am curious. Why do you do it?"

"Let me ask you a question. How much do you make an hour at that tele-what's-its-place? Six and a quarter? Six and a half an hour?"

"Six and a quarter," Mom whispers.

"You're good-looking, nice figure and all, so there's probably somebody, a supervisor or some such, who's after your ass, right? Yeah, I've been there. Listen. All my life these nice big bosoms of mine have gotten me in trouble. Now I make them work for me 'stead of against me. And on a really good night, I can make a thousand bucks, that's six hours of work, five to one AM, including dinner and potty breaks."

"A thousand dollars, really? How often do you have a really good night?"

"Frankly, not all that often, not lately, but it does happen now and again."

"How much on a bad night?"

"Don't ask. But during the school year, I am here to kiss Chablee good-bye in the morning and help her with her homework in the afternoon. Besides, I won't be doing this forever."

"How long have you been doing it?"

"Well, too long. But I'm almost there. Pretty soon I'll have enough money saved for the down payment on a sweet little town house. I've already started a college fund for Chablee—got over $3,000 saved. When she starts high school, I'm going to go to school myself, part time. Study to be parasomething."

"A what?"

"You know, paraprofessional. Paralegal, paramedical, one of those paras, or maybe I'll take up real estate. There's a lot of money in real estate. I'm not sure which one I'll do, but when I become one, I'll quit dancing."

"Well at least you've got a plan. I wish I had one."

"Wishful thinking is better than no thinking at all, I guess."

My mother laughs, but it's the kind of laugh she makes when things are not all that funny.

Eden goes on and on about her plans for about three hours and I'm only half listening when she says, "So now that you know my life history, tell me about you. Why'd you leave your husband?"

Mom says just a minute and I hear her get out of her chair. In a flash, I am in bed and practically snoring when my mother comes into the room. She kisses the top of my head softly and closes the window. "Good night, Sammy," she whispers and I don't know whether I've been caught or not.

What could be so bad she doesn't want me to hear, I am thinking. And I figure it must have something to do with sex, right? If I can't hear about it, what else could it be? I'm tempted to open the window a crack, but it's one of those creaky old wood framed ones.

"Shit!" I whisper in the dark. The word feels good in my mouth, sort of powerful and mature, so I say it again a few times.

Part of me is grossed out by the things Eden told my mother, but there's another part of me that's all thrilled and delighted, because that part can't wait to tell Audrey. Still, there is another part of me that wants to keep everything to myself.

This is all too much to think about. For a long time, I can't sleep and even though the light is on in the living room, the word vampire pops into my head. Before I can give this much thought and get all scared, I try Dee's alphabet method. After about five attempts, I make it through without a single mistake. Somewhere on the seventh or eighth run through, my mind stops thinking.

* * *

There's this broken down tool shed facing the alley behind the motor court. It was after dinner one night; Audrey, Chablee, and I were taking turns shooting a soccer ball through a bent and netless hoop some caveman had nailed above the shed door about a million years ago. The person who made the most baskets got to have Justin Timberlake for a boyfriend and I was waiting my turn.

I saw him first. He was just standing there watching, smiling at us with these perfect, white teeth. Pretty soon Chablee and Audrey noticed him too. They start nudging each other with their elbows like two idiots because he's such a fox, and I can tell he thought it was all pretty amusing. For once, Audrey and Chablee are the clueless ones.

Then he asks if he can take a few shots, makes ten out of ten, then tosses the ball to Chablee who makes five. It's Audrey turn. She makes six, then it's mine. Usually, I can make two or three, despite my height, but this time, I'm trying too hard and don't make a single shot. My face is hot, glowing red, and it's not heat. Then it happens.

The fox says, "Here, let me help you." He picks me up and I drop the ball through the hoop. "My name is Eddie," he says. "What's yours?"

"Sam," I say. My voice is calm, but I am shaking inside.

Chablee throws her chest out and steps in front of me. "I'm Chablee," she says in that phony honey voice she uses when she doesn't want someone to know what a snot she really is. "And this is my friend, Audrey."

I'm mad because I saw him first and it's me he lifted up to make the basket. Now Chablee is butting in with her big butt, as usual. I want to say "shit," but I don't, because this boy is way in high school and too old for any of us anyway.

But Chablee goes, "I think I know you. What school you go to?" And I am thinking Chablee is such a liar.

"Tucson High," says Eddie.

"I'll be starting there in the fall," she says and I want to scream, because she'll be in grade seven in the fall, just like me.

Eddie smiles and tosses another basket. Chablee and Audrey are climbing all over each other to get to it, but I just stand back and watch them make fools of themselves. Chablee has the ball and Eddie is tickling her middle so she will drop it. She's yelling no and stop, but doesn't drop the ball, of course. Audrey tries to join in the fun, but trips over Chablee's big foot and goes down hard.

Right away Eddie is kneeling at her side and examining her skinned knee. "Are you okay?" he asks, really sweet.

"Oh yuck," Chablee says when she sees the blood and hanging skin. "Oh yuck. That is so totally gross. I can't stand the sight of blood." She is practically fainting, and I'm thinking, what a phony.

Eddie helps Audrey to her feet, one hand on her upper arm, the other around her waist. She leans against him, limping and laughing like it is nothing, "I'm like such a klutz," she says, but I can see it really hurts and she's just trying to cover up because she's embarrassed.

"I'll get Mom," I say, even though I know nobody wants me to.

By the time Mom and I get to the alley, Eddie is gone.

Later all Chablee and Audrey can talk about is what a hellafine, foxy dude he is. It's ohmygod that skin? Ohmygod his eyes, his teeth and lala lala lala. And they say I'm immature.

Anyway, every day for the next week we go out to the shed after dinner to shoot baskets, but Eddie never comes. Who could blame him?

* * *

On the 4th of July, the temperature hits a record-breaking 250 degrees and even after the sun goes down, it's still about 248 outside. We're sitting on lawn chairs in back of Chablee's apartment and listening to oldies on the radio. Eden, who is wearing a tube top and cut-off jeans, has been barbecuing hot dogs on her Hibachi. All of a sudden, she dumps a glass of water on her head, then drags Mom out of her chair. They start to do some oldies dance and they're laughing. Pretty soon, Audrey and Chablee start dancing too. I don't have a partner, so I just sit there, sucking on an ice cube. Who cares, anyway? It's too hot to dance.

Back in Santa Rosa, I'd be swimming in Tammy Gardner's pool with the whole neighborhood. There would be homemade ice cream and Red Devil Fireworks. Fireworks, even sparklers, are illegal in Tucson. I guess they're afraid the town might catch on fire. One spark is all it would take. So what? If the whole place burned to the ground, I, for one, wouldn't even notice the difference.

Mom has made her so-called famous potato salad. This is a big improvement over Rosarita refried beans, and I'm supposed to feel grateful. She and Eden are drinking beer, which is why they are acting so weird and happy.

"Oohwee, girl," Eden says to my mother who is no way a girl anymore. "I got to sit down."

The hot dogs are beginning to burn. I roll them over with a fork. So now we're just sitting around, burning the hot dogs and listening to oldies—having a real hot time, not that there is any other kind of time here in hell—when this totally disgusting old drunk guy kind of weaves down the alley, stops and just stares at us for awhile, a stupid grin on his face. Really, he's almost drooling and he says, "Any of you girls care to join me for a drink?"

"Uh oh," Eden says. "Looks like some village has lost its idiot."

"Maybe we better go inside," Mom says, touching the little scar on her chin, which is practically glowing like a taillight.

"Not on your life. We live here. It's this son of a bitch has gotta go." She gets up, grabbing an empty beer bottle by the neck.

Chablee leans forward and whispers, "Mama's going to set him straight. You watch."

Next thing, the guy's apologizing and weaving on down the alley.

"You ever notice how God made more assholes than asses?" Eden says, and everybody, even Mom, is laughing. And I'm wishing I could be like that, wear a tube top and say funny things and never be afraid of what people might think. When you look like Eden, you can pretty much do or say what you like. Unlike my mother, she doesn't take any shit from anybody. I guess in a way that's good.

When it gets dark, we take the ladder from the shed and climb up to the roof so we can watch the fireworks, which are legal, I guess, if they are set off by some certified professional fireworks expert at the golf course. Anyway, we've got a pretty good view of them from the roof. The silver and gold sparks fall like water or burst open like dandelions, and we can hear the pop, pop, pop as each one explodes against the black sky.

It's cooler on the roof, and for once, nobody is saying much, except the kinds of things people always say when they're watching fireworks, like that's the best one yet, the kind of thing you don't really have to listen to. I lay back, the roof tiles cool and bumpy against my back, and I can't help thinking about how there are no dads around. Not here on the roof, not anywhere in the court. I wonder if anybody else notices, or if it's only me. Even though I'm not alone, it feels lonely. But it's not just loneliness. When there are no dads, it makes you feel creepy in a way. It's hard to describe, but it's like there is an important part missing, and this makes you different, and not in a good way, from every other person in the world who has that missing part.

Audrey says she doesn't miss Dad. It's true, he wasn't a great Dad. He was mean to us a lot and sometimes scary-mean. But if he were with us tonight, I bet he'd be saying which firework was the best just like a normal dad and things would feel a whole lot better up here on the roof.

* * *

The weather is changing from hell and blue sky to hell and gray sky and it's instant sweat if we so much as move a muscle. "It's the monsoon coming," Eden tells us, whatever that means. Anyway, even the cemetery is buggy and sticky, the air thicker than at the motor court, so there's even less happening than usual. Chablis and Audrey are doing their thing, which is so much like nothing I can't tell the difference, so I go over Dee's, who answers the door wearing a pair of triple X overalls and a baseball cap turned backwards on her head.

"Come on in," she says.

I do and I can't believe my eyes. Dee's place is always so neat and clean, that's one thing I really like about going there, but now a wet towel, two Burger King wrappers, an empty Big Gulp and a carton of Fudge Ripple ice cream, also empty, are just tossed on the floor. The table is covered with paper, some balled up, some stacked. There is also a half-finished ink drawing of a hot rod and LeRoy is barking his little head off in the bathroom.

"Why's LeRoy in the bathroom?" I ask.

"To keep the little fart out of my way," Dee says, so I know something strange is going on again and I'm feeling weird about it.

"What's the matter, Sam? You look like somebody just shit on your Wheaties."

"What?"

"I said, did somebody just shit on your Wheaties?" Dee starts laughing and I have to laugh too.

"Can I let LeRoy out?"

"Go ahead," she says drawing a curl of flame on the side of the hot rod. "Just keep him off my lap."

When I open the bathroom door, LeRoy wags his tail, but doesn't move from his blanket, which is folded next to his water bowl. He rolls over, legs straight in the air like a dead rat, and I scratch his belly until my hand is about to fall off.

Back in the living room I pick up a finished picture. "I didn't know you could draw," I say. "These are really cool."

"Yeah? You like to draw?"

"I'm not any good at it."

Dee shoves a pencil and a few pieces of paper my way. "It takes practice."

I pick up the pencil and slowly begin to copy one of Dee's drawings, but my lines are already beginning to wobble. "Do you have a bigger eraser?" I ask.

Dee opens the canister on the table. Inside is a jumble of pencils and crayons and tightly folded slips of paper. She hands me a gum eraser. It is then I notice the red double crescent on her left arm, just below the inside of her elbow. "What happened to your arm?"

Dee examines the wound. "Got bit."

"LeRoy bit you?"

"LeRoy?" she makes a face that says get real and turns her attention back to her drawing.

"Does it hurt?" I ask, which is not really what I want to know. What I want to know is who bit her, but I'm embarrassed, not for myself exactly, but for Dee. There's something embarrassing and funny, and I don't mean funny ha ha, about Dee, her overalls, her hat, and the bite on her arm.

Dee shrugs. "She just does it for attention."

"Who's she?"

"You know. You played cards with her last week, didn't you?"

"I play cards with you every day."

Dee pushes her drawing aside and goes into the kitchen. I follow. "*Get thee behind me Satan*" is still on the refrigerator, I notice. It's been there for the past three days. Dee pauses in front of this message and rearranges the letters until they read *Get me behind thee Satan.* Then she takes a jar of salsa from the refrigerator and just pours the whole thing directly into a bag of tortilla chips.

"No muss, no fuss," she says and we spend the rest of the afternoon eating chips and salsa and drawing hot rods. By the time we finish the second bag of chips, I'm getting pretty good at hot rods.

* * *

When I get home from Dee's, Chablee is gone, but Audrey is right where I left her, that is, on the couch watching TV. First thing out of her mouth is, "You have to clean the bathroom."

"It's not my turn."

"It's your turn, because I washed the dishes. Just deal with it."

"I won't just deal with it. Nobody asked you to wash the dishes. I was going to wash them right now. I'm not trading washing dishes for washing the toilet."

"If you wanted to wash the dishes instead of the toilet, Miss Piss, you should have done it before you left."

"That's not fair. I'm not going to do it and you can't make me." I say and am pleased when Audrey's face turns red. "What's wrong? I add sweetly. "Somebody shit on your Wheaties?"

"Oh yuck. That is so gross. Do you actually eat with that mouth?" she says, but I am already in the bedroom, slamming the door behind me. Audrey jiggles the handle. Too late. I've locked the door.

"Wait 'til I tell Mom," she yells.

"What's she going to do? Send me to my room?" I yell back, feeling pretty smart and happy about telling old Audrey off like she deserves for a change, but then she says, "Wait until the next time you ask to sleep with me. You can just forget it."

And I am thinking, that's just so unfair. A person's phobia should be off limits. I'm also mad at myself for having such a stupid phobia to begin with. A fear of heights or snakes or airplanes would be a much better phobia to have, one some blackmailer, namely my so-called sister, could not take advantage of so easily.

I take out my list of Advantages and Disadvantages of Tucson. Sleeping with Audrey is the second place advantage right after Eddie. I erase it and move it to the Disadvantages side. Satisfied, I put the notebook away. Still, I can't stop thinking about what will happen the next time I wake up in the middle of the night. Part of me wants to ignore her threat. After all, I might never need to sleep with her again. It's been weeks since the last time. But the other part unlocks the door, and without saying a word, goes into the bathroom to clean the toilet.

After I'm finished, I'm so mad I slam outside before I remember I have no place to go. I've already been to Dee's, I can't go to Chablee's without Audrey, and I'm not about to go back inside. I want to scream. I hate this motor court. I hate Tucson. I hate Audrey and Chablee, but mostly I hate myself for being so stupid in the first place. If I had the soccer ball, which I don't because it belongs to guess who, Miss Fat Butt Chablee, I could at least shoot some baskets. I go out to the shed anyway and sit, my back against the door, which is shaded by a scraggly mesquite tree growing through the asphalt, and pretty soon I am crying. I think I've cried more times since we left Santa Rosa, than I did in the entire fifth and sixth grade combined. After a while, I don't know how long, I stop crying. When I open my eyes, he is standing right between the mesquite and the broken shopping cart someone dumped there last week.

"What's the matter, Sam?" Eddie says. "Have a fight with your friends?"

I shake my head, tears starting again. "I don't have any friends."

"Ah come on, Sam. Sure you do," he says, voice sweet, soft. "I'm your friend. Can I sit down?"

I scoot over to make room in the shade for him, even though I'm not so stupid to think when he says he's my friend, he means a real friend you can do things with, or a boyfriend, or anything like that. But it feels good in a weird way just to know that he remembers my name. Feels good that somebody like him wants to sit next to somebody like me.

"I bet I know what you're thinking," he says, and my face gets hot, embarrassed that he might actually know how much I like him. How much I want him to like me.

"You know how I can tell?" he goes on. "I had a little sister once just like you and I could read her mind like a book. Knew what she was thinking, knew what she wanted before she even knew herself. You've got the prettiest hair, Sam. So shiny." He reaches over. With one finger he tucks my hair behind one ear, leaving the other side to fall across my face. For awhile we don't even talk, just sit side by side, not quite touching, and I feel tight inside, like I've just done fifty sit-ups, only it's the inside muscles that are stiff. His breath smells exactly like watermelon chewing gum. I can feel it on the top of my head, a fraction hotter and damper than the air.

"Your hair is like corn silk. So much like my little sister's. We were so tight, my little sister and me. She was the best little kid ever, sweet and pretty, just like you."

Hot prickles rise on my scalp at the word pretty. "So where's your little sister now? You talk like something's happened to her."

"There was an accident . . . it was a car accident. Both my mom and my little sister. . . ."

Eddie stops talking then, almost stops breathing, and I'm afraid to look at his face. Afraid he might be crying. I sneak a peek. He's got his hand over his eyes.

"I'm sorry," I say.

Eddie takes my hand in his and holds it to his chest. His hand is smooth and hard and much bigger than my own. I don't move, don't speak, just feel the thump of his heart against the palm of my hand. Part of me wants to stay, Eddie holding my hand against his chest. Part of me wants to run away, it's all so weird. Finally, I say, "She was lucky to have had a big brother like you."

"You think?"

I nod my head, and he seems to cheer up.

"I know what your problem is. Chablee and your sister are best friends, and you get left out. Right?"

I shrug.

"See, I can tell how you feel just by looking at you. Felt the same when I was your age," he says, still holding my hand. "My big brother was good at everything, had lots of friends. I felt left out too."

"What did you do?"

"I waited. Pretty soon things got better because I found a special secret friend," he says and kisses the back of my hand lightly. Now I've got the prickles all up and down my arms and my scalp. For a long time we sit like that, in the speckled shade, holding hands.

Finally, he gets up; says it's getting late. "We'll be secret friends, okay?" And before I can even say okay, he kisses me right on the mouth. Just a little kiss, like Mom might give me, but it feels different, like a tiny shock of electricity.

* * *

As soon as I walk in the door, part of me wants to run and tell Audrey all about Eddie, but part of me wants to keep it secret, because she'll say I'm lying, or worse, she'll twist it all around. Part of me is afraid she'll tell Mom. No way are we allowed to have boyfriends before we are fifteen, not that I think Eddie is my boyfriend, but still. . . .

So when Mom gets home, halfway just to make conversation and halfway just to keep from talking about Eddie, I tell her I how much I miss Dad. Ask if we'll ever go back to Santa Rosa, even though for the first time since we got here, part of me wants to stay.

"I can't answer that right now," she says. Bam. End of discussion.

Somehow the tone of her voice, flat and not the least bit interested in what I may think or want, hurts more than her words, and out of the blue I am crying again. I tell her how I hate it here, how boring it is, how I don't have any friends except Dee, and she's only my friend because of Jesus.

"I know it's been hard," she says, like all of a sudden she notices I'm in the room. She pulls me onto her lap, which part of me hates because it makes me feel like such a baby. The other part of me is too busy crying against her neck to care. "Things will be different when school starts. You'll make new friends and have lots to do," she says.

"Oh right," I say. "And where am I going to invite all these new friends to go? Nobody will want to come here. You promised that this place would be just temporary."

"Sammy, right now I can't help where we live. I'm doing the best I can."

"No you're not." Suddenly furious, I am screaming. "You are not doing the best you can at all. If you were doing your best, we'd still be in Santa Rosa with Dad." I am screaming these things at her. I don't know why I'm so screaming mad, because a big part of me understands she is doing the best she can. A big part of me knows why we can't go back, but it's like I don't want to know it, can't stand to think that the way things are now, are the way things are going to be for a long, long time.

"Sammy, you don't understand."

"Stop saying I don't understand. I do understand. I do. So stop saying I don't." I am screaming and crying at the same time. I know I should stop, but I can't. "You're just being a selfish B."

"Sammy, listen to me. . . ."

"No, you listen to me," I scream, and watch the scar under her lip turn pink. "I'm sick of this shit."

There is a long moment of silence. "Go to your room, Samantha," she says, really quiet, really calm.

"Oh sure," I yell. "Go to my room. That's your solution to everything, isn't it?"

"It's not my solution, Sammy. I don't have any solutions," she says and walks out the door. Just like that. And I am alone even though Audrey is with me, but Audrey doesn't count, and I hate to be alone. Then I feel bad, ashamed, because I remember my mother doesn't have any place to go, and I know what that's like. I want to run after her, partly because I am scared, partly because I am sorry, but there is something hard in my heart that I hate, and it keeps my legs from moving.

Audrey's mad at me too because of Mom. We're in bed, but not asleep, and I feel like my whole body is stiff as a board or more like a frozen corpse.

When Mom finally gets home, I want her to come in to say good night, or just look in the door to see if we're okay, but she doesn't, and I wish I could be invisible because that would be better for everybody. I know Mom would be better off. That's for damn sure.

I close my eyes tight and wonder what God has in mind for me. Why am I here rather than nowhere? Being nowhere, being nothing, it seems, might be better. At least it wouldn't be scary or painful. Really, sometimes I wonder what God was thinking, if he was thinking at all, when he put me on Earth.

* * *

The next day is Saturday and we are walking down Miracle Mile on our way to the ABCO. Even though it's still early and the sky is gray, it's already hot. Mom says it will rain this afternoon because it's so sticky-hot. An old lady is sitting at the bus stop. There's no bench, so she's just sprawled on the sidewalk, like a kid at the beach. Her hair is stiff from yesterday's sweat. Despite the heat, she is wearing a faded denim jacket. When we get closer, I see she's not so old. She just has that dried up look people around here get when they've spent too much time at bus stops and in the medians holding up signs saying *Will work for food*, and she is whispering into her Big Gulp like this is a totally normal thing to do.

"Oh, no you don't," she whispers into the cup and gives the cup a little shake for emphasis. My mother is busy ignoring her— she's gotten good at that. But Audrey and I take one look at each other and begin to giggle. Even though we know this is probably a homeless person who is crazy and even less fortunate than we are, we can't help ourselves. Mother shoots us this look that says if you don't quit laughing, you'll be sorry, and that just makes us laugh harder, until tears are coming out of our eyes from the effort of trying not to laugh. With that, my mother turns on her heel, opens up her wallet and pulls out two five-dollar bills. Two! Hands them over to the lady who stops talking into the Big Gulp and is looking at my mother as if she is Jesus or at least Dr. Martin Luther King.

"Thank you," she says into the Big Gulp, and you can't tell if the lady is thanking my mother or the Big Gulp.

"Have a nice day," my mom says and we continue down the street. Audrey and I are no longer laughing because we figure Mom has just given the lady our allowance.

Now I know we shouldn't have laughed. It's probably not that lady's fault that she talks to a Big Gulp. But it's not my fault either, and I bet anybody would think a person talking to a Big Gulp was at least a little funny except my mother, of course, who has no sense of humor anymore. It's not like I don't understand that the Big Gulp lady needs our allowance more than we do maybe. It's just sometimes my mother can be such a snot. I mean, she could have at least asked if we wanted to help the lady out or maybe just given her half of our allowance to make us think twice. After all, we're only one paycheck away from homelessness ourselves, as my mother loves to remind us every time we need something that's not in her so-called budget. "You think you need that? Well, use your allowance," she's always saying. Now what are we supposed to do? I want to tell her, thanks a heap for your generosity to a complete stranger when your own daughters eat Rosarita Refried beans nearly every day, breakfast, lunch, and dinner. It's really so very touching. But as usual I don't say anything.

So that week I can't buy a new paperback and Audrey is unable to add to her growing collection of designer make-up products, which are a waste of her money anyway as far as I am concerned because you can't tell a bit of difference between the before and after.

The worst part comes after we get home. I start whispering into my ice tea glass. Audrey tells me to shut up and pinches me on the arm. A person can't even make a little joke around here anymore. But I don't say a word, just get up and go to my room and close the door behind me. I guess losing your sense of humor is catching because now Audrey's lost hers, and I am not feeling so ha ha ha, myself.

So what I want to know is why Mom thinks Tucson is better than Santa Rosa if all we do here is make each other mad and hurt each other's feeling? Not that I think anyone notices when my feelings get hurt, which is like every day.

Mr. Danner used to say, "You can be part of the problem or part of the solution." It seems now everybody thinks I'm part of the problem, even though I don't mean to be.

I take out my notebook and practice writing Eddie over and over until it's just about perfect. If I knew his last name I could practice writing that too. Then I draw a hot rod. It turns out pretty good, so I name it Eddie.

* * *

Once the monsoon started, which I found out is nothing more than thunderstorms, we spent a lot of time sitting on the stoop just watching them, which is less than thrilling after about the first hundred or so. But at least things cooled off after a storm and we could actually go somewhere, the Circle K maybe, or the cemetery, without melting.

One afternoon, the three of us are just sitting on the stoop. Audrey and Chablee, who spent the last five hours styling their hair and outlining their lips are all, "Ohmygod I'm so fat" and "Ohmygod you're kidding," while I watch them apply eye shadow which is supposed to make their eyes dewy and mysterious.

"You should always put your eyeshadow on in natural light so you can see how it really looks," Chablee says, like she's the eyeshadow authority of the universe. She pats Pillow Talk, "from lash line to crease," with a special sponge she has just for eye shadow, then it's up to her eyebrows in Mauve Moiré.

"Now I'll do you," Chablee says, and it takes a minute for me to realize that she means me. She selects Ocean Mist and pats it on.

"You look so hot," she says. "Doesn't she look so totally hot, Audrey?"

Audrey, who's too busy spreading Peach Caress under her eyebrows, which are still red and puffy where she plucked them down to two pencil-thin lines, doesn't even look up. The weak thing is, the whole time they're talking and gobbing on eye shadow, they're both holding their make-up mirrors so they can see over their shoulders without turning their heads, just in case somebody foxy might be watching.

Dee comes out to check her mail.

"There she blows," Chablee says, and everybody laughs, even me. I don't want to laugh, but it's like the tenth time Dee's been out to the mailbox, and every time Chablee says something. After awhile you have to laugh even though it isn't nice. Thank God, Dee's finally got some mail so she can quit checking, I'm thinking, because I really don't like it when Chablee and Audrey make fun of her. They don't even know her. It's what's on the inside that counts, and inside Dee is just like this normal . . . well not normal exactly, but on the inside she's much thinner than she is on the outside, and better looking too.

But then we see the Sidewinder. He walks right up to Dee and they start having this big conversation like they're best friends.

"Ohmygod, ohmygod," Audrey whispers. She is watching the two of them in her mirror.

Chablee arranges her mirror so she can see too. "Looks like Shamu's got a boyfriend."

"Do you think they're doing it?" Audrey says.

"I totally think they're doing it."

"Oh yuck," Audrey says.

Then to make it worse, Dee and the Sidewinder go over to his place and shut the door. Well, Chablee can't stand it and she's all, "See, see, see. What did I tell you. They're doing it. I wonder if she takes off her muu muu or if he just lifts it up and sticks his crooked old thing underneath."

"Oh gross," Audrey says, and she and Chablee are really yucking it up now. I don't say a thing, even though I should tell them to shut up and mind their own business. I hate Chablee and Audrey. Really, I hate them. They think they are so cool, with their dewy, gooey eye shadow and skinny eyebrows, but I don't say one damn thing about it. Suddenly, I can't stand to sit there another minute. "Got to pee," is all I say, because I don't have the nerve to tell them I think they're nothing but stuck up B's.

Back home, I am standing in front of the bathroom mirror, trying to see myself the way Eddie would see me. Are my eyes dewy? Do I look hot, like Chablee says?

I roll a hand towel, slip it under my tee shirt, then twist my shirt where my nipples should be. Arching my back, I pull my hair behind one ear and raise my left eyebrow. "Am I hot, Eddie?" I whisper, then kiss the mirror, touching it lightly with my tongue.

* * *

Whenever I go over to Dee's, I always check out the refrigerator door to see what kind of a day she is having. If it says something like "His light is beginning to shine," I know Dee is feeling like herself. If it says something gross, but kind of funny, "t-i-h-s spelled backwards is s-h-i-t," for example, I know we'll spend the afternoon drawing hot rods or superheroes and eating chips. When the message is spelled wrong or it doesn't make sense, I have to play about half a million games of Go Fish, which is still better than staying home.

This one day the message is "We are here to awaken from the illusion of our separateness." I read it twice and wonder what kind of a day it means. But here she is, smiling, red curls all jiggly, she's so glad to see me. LeRoy seems his normal self too, toenails ticking on the linoleum, so I figure everything is okay.

"Got something for you. It's in my God Box," she says, dumping the big cookie canister out on the table like I would my old jewelry box back in Santa Rosa. Used to be, when I opened my jewelry box, a ballerina would pop up and twirl to the Blue Danube Waltz. It was filled with all the junk that was too babyish or broken to use, but too good to throw away. Every once in awhile, I'd dump it out on my bed and sort it into categories. The foreign coins, some from Mexico and Canada, one from France, went in one pile. Barrettes went with barrettes. Rings, bracelets, and necklaces were lumped together in another pile. There was a big seed with a hand painted Chinese village on it and the collection of glass animals I'd had since I was about six: a giraffe, an elephant, a whale, a ladybug, and the bluebird of happiness. But the ballerina got broken and the waltz hadn't played for a long time, so I left it behind in Santa Rosa. Didn't think I'd miss all that stuff, but sometimes I do, especially the bluebird of happiness.

But now Dee is sifting through the contents of the God Box. There are the assorted crayons and erasers I've used, a card with Jesus standing on a blue cloud in a shower of golden light, several folded slips of paper. I notice a crucifix, a gold charm, and a piece of something floating in a tiny bottle. I hold the bottle up to the light.

"That's a sliver of the true cross." Dee says, adjusting her copper bracelets.

"The one Jesus died on?"

"One and the same."

"What's it floating in?"

"Real olive oil from the Promised Land."

It looks just like a big old splinter to me, nothing special, but you never know. I cross myself like I've seen people do on TV when there is some sort of miracle or sacred event, then lay it carefully in the bottom of the box. Next, I pick up the charm. It looks like it's made of real gold. Engraved on one side is the name Michael. I turn it over in my hand. The date 5/14/75 is on the other side. "Who gave you this?"

"Gave it to myself."

"So who's Michael?"

"Someone I love." She takes it from my hand and places it back in the box, all gentle.

I take this to mean she doesn't want to discuss it, so I change the subject. "Why do you call this a God Box, Dee?"

"It's just something we came up with. We write out our prayers and put them in the box along with a few odds and ends, my God things."

God things? Looks like just like a pile of stuff to me, and I'm wondering who *we* is. Her and Michael or maybe LeRoy? But I don't ask. Dee is always saying weird stuff like that.

"See?" She picks up one of the papers. "Here's a prayer." She unfolds it and reads, "Please take the pain from my right knee."

Wrote that myself just the other day and today my knee is definitely better." She crumples the paper and drops it in the trash. I guess once the prayer has been answered, there is no need to keep it.

"But that's not what I wanted to show you," Dee says and picks up a little cross. It's one of two. "They were giving these out to the Sunday school kids over at church. I picked up two. One's for you and one's for another little friend of mine." She hands me mine.

It's made of white plastic and no bigger than the palm of my hand. "Thank you. I've been wanting one of these," I say, but I am thinking that it's just the kind of thing I would have put in my old jewelry box, junk in other words.

"Well, I thought you could use it. Glows in the dark," she says, as if that makes all the difference in the world. Dee points to the closet. "Go try it out."

This suggestion makes me feel funny, but I don't want to hurt her feelings so I go stand in the closet.

"Close the door," she says.

Part of me is really feeling funny now, that old hollow, hot feeling I get, but the other part is telling me to quit being such a baby. My fist is wrapped tight around the cross. I close the door and shut my eyes so I won't see how dark it is, a sick feeling growing in my stomach. Finally, I open one eye. Pale blue rays are glowing from between my fingers, like I'm suddenly radioactive. I open my fist. The cross glows so bright, I can see the palm of my hand. For awhile I just stand there and stare at the cross, my hand feeling almost warm where it touches my skin. At that moment, something happens in my chest. Relief and confidence are opening up inside my ribcage like one of those time-lapse photographs of a big rose—bud to full bloom in seconds. One thing a vampire is afraid of is a cross, and a vampire could see this one even in the dark. I slip it into the pocket of my shorts where I imagine it glowing against my leg.

"Well?" Dee says when I come out of the closet. "Will it work?"

"I think it will work," I say and give Dee a hug. This is the first time I have ever touched her on purpose. My arms can only reach so far, but I am amazed that beneath her circus tent, she is both hard and soft at the same time. Dee is hugging me too, not all tight and desperate, but not all loose and iffy either. And I think if it weren't for Dee, I would be invisible for sure, because she is the only one who sees the real me. Dee, and maybe Eddie.

When we finish hugging, Dee goes to make my snack: A peanut butter, banana, and mayonnaise sandwich cut in four equal triangles. It's my current favorite.

"Put that stuff back in the box, Samantha, will you?" She calls from the kitchen.

I start to do just that. There is a Saint Christopher medal. I drop it in the box. The silver crucifix. In it goes. An Energizer battery, crayons, pens, pencils, the gum eraser, two paper clips, another medal, this one the Virgin Mary kneeling before an empty cross, all go back in the box. I examine the charm once again; feel its weight. Real gold for sure. Michael. Maybe an ex-husband or an old boyfriend? How old would Dee have been in 1979? Too young to have a husband, I think, and I drop it in the box.

The only items left are the tightly folded prayers, and I start to gather these up. I can hear Dee in the kitchen and wonder how far along she is in the sandwich process. I roll the prayers in my hand. They remind me of tiny Chinese fortune cookies, each containing a message, a clue to the future maybe, or an answer to an important question. Though it's none of my business, it's like I suddenly have this burning desire to know what Dee prays for. Carefully, I unfold a prayer. It is addressed to Jesus and written in a loopy cursive. "Let us all live together in peace," it says. I refold it exactly like it was, drop it in the box, and open another. "Dear God, remind Dee we're out of salsa and chips," it says in tight, perfect block letters. The last prayer is written in a pink Crayola scrawl. "Dear God," it says. "Hep me stop bit Dee." And I remember the bright crescents on her arm last week.

Dee comes back with my peanut butter and banana sandwich and I cup this last prayer in my hand so she won't know I've been reading it. I look at the bite on her arm. Now it's only a series of small, dull bruises, each no bigger than the eraser of a pencil.

"Thanks," I say, biting a point off the sandwich. It has just enough mayonnaise to make it slide easily against my teeth.

"Well, I finally got rid of the old station wagon," she says with a sigh. "Gave it to Junque for Jesus. Ever see their billboards?" She gathers up the prayers, reading each quickly. One she tosses into the trash. The others, she refolds, puts back in the box and closes the lid.

"You just gave it away?" I say, eyeing the box. "Couldn't you fix it?"

"Didn't need fixing. Still ran pretty good."

"So why didn't you sell it?"

"None of those used car slickies would give me what it was worth. So rather than let them have it for a song, which was an insult to a perfectly good car, I just gave it to the Lord, so to speak."

"Well, it was getting kind of old," I say to be polite, but I'm thinking it was an ugly old heap that even the Lord wouldn't be caught dead driving.

LeRoy is prancing around my ankles begging for a bite of the sandwich he knows I'm eating just as if his eyes were 20/20 instead of zero/zero. I break a triangle in two and hold a piece out to him. He takes it neatly between his front teeth and withdraws to the kitchen. "What kind of a car are you going to get now?"

"I'm not going to get another. At least not any time in the near future."

For some reason this announcement makes me feel sad, like Dee has been made suddenly pitiful by her lack of a car. I know this is not rational; we don't have a car either and we're not pitiful, not exactly. Still, I wonder how she'll get around now, Dee not being the walking type exactly.

"Should have done it long ago," she says, not at all concerned. "Kept losing it."

"What do you mean, kept losing it?"

"For instance, I'd drive it to the mall in the morning, come out later, sometimes it would be dark, and I wouldn't know where the car was parked. You know what I mean?"

I don't have any idea what she means. Oh, I know my mom sometimes used to forget the exact spot she parked our car and had to look around a little. That happens to people all the time.

But how could Dee lose a great big station wagon the color of old dentures? It would stick out a mile.

She pauses, adjusts the bracelets again, and says, "It was as though one person had driven it to the mall and a different person was supposed to drive it home, but the first person forgot to tell the second person where the car was parked. You see? Worst thing was, those people might not even be licensed drivers!"

"You're letting someone drive your car who doesn't have a license?" I say, now totally confused.

Dee shakes her head. "I'm saying it's like that when I drive. So Big Dee says sell it and leaves me to take care of the details. That's why they're called Dee Tails," she says laughing. "You got to laugh," Dee says. "You absolutely got to."

I smile, but now I'm really confused. Big Dee? Is there another Dee who's bigger than Dee, one who tells her what to do? I pick up my last triangle and take a small bite out of each corner. My mother calls Dee an odd duck. I guess she is, but that's okay. I am definitely not the type who would turn my back on someone just because she's an odd duck. Beneath the table, I refold the prayer tightly, drop it on the floor, and hope for the best.

* * *

When I get home that afternoon, Audrey is lying on her bed. Her eyes are closed, and she's looking pale. I tiptoe past the bedroom door so I won't wake her.

"I'm not asleep," she says, in this weak voice that is meant to let me know just how weak she is.

"What's wrong?"

"I started my period this afternoon," she sighs and waves her hand towards the dresser over which is spread the contents of her little emergency supply kit, a pink plastic make-up bag that mom filled with Modess pads, a small bottle of Midol, and a pair of pink nylon bikini underpants. She presented it to Audrey on her last birthday, like it was some special deal, so she'd be ready for the big event. Now it's come and Mom's not here to share the news with. If this were Santa Rosa, she'd be sitting on the edge of Audrey's bed, probably.

Technically speaking, Audrey is now a woman. She's even eligible to have sex, because once you start your period, you could, though at the time, I'd never known anyone her age who actually had. "Does it hurt?"

"Bad. I took two Midols, but they made me sick and I puked my guts out. I wish Mom was here."

"You could phone her."

"Right, like she's going to tell her boss she's got to rush home because her daughter's started her period."

I can see tears in her eyes and I figure she's not just trying to be all dramatic, like usual. I should be nicer to Audrey. After all, somebody's got to be nice around here, and I'm better at it than she is. "Can I get you anything?" I ask, thinking what Mom would do if she were here? "I could make you some hot tea."

"It would make me throw up."

"What hurts?"

"My back, my stomach, between my legs. It's the cramps."

The cramps can be pretty bad. I know from personal experience because Tammy Gardener started her period last year and had to stay home from school the first two days every time she got it. "Tammy Gardener has bad cramps," I say in order to remind her that she is not the only one in the world who has started her period.

"Tammy Gardener has her period?"

"She started when she was ten and seven months. It's supposed to be a secret, but I guess it doesn't matter now. Want me to rub your back?" Audrey rolls over. "Where does it hurt?"

"Down low, I guess. Just above my tailbone."

She is wearing shorts and a T-shirt and I massage her back through these, pressing outwards from her spine with the palms of my hands, like Mom used to when one of us had the flu. "Audrey?"

"Hmm?"

"Do you think we'll ever go back to Santa Rosa?"

"I don't know."

"But you want to, don't you?"

"Sometimes."

"I do. All the time. I hate it here. I don't have any friends. It's hot. It's ugly. I hate this apartment. It's ugly and dirty and small."

"It's not dirty."

"There are cockroaches," I say to prove my point. "We never had cockroaches in Santa Rosa. Do you think Dad misses us?"

"I doubt it. If anything, he's probably happy we're gone. Don't press so hard, Sammy. You're making it worse."

"Sorry," I say, switching from my palms to my thumbs. "How's that?"

"Better."

"Well, I think he misses us."

"Whatever."

"And I think Mom still loves him. She's just being stubborn."

"Listen, Sammy. . . . Oh, never mind."

"I hate when you do that. What you were going to say?"

"Nothing."

"Yes you were. What?"

"Don't get your hopes up, that's all. Even if Mom still loves him, which I seriously doubt that she would after all the terrible things he's done to her, to all of us, she won't go back to him, not ever. You're just going to have to learn to deal with it."

"Would you quit saying that? You keep saying that. Just deal with it, deal with it, deal with it, like a broken record. Besides, you don't know everything. You can't tell the future."

"No, but I can tell the past. Dad's crazy and Mom won't go back unless he gets help, mental help, which of course he would never do because he thinks he's perfect."

"He's not crazy," I say, my throat beginning to tighten, which is a bad sign. "He just has a lot on his mind. Mom says a person who's in real estate. . . ."

"Yeah, Dad has real important things to think about, especially when he was home, like who moved the remote control, or why there's not a beer super-chilling in the freezer the moment he walks through the front door, or how many times he can jiggle his knee in sixty seconds. Did you ever wonder why he jiggles his knee?"

"So, he's got a habit. You chew on your cuticles."

"You don't think it's crazy that he hits us for nothing?"

"Only when we've done something wrong."

"You mean like the time Dad pinched your arm so hard it left a big old purple pinch mark because you didn't get in the car fast enough?"

"So? You pinch me hard for nothing all the time."

"Yeah, but I'm not a grown-up. Grown-ups don't go around pinching their kids unless they're nuts. And what about Mom? You think she's just clumsy? Don't you think it's kind of funny that she hasn't cut herself on a chipped glass or tripped and fallen on her face even once since we got here? She used to do it all the time in Santa Rosa. Think abut it, Sammy."

I don't want to think about it. What good does thinking about that kind of stuff do anyway? Just makes me feel weird is all. It's clear that Audrey wants to make me feel stupid, like always, because I still love my father. And I do feel stupid. I can't explain why it doesn't matter if he sometimes hit us when we didn't deserve it. I know he hit Mom. I'm not blind. But I love him anyway. "I'd rather get hit or pinched once in a while in Santa Rosa where we at least have a nice house and friends and there's something to do besides watch TV and hang around the stupid cemetery," I say.

"Look, Sammy, Mom told me not to tell you this, but I'm going to anyway. It's for your own good," she says sitting up on one elbow and making her face look all sad and concerned. "You remember the mama cat and her kittens?"

"Her name's Miss Tippy," I say, thinking I should not stick around to hear about this thing that's supposed to be for my own good.

"Whatever. Did you ever wonder what happened to her?"

"Dad took Miss Tippy and the girl kittens to work and gave them to somebody who didn't have any cats, and we got to keep Willy and Nilly," I say.

"Dad didn't give them away. Dad put them in a pillow case and did something to them."

"You're lying. Mom said . . ."

"She just made that up so you wouldn't get all freaked out. I ought to know. I was there when he did it. He just dropped them into a pillowcase like they were stuffed animals, not real live cats."

"Then what did he do?"

"I think he killed them."

"He did not. He wouldn't. You're making this up." This is what I say, but I am not so sure. Sometimes Dad could do really mean things, like the time he smashed Audrey's Walkman with a hammer, I can't remember why. Audrey got in trouble a lot more than me, but that was because she never listened the first time. I am crying now, so I just get up and leave. I don't want to have to say another word or listen to another one either.

What I want to do is hide. I know that sounds immature and stupid, but I don't want to see anybody and I don't want anybody to see me. If this were Santa Rosa, I'd just go into the back yard and crawl behind the mock orange hedge and stick some mock orange right under my nose. Nobody ever thought to look for me in that hedge, and I could stay there as long as I wanted, cry if I wanted, the mock orange cool and sweet against my face, because nobody could see me.

Outside the clouds are thick and yellow, and there is not one bit of a breeze. It has just started to rain—only a few big, slow drops. I tip my head back so they can fall on my burning face. There is this smell in the air. Part of it's wet pavement, and is familiar, but there is something else, like the smell of a cough drop, the green ones that open up the inside of your nose so you can breathe. I breathe in the smell of cough drops and wet pavement. It's not anything like mock orange, but the ache loosens in my throat a little. I head to the shed where I can be alone. My secret hope is that Eddie will find me there.

The rain has picked up. It sounds like somebody's throwing pebbles on the tin roof and there is lightening too. At first it's a long ways away, but each bolt lights the shed a little brighter and each crack is louder. In one corner, there is a bucket. A rake and an old rusty shovel lean against the wall. I turn the bucket over and sit down so I can cry in comfort. Part of me is crying for Miss Tippy and her girl kittens, which I hadn't even named yet, but part of me is also crying because at that moment, I hate Audrey so much there is only one thing I can do and that is cry. I know it's my father I should hate, but I can't help that. And I hate to cry. Everything inside my head swells up and aches when I cry and it's like I do it practically every damn day, thanks mostly to my dear sister who's always telling me things for my own good. Deal with it, she says, like my life is a deck of ratty old cards. I'm sick of dealing with it, and I'm sick of her.

It's true, I miss Santa Rosa, but it isn't just Santa Rosa. It's more than that, more than Dad, more than the house we lived in or my friends, or even that I'm bored or lonely, but I can't say exactly what it is, so I have to cry. How do I explain that hollow place that opens up in my chest, or the sick feeling in my stomach that's not something I ate or the flu or a case of the jitters, but something deep and scary that comes over me if I let myself think about things I don't even have names for? I say I'm lonely or bored when that is not what it is. It's irrational, like vampires.

After awhile, I stop crying, even though I don't want to, because I don't have anything else to do, and crying is better than nothing. Inside the shed is not much better than outside, because there are serious empty places where the boards in the walls are cracked or missing. The wind's come up and it whistles through the walls. The lightning is right here, and there is the crack-boom of thunder. I am sure the palm tree out front has been hit, and I wonder what would happen if it came crashing down on the roof of this shed. I'm beginning to wish I were back in the apartment where I'm pretty certain I'd be safe from the lightning at least, if not the cockroaches and Audrey.

I take the plastic glow-in-the-dark cross out of my pocket. Though it's not dark enough in the shed for it to glow, I rub it, like Aladdin's lamp. "Dear God," I start to pray, but stop. I really don't know what I should pray for. I want to go back to Santa Rosa. I could pray for that, I guess. Could pray for Dad to change, but even if he did, it wouldn't bring Miss Tippy and her kittens back, and how would we know if he's changed unless we went back to Santa Rosa which we can't do because of the way he is. I think of my cats Willy and Nilly and wonder if they are safe or if Dad has put them into a pillowcase too.

"Dear God, protect Willy and Nilly, Miss Tippy, and her babies." This is what I say out loud, but inside I am praying for Eddie to come and kiss me again like a real boyfriend.

I look around the shed, hoping to find something, maybe an old newspaper or catalogue to read, to make the time pass. That's when I notice a few little twigs sticking out from a corner shelf. I stand on the bucket for a better look. There's a pigeon sitting absolutely still. She pretends not to see me as if she wants to be invisible too. Lightning strikes again, but the pigeon doesn't even twitch. She's a soft pretty gray, with bright pink-rimmed eyes.

"It's okay, little bird. I won't hurt you," I say, but she continues to stare at the wall, and I wonder how many eggs she's sitting on. After they hatch, I'm thinking, maybe I could train them to sit on my shoulder and eat out of my hand, come when I whistle. If I could just give her a little nudge, say with the handle of the rake, I could get her to move over so I could take a peek underneath. Rake in hand, I stand on the bucket and give Mrs. Pigeon a little poke with the handle, but it's not exactly a little poke because I lose my balance and sort of thunk her on the head by mistake. She gets all upset and flies out of the shed through a crack, leaving not eggs, but two chicks, live and featherless, exposed to the elements, namely me and the wind coming through the walls. How long does it take a baby pigeon to die of exposure, I am wondering. Just then, the shed lights up and there is another crack-pop and the baby pigeons are shuddering, or maybe it's the walls shuddering in the wind, but one of the chicks raises its head and looks straight at me, like it's saying, *why are you just standing there like an idiot?* I figure I've got to do something quick.

The ladder is outside near the basketball hoop where it's been since the 4th of July. The rain is coming down like needles, only sideways, as I drag it inside. Once I'm at eye level with the baby pigeons, I reach for the nest, but I guess pigeons aren't such great nest builders. The only thing holding it together is pigeon poop, and it falls apart as soon as I touch it, leaving the babies sitting on the bare shelf where they could roll right off if they just thought about trying to move. With great care, I pick each baby up. With their bulging eyes and wobbly, bald heads, they look more like little old naked men than birds and I wish I had never touched the mother, wish I'd never come into the shed in the first place, wish I weren't so stupid. Mama pigeon is probably wishing the same.

Carefully, I put them in the bucket where they'll be safe, but I am dripping on them, and I know I need to take them someplace warm. Lightning is still striking close by. I'm scared, but I put my hand into my pocket and feel my glow-in-the-dark cross. It's warm to the touch. After the next bolt of lightning strikes, I make a run for it. By the time I hit our front door, I am soaked and the baby birds aren't so dry either.

* * *

Mom is standing over the bucket, which is lined with a dry towel and sitting on the oven door. She turns the oven down from 350, to warm.

"You should know better, Sammy."

"But they would have died."

"The mother would have come back if you'd just left well enough alone."

"No, she wouldn't have." I say, though I'm pretty sure my mom is right. "It was the thunder and lightning. She got too scared."

"So tell me again. You went into the shed because of the lightning and she just flew out the door?"

I shake my head yes. The truth is too humiliating. "What do pigeons eat?" I ask moving to a safer topic.

"Garbage," Audrey says, then adds, "Pigeons are flying rats."

"Shut up," I say, remembering the mama pigeon's soft gray feathers.

"Don't you two get started," Mom warns.

"But she's such an idiot." Audrey says, eye rims turning red.

Mom just looks at her without saying a word. If I had said that to Audrey, Mom would have sent me to my room for the millionth time. "Let's try some bread soaked in warm water," she says, and gets a package of hot dog rolls out of the refrigerator.

"Those guys are going to die. I'm going back to bed," she says. slamming the door behind her.

"Are they going to die?" I ask.

"You know how it is with baby birds, Sammy," is all she says and then goes in to comfort the invalid. As usual, I'm left alone. I soak the bread and offer it to each baby, but they don't even lift their heads.

* * *

First thing in the morning I am out in the kitchen. The pigeon babies are still warm to touch but that's because they've been sitting on the oven door all night. When I pick one up, its head flops to one side like its neck has no bones to hold it up. I wrap the birds in a paper towel. Still in pajamas, I go to the shed for the shovel. Up in the corner sits the mother. This time she ruffles her neck and looks straight at me. I hold her babies behind my back so she can't see that they're dead.

I bury the babies in the cactus garden, making a cross of quartz rock over the top.

Later in the afternoon, I go by the grave and red ants are tunneling though the dirt. It makes me sick to think about what's going on down there, ants covering the naked babies like the feathers they never lived long enough to grow. I consider digging them up, but then what would I do? Put them in the garbage? They are better off with the ants, I think. At least that way they'll be of some use. The pigeons will feed the ants and the ants will feed whatever eats ants. Do pigeons eat ants?

I should have put the dead babies in a Ziploc bag, maybe made a deeper hole. Should never have disturbed the mama pigeon in the first place, or taken her babies out of the nest. Mom was right, I should have known better. Now I understand how people can do bad, stupid things without really meaning to. I'm pretty sure Dad never really meant to hurt us either.

DEE

The Bible tells us to fight our demons. This is one of those places I think the Bible is wrong. Oh, I know it's supposed to be the word of God, but there are too many words in there that are just plain mean and low spirited to be His. Those must be words man has put in God's mouth, is the way I see it.

Now Samantha has demons she's struggling against. It seems the more she struggles, the more she hates herself. But God doesn't want us to hate ourselves, because when we do we act in hateful ways, like with Little Girl in the shed that day. That part seems pretty clear to me. So maybe Samantha has to accept her demons, sort of like me. Learn to love them because they are part of her. They say love the sinner, hate the sin. I think it's sort of like that.

The devil will take them all.

Not all.

Every last one will swim naked in the boiling seas of hell.

Enough about hell and the devil!

You're going to meet the devil in hell, close up and personal, if you mock the Bible.

I'm not mocking the Bible.

The Bible is God's WORD. The Bible tells us so.

Leave me alone. A person can't even think.

So one afternoon—this was after all the trouble and school had already started—I am fixing Samantha a peanut butter and mayo sandwich. She's rummaging through the God Box, which she's done a dozen times. Opens each prayer, reads it, returns it to the box neatly folded. Whatever she is looking for, I don't think she'll find it in there, but there's no point in my saying so.

I cut the sandwich into four equal triangles, like she likes it, and arrange each triangle on one of Gerralee's little flowered plates.

"How was school today?" I ask.

Samantha shrugs those thin shoulders of hers and picks up the bottle with the sliver of the true cross floating in olive oil from the Holy Land. She gives it a shake, watches it bob to the surface, shakes it, watches it bob, shakes it, watches it bob. Does this with great concentration as if she were conducting some scientific experiment.

"Make any new friends?"

"No," she says, tossing the bottle back in the box.

"It will happen," I say, knowing maybe it won't, at least not real soon, the way she's acting. "It's hard to be the new kid in school, but you'll make friends if you just open yourself to it."

"I don't want any friends."

"Chablee's your friend. Maybe her friends will be your friends too," I suggest, but she just shrugs those shoulders.

"You going to eat your peanut butter sandwich?"

Samantha takes a small bite out of one corner, slips a bite to LeRoy, then says, "Do you think God is a man or a woman?"

"Well, there is certainly a lot of talk about that. To my way of thinking, God is not one or the other."

"But you always say Him or He."

"That's just habit. If I call God He, it's only because you can't call God It."

"Why not?"

"Are you going to eat your sandwich?"

Samantha takes another bite. "Why can't you call God It?"

"Seems to me, you call animals it, but God is not an animal."

"Humans are animals."

"Sure, but God's not human. God is something else. You could call God She, I guess, but that wouldn't be any righter than He. Call God what you want. Any name you can think of, lots of people call God different names, but if you got God in your heart He or She or It will answer when you do."

While Samantha is thinking this over, she nibbles at her sandwich. One thing for sure, she doesn't believe in something just because you say so. Likes to figure things out for herself.

"So why do you think It does what It does?"

"What do you mean?" I ask, pretending not to notice the ugly tone in her voice.

"Why do you think God makes people suffer?"

Only now am I beginning to understand where this conversation is going. I'd like to say something to her that would make a difference, something reassuring, but this is a question I still catch myself asking. "There's lots of people smarter than me who've tried to answer that question." I say. "It's like asking what's the meaning of life."

"So what is the meaning of life?"

"Oh Samantha. I don't know the answer to that one either, but let me tell you something I do believe. We all have to find our own way. Now don't roll your eyes, let me go on here a bit."

"Sometimes, when things are bad in my life, I think this is not my real life yet. My best, real life hasn't started yet. But that's not true. I'm living my real life right now, every day. I think, life's made up of bests and worsts and all we can do is put one foot in front of the other.

"And sometimes we step in a big pile of dog poop."

I have to laugh at this and even Samantha's lips kind of quiver like they do when she's trying not to smile. "Yes, we do," I say. "And when that happens all we can do is keep walking until the stink wears off. But sometimes we step on. . . ."

"Cool green grass."

"Right. We step on cool green grass. Then we get to take off our shoes and wiggle our toes in it as we walk. The point is, to keep walking no matter what. That's what God intends us to do. Keep walking from beginning to end, enjoy what you can along the way, learn from it, and leave the really worst things behind you like a bad stink."

"Is that what you do?"

"Well, it sounds easier than it is, but yes, that's what I try to do."

"I want to write a prayer and put it in the God Box, but you got to promise not to read it."

"Okay, I promise. You better mark it special with a crayon or something so I won't look at it by accident."

When she is finished writing, she folds the prayer again and again until it is about the size of a postage stamp. She prints S across it with a purple crayon and buries it inside the box beneath all the other odds and ends of my life.

After Samantha finally goes home, I feel grateful and relieved. Jesus was truly with me when I needed him. I go to the refrigerator, spell out: Let Jesus be your voice. It's a message we ALL should take to heart.

It's Satan you've taken to your puffed-up heart. Read the Bible each day to keep Satan away.

So read the Bible if that's what turns your knobs.

Even Satan can quote scripture if it suits his purposes. If you follow the example of Jesus and listen when he speaks, then the Bible isn't all that necessary, is what I think. Jesus, after all, did not write the Bible.

What about the parts in red?

Okay the parts in red, then, but even those are hearsay.

Hearsay heresy. Is hell hearsay?

To me the Bible is . . . but there's too much buzzing. I'm too tired to keep this up. Doc says each of us needs to have our say; share our stories. What I don't remember, the others will. Maybe that's true, but sometimes I think I've had more stories shared with me than I can stomach. My own story, the one that begins with my mother leaving and ends who knows where, maybe in hell since a certain someone is so determined to send me there . . .

Whores burn in hell. Uncle Birdie made you his whore.

At least he loved me.

You call that love?

Uncle Birdie saw something of worth in me.

Your hole.

There was more to it than that. What he did was wrong, worse than wrong. But he loved me, as selfish as that love was. I know he did and it was better than no love at all. If that makes me a whore, so be it.

So finally you admit you were his whore.

I was his child. Wherever he is now, with the help of the Lord, I have forgiven his trespasses against me, but Aunt LeeAnn. . . .

She took us in when nobody else wanted us.

She took everybody in but me. I tried to be good, but I just was never fast enough or smart enough or pretty enough to please her. Many times she hurt me.

You were always asking for it.

Asking for it? Asking to be hit and punched and scratched and burned and locked up and told every day of my life that I was dirty and stupid? I've prayed about it, but I can't seem to forgive her.

If we can't forgive, we can't expect to be forgiven.

Well, I've said the words many times, but I don't feel them in my heart and if forgiveness doesn't come from the heart . . . well what good is it? Just words is all and empty.

She's still alive and well, Aunt LeeAnn. Frank and Lollie keep in touch with her. That's okay for them; she's the only mother they remember. I know she tells them I must be crazy since nothing like THAT ever happened. NEVER HAPPENED. Of course, they want to believe her. I can't fault them for that. I'd like to believe it never happened too. For a long time I did. But I can't deny what I know to be true any more.

Why it was only me, I'll never know. Frank and Lollie had a totally different childhood than I did; have a different set of memories than I do. "Don't you remember our trip out to California? We all had such a great time," they say. How can you forget Disneyland? The ocean?" When they say we were all there together, I believe them. They're my little brother and sister. I love them, spent my childhood trying to protect them. They have no reason to lie about it.

I do believe that somebody got to go, somebody took a trip to the ocean, got to jump in the waves and play in the sand. Who? Brad and the twins, maybe. But when we came home from all those good memories that I don't have, I was left to do the hard, sad work. Those are my memories, and they have nothing to do with rides at Disneyland or a California beach.

So where was I, where was Dee, while Brad or the twins played in the surf? I honestly don't know. Hanging out with Little Girl and Big Dee I guess, twirling in space, out to lunch, just gone, gone,

gone. If Brad and the twins got to go to the movies, it was Big Dee, Little Girl, and me who paid the price of admission.

There are parts of me that remain optimistic, parts that can play, parts that have been spared. But when I'm running on the last fumes before empty, it is only Jesus who keeps my engine going.

I've had no contact with Aunt LeeAnn since I began my recovery and I won't until she tells the truth or I am able to forgive her, whichever happens first.

We won't hold our breath.

Don't. God forgive me—everybody, but not Aunt LeeAnn. Funny thing, for a woman who had so much trouble with the truth, when it came to my mother, Aunt LeeAnn had no problem telling a five-year-old all about it.

That first day we set foot in her house, the three of us surrounded with brown paper shopping bags full of clothes and toys and Daddy already out the door, I told Aunt LeeAnn that Mommy was with Jesus just like Daddy said.

I can still hear her laugh, not a happy laugh, but ugly, hard. "With Jesus? Your mother? She ran off with a nigger, not a spic." Her exact words. If I knew what a nigger or a spic was back then, I can't say. Only recently have I understood exactly how mean-hearted those words were to a little child who'd lost her mother. But even if the significance of her words were lost on me as a child, her laugh said everything. I told her I hated her right then and there. So maybe I did ask for all that came later.

Don't get yourself started thinking that way, Honey.

Right. Right. Right. If I do, I'll finish the job Aunt LeeAnn started. And I promised God I'd never try that again. I take my copper bracelets off then, rub the ridged surfaces of the white crosses I carved deep into my wrists.

You'll end up in hell yet.

I guess that would suit you, Miss Queen of Morality and What's Right and What's Wrong in the Universe. You think you've got the very corner on Christian Faith, don't you. Would slice off your own lips rather than blaspheme, but let me say this. You never lifted one damn finger that night. Was Brad who called 911. Was Brad wanted to live. The rest of us didn't give a goddamn, you included.

You know, there's a difference between knowing something and taking it to heart. There's lots of things I know, but can't seem to take to heart. When I think of all that happened in my life, the single worst one was getting left behind by my mother. Though I know it, I just never could believe it. It's always been easier to think that she's dead. A dead mother is a mother I can imagine loved me. If I think of her as alive and well living some place, maybe some place close by like Phoenix, then this is a mother who didn't love me because I wasn't good enough. How am I supposed to feel about that mother? How am I supposed to feel about myself?

Damn her to hell where she can get to know Aunt LeeAnn and Uncle Birdie.

Now don't you start. She's my mother and I forgive her.

Is that so?

Yes, it's so. Damn it! You can take all the others to hell with you, but her.

Like Christ, we suffered to save the children. Lay the burden at his feet and forgive.

Amen. It was a long time ago. I wish we could let it all go once and for all. There's sometimes I think, with Doc's help and the help of the Lord, we're making progress in that respect. But there's other times I think we hold on tight to all that ugliness, hold on for dear life, just because if we let go, we're afraid there'd be nothing left of us.

That's the devil speaking!

That's Dee speaking. That's me.

* * *

I'm having one of my days. All I can do is sit back and hold on. Can't let go for a moment. Don't want to sleep, but I guess it happens anyway. There is a click, then a whisper, like a secret told close to my ear. I feel sick and cold as the bed falls out beneath me. I cover my eyes, my ears, but the video starts running. I see a light shining across the foot of a bed, hear her voice coming from the kitchen—whispery, dry as April weeds in June.

"Not my fault," she's saying. My head is still half-opened, half-closed. I push it back into my little pillow, but my bottom is wet. I'm too big to wet my bed. I get up, dragging my blanket behind me and go into the kitchen.

They are sitting at the table. At first they don't see me. The brown linoleum is sticky under my bare feet. I lift one foot, then another as I wait, cold in my wet pjs. I begin to cry.

Mommy starts to get up, but Daddy grabs her arm and pulls her back down. "Go back to bed, Little Girl."

I don't move.

Daddy picks me up. Pulls my thumb out of my mouth. He doesn't hug me or ask what is wrong. He doesn't say a word, just carries me back to my room, tosses me on the bed.

"But it's all wet and cold." I am crying hard now.

"You're too big to pee the bed. You can just sleep in it, Little Girl."

Mommy is at the bedroom door. I start to get out of bed.

"You get out of bed one more time, Daddy's going to have to get the belt. You understand that Little Girl? Don't make me get the belt now," he says and pushes Mommy out of the room.

I lie in bed and listen to Mommy and Daddy, their voices low, buzzing. Sometimes I hear Mommy crying, but mostly, it's just buzzing, like bees. I lie there for a long, long time listening. Then I remember what Mommy taught me to do when I can't sleep. ZYX, WVU, TSR, QP, ONM LKJI, HGFE, DCBA. I say this over and over.

In the morning, Mommy is supposed to come in to get me up for school. I'm scared to get out of bed, scared of Daddy's belt. I wait and I wait, but she doesn't come. The sun is already shining through the yellow shade, dust fairies floating in the sunbeams. God takes me for his sunbeam, I sing loud as loud, but she still doesn't come.

"Mommy," I call. Again and again I call for her. After a long time, Daddy comes in. Sits on the side of the bed and gives me a hug. He is hugging me and kissing the top of my head, my face.

"Mommy's not coming, Little Girl," he says. "She's gone."

I'm worried because I don't want to miss school and Mommy has to comb my hair. "When's she coming back?" I ask.

But Daddy doesn't answer me. He is crying now. The sound he makes is scary. He is hugging me too hard, but I don't say let me go. I say, "Don't cry, Daddy."

"Mommy's gone away for good, little girl; She's gone to live with Jesus, Dee darlin'."

"I want to go see her."

"Jesus lives far away in heaven," Daddy says. "It's too far to visit."

I hate him for saying this. I want to kick him, scratch him, take the belt to him. He is hugging me, my face pressed against his chest. He smells bad. Worse than pee. It's hard to breathe, but I don't push him away. I'm too scared. I turn my head and I bite my shoulder. Bite my shoulder hard. Bite until he stops crying and lets me go.

When he's gone, I pull the sheets off the bed. I've been bad, so Mommy went to live with Jesus instead of us. I stop to look at the teeth marks on my shoulder. They are red and just right.

CHABLEE

Audrey, I'd have to say, is my best friend, because she's the only one I can really be myself with, mostly. But before we got to be tight, I told her a lie about my daddy. Said he died in a fire trying to save my life. Well, I didn't know we were going to end up being tight, so I thought it didn't matter what bullshit I told her. Where my daddy is, is no business of hers, is what I was thinking at the time.

This one time, it was still last summer, Audrey asks about the chain I always wear around my neck. I pull it out and show her the ring.

"Where did you get it?" she asks.

"My daddy gave it to me," I say, without even thinking.

"How can that be if your father died saving you from a fire when you were a baby?" she says and cocks her head in a way that means she knows I lied to her.

I just cock my head right back at her. "So what?" I say, and you know I am hating her bad at the moment.

"So, nothing," she says. "I know your dad's in prison."

"How do you know that?"

She tells me Sammy heard my mother tell her mother all about it. Then she says, "It's no big deal. I wish my dad were in prison." Tells me, "That's a nice ring. I bet it cost a lot of money."

"Thanks," I say. "So why do you wish your daddy was in prison?"

"Well, mostly he was never home, but when he was all he did was sit in front of the TV jiggling his foot, surfing with the remote and bossing us around. If you didn't do what he said the instant he said it, or if you got in his way by accident or said some little thing, he'd get so mad, and his mouth would get all foamy and gross at the corners. And it was like he couldn't make a point without hitting or pinching or kicking or poking hard with his finger, poke, poke, poke," she says and pokes me in my arm, her mouth a hard, straight line, just to show me how it feels.

"Ouch," I say, and slap her hand away before she can poke me again.

"Somebody that mean should be locked up."

"What made him so mean?"

Audrey throws her head forward so she can examine her hair, like she's looking for split ends. "Just mean, I guess, or maybe it was drugs. That's what my mom says."

"My daddy's a Muslim, that means no drugs, no alcohol, no coffee, no cigarettes, nothing like that. He never hit me even once, Mama neither," I say. Then I tell her all about my father and how his name used to be Terence Duwayne Edwards, but now it's Mukisa Abdul Muhammad, Good Luck Son of the Profit of God.

"Cool," she says. "I wish I could change my name. I hate Audrey."

"I hate my name too," I say, which is just another lie, of course, but what are you supposed to say to somebody who has a name like Audrey?

"Chablee is like so cool," she says. "You should never change your name."

I tell her that Audrey is cool too, and that's when we started getting tight, which probably wouldn't have happened if I always told the truth like Mama says.

* * *

Right after Audrey had her first period, she's over and I'm giving her a French manicure to celebrate the big event. She's got one hand soaking in Ivory and I'm working on the other, when all of a sudden she asks me why I'm a year behind in school. Now you think I'd wouldn't need to be lying to Audrey anymore, but back then, I was just so used to making up my life, that I said the lie before I ever gave it any thought.

"I had cancer when I was little and had to spend a whole year in a hospital."

She's looking at me like, is she telling the truth, so I add a few details. "The cancer was in my stomach. They way they discovered it was I couldn't eat, not even ice cream, my stomach hurt so bad."

She's still looking at me funny and so I tack on some more. "I had all these tubes up my nose and in my arms, but the doctors and nurses were really nice and I had my own private room with a TV. Was when I was seven," I say and then I get to thinking, why am I such a big liar? Still, I've started the lie, might as well finish it. "So I missed most of second grade." That part of the lie was true.

It was when I was in second grade my daddy was arrested for selling crack cocaine. Then some men came and took our car, our house and furniture. Even took Mama's diamond engagement ring right off her finger that was supposed to be mine when I graduated college. I still don't understand how they could do that to us. Mama and me never did anything wrong. Anyway, I guess you could say we were homeless, not that we ever had to live on the streets. We lived in one of those shelter places for awhile, until Mama couldn't take all their rules and bullshit any more. That's when she started dancing again. By the time we moved into the Oasis Apartments, the school year was almost over, so Mama didn't bother to send me back, figured I'd be better off starting second grade again the next year.

This one afternoon, we're just sitting on my bed, looking through my collection of barrettes and clips—some, like the bows and teddy bears, I've had since I was a baby—when Audrey starts to nibble at the skin around her fingernails, like she does. Then she just asks straight out. "So really, how come you're in seventh grade instead of eighth?"

At first I just pretend I don't even hear her. Pick up my yellow butterfly barrettes and try them on.

"I mean, did you flunk, or something?" she says. "Cause if you flunked, it's like no big deal. I almost flunked third grade because I practically couldn't read t-h-e."

"Stop biting your damn cuticles," I say, pulling her hand away from her mouth. "How'd you know it was a lie?"

"Like I heard around school that your mom's got cancer. I know that's a lie, so when you told me you had cancer too, I just figured it was just another lie."

"Lying's sort of this thing I do, like a habit? Kind of like how you chew on your cuticles? Anyways, sometimes I don't even know I'm going to tell a lie until it's out of my mouth. Then once the lie gets started, I feel I have to finish it. Like you can't switch over to the truth right in the middle of a lie."

"So why did you? You don't have to say if you don't want. Say you don't want to discuss it; that's cool, but don't lie to me, okay? It's like so rude."

"The reason, and this is the truth—the reason I didn't want to say was because it has to do with my daddy going to jail."

"I know your dad's in jail," she says.

"Yeah, but you don't know why."

"So tell me why; that is, if you want me to know."

"Your daddy's a crackhead, right?"

"So?"

"Well, my daddy used to sell crack cocaine, all that shit."

"I thought you said your dad didn't do drugs because he was a Muslim."

"That's true. He wasn't taking the drugs himself; he was just selling them. It's kind of complicated, but when he was in jail the first time. . . ."

"He's been in jail twice?"

"Yeah. The first time he was doing drugs and was breaking in houses so he could buy his shit, you know?"

"So your dad was a druggy."

"Yeah, but that was before he became a Muslim. I told you it was complicated. Anyway, he became a Muslim when he was in jail because he learned that the CIA or maybe it was the FBI—anyway one of those three letter dudes—is flooding black neighborhoods with all kinds of drugs so black folks will kill themselves off or something like that. So when he got out, he started selling drugs, but only to white guys, see? It was like a political protest, but instead of marching. . . ."

"He sold drugs only to white people."

"Right. That's why he's in jail. Well actually, he's in jail because they say he killed some dude, but it wasn't him who killed the dude, but this other dude who just happened to be there at the time my daddy was trying to get the dude who ended up dead to pay him what he owed. See? It's kind of complicated, but my daddy was definitely not the one who pulled the trigger. That would be against his religion."

"So why did you lie to me about it?"

"Well, I just didn't want you to know that my dad was the kind of dude your dad got his shit from."

Audrey is thinking this over and I have to pull her hand away from her mouth again. "What your dad did and what my dad did, doesn't have anything to do with us," she says finally, and I know we're cool again.

"I'm going to style your hair," I say, pushing it back from her face. Audrey's hair is sort of like my mama's, thick and wavy, only shorter and a darker brown. I comb my fingers through it, and it's all silky-like and heavy. "I'm going to style your hair black," I say, picking though all the clips and barrettes until I have a handful of solid butterflies.

* * *

Every day, we take the school bus back and forth to Desert Corner Middle School, which is grades seven through nine. For awhile, these two eighth grade dudes, Jesse Contreras and George Balderon, sat behind us. Then one afternoon, we kind of switched places, and it was me and Jesse and Audrey and George. When we got off at our stop, Audrey was pissed because George was like leaning all over her. Sammy was not all that happy either because she had to sit alone. Audrey thought it was all my idea, which was not the case.

"It was George," I tell her. "He thinks you're hot."

Audrey takes a minute to think about this. "You are such a liar. Besides, he's too young for me." She says this, but you can tell she's all thrilled that somebody, even George Balderon who is the shortest boy in the eighth grade and like two feet shorter than she is, thinks she's hot.

"They want us to meet them at the mall Saturday."

"You are out of your mind," she says. "Besides, what about Sammy? Sammy has to come too."

But I've got it all figured out. "Jesse's got a little brother," I say. "Him and Sammy can hang out at the Arcades while you and George and me and Jesse hang out." Audrey looks at Sammy to see if it's okay, and Sammy shrugs like she doesn't give a damn one way or another. So it's all set for Saturday, which is cool. It's already the forth or fifth week of school. I don't even have a boyfriend yet and Jesse is totally hot—everybody says so.

That Friday night before we're supposed to meet Jesse and George at the mall, Audrey is sleeping over at my house. We've got my lipsticks, lip-liners, blush, eyebrow pencils, highlighter, and make-up brushes, the fat one for blending blush and powder and the small one for blending eye shadows, and the skinny one for doing lips, spread out all over my vanity, Scrunchies pulling our hair back from our faces so we can really concentrate on our plus and minus areas.

I'm dotting concealer over Audrey's zits when she asks have I ever French kissed.

"First time was in fifth grade."

"No way! In fifth grade, you were what? Ten?"

"So what's your point?" I say, filling my lips in with Underworld, which is exactly one tone lighter than the Burgundy I outlined them with.

"Isn't that a little young to be French kissing?"

To be honest, that first time, it was not really French kissing because all we did was touch tongues, but you've got to start somewhere. "You should always put the darker color on the outside and the lighter color on the inside," I tell her.

"Who says?"

"Everybody says."

"Why?"

"Hell, I don't know why. That's just the way you're supposed to do it."

"French kissing is so totally disgusting," Audrey says, brushing on a layer of Peach Glacé.

"I think it's sexy. You never French kissed? No? Tell me this. Have you ever even kissed regular?"

"Once. Last year I went to a make-out party with my best friend. I'm not allowed to go to parties, at least I wasn't last year; it hasn't come up so far this year. Anyway, last year, I wasn't allowed to go to boy/girl parties, so I lied and told my mom I was just staying over Lissa's house; that's my best friend from Santa Rosa. The party was stupid. For the longest time, we just stood around in the dark. Finally, this guy who I didn't even like, asked me to dance, and I knew he was going to kiss me. Like, you know how you just know?" She says and makes a face like something in the room smells funny.

"Yeah, it's like they just come up and start breathing on your neck. Why do they do that? It's like so not sexy."

"Anyway, I was real nervous, and I like forgot what I was supposed to do. So when he goes to kiss me, I kiss him the same way I kiss my mother, or something, and we kind of miss. Like I hit the corner or his mouth and he hit my nostril. And I couldn't help myself, I like kind of snorted."

"Ohmygod! He's kissing your nostril and you snorted?"

"Yeah, well, I couldn't help myself. It was funny and sometimes when I laugh, especially, when I'm nervous, I sort of laugh out of my nose or something and it comes out like a snort."

Now we're both laughing and for the first time I notice that when Audrey laughs, she does kind of snort, and I point this out.

"Ohmygod! That is like so gross! I'm snorting?"

"A little, but it's not bad. It's kind of cute."

"Really? You're lying."

"No, I'm not. It's kind of cute. So what happened when you finished snorting?"

"You mean at the party? Nothing happened. After that, nobody else asked me to dance, of course. I stood around in the dark for awhile, waiting for Lissa who was off somewhere making out. Finally, I got bored and walked home by myself. Told my mother Lissa's dad brought me home because she all of a sudden got the flu and was throwing up."

"So technically, you've never kissed anybody yet."

"Well, technically, yes. I kissed that guy at the party."

"That doesn't count."

"Okay, so technically, I've never kissed anyone. Do you think I'll have to kiss George at the mall?"

"Not if you don't want to."

"What if I want to?"

"Just don't snort."

"But I'll get all nervous. What if I miss again?"

"Just practice. Here," I say, handing her my magnified make-up mirror. "Pretend this is George."

"Hi George," she says giggling and snorting. "See, I'm going to snort."

"Quit that," I say, laughing. "Kissing is supposed to be all serious. Now close your eyes." She closes her eyes, but her lips are twitching at the corners. "Relax your lips. That's all you have to do. It's the dude's job to do the rest," I say, pushing the mirror until it's against her lips.

"Kissing a mirror is like so pathetic," she says, looking at the perfect pink imprint.

"Okay. Then you pretend I'm George."

"Like I'm going to kiss you?"

"Why not? It's just pretend. Close your eyes and think of George," I say, but she doesn't close her eyes. Our lips get closer and closer and our eyes are open until the last second.

"There. How was that?" I ask.

"Weird. How did it seem to you?"

"To be honest, you were kind of stiff, and you can't just let your arms hang limp at your sides. You got to put at least one arm somewhere, like on his shoulder or at the back of his neck. "Like this," I say, putting my hand on her shoulder. "And loosen up your lips. They've got to be like soft little pillows."

"Like this?" she says pooching out her lips a little.

"A little less pooch. There. That's good. Now, let's try it again." I cup the back of her head in my hand. She puts hers on my shoulder, and I tilt her chin up a little with my finger. We kiss, not just once, but three or four soft little kisses. Audrey's eyes are still closed. I kiss her again, longer this time, just like in the movies, except we're girls. I step back to see the effect. I've been told I'm a good kisser.

Audrey opens her eyes, blinks. "Well, now what?" she says.

"Well, now you're ready to try it out with George."

"What if he tries to French kiss me?"

"You want to practice that?"

"I guess we'd better."

"Okay, this time, you got to keep your lips relaxed and your mouth open just a little. Ready?"

"Ready," she says, closing her eyes. I look at that mouth, soft and pink, and realize how much I want to kiss her. Though it feels scary, that doesn't stop me from slipping my tongue between her teeth, letting my tongue play with hers. I only french kiss her once. Once is enough to make sure she knows how to do it, is what I tell her, but I stop because it feels as nice to kiss Audrey as it does to kiss Jesse and that is just too weird.

After our kissing lesson, Audrey asks me can she comb my hair. I sit in front of my vanity. Each time she draws the pick through my hair, I feel the tingles walk down my spine.

"Your hair is like, I don't know. Soft but crisp."

"My hair is nappy."

"Nappy then. Soft, crisp, and nappy," she says. Then she does something so totally weird. Puts her face right in my hair, breathes in deep. "Smells like butter," she says. "Melted butter."

"Melted butter, *café au lait*, I must be good enough to eat," I say, without thinking. But Audrey's so busy messing with my hair, she doesn't pay any attention. Thank God. Probably doesn't know what it means anyways, and I'm not going to be the first one who tells her about it, either.

* * *

It's funny how you think you want something and then when you get it, you want to get rid of it. That's what it was like with me and Jesse. He'd given me a necklace with a heart and a real diamond, so we were going steady. That meant every night I'd have to talk to him on the phone for like an hour or else he'd get pushed out of shape. I didn't think it would last much longer. So far, my record is five weeks, but that was when I was younger.

It didn't work out for Audrey and George either. At the mall they made out for about an hour, but he tried to put his hand up her shirt and she like freaked. It would never have lasted anyway, him being so short. In a way, she was lucky it was over so fast. At least she could watch TV without having to miss all the good parts because she had to be talking on the phone.

We don't talk about the night we practiced kissing, though I still think about it. I wonder if Audrey still thinks about it and if she does, what she thinks. What I liked about kissing her was that I was the one in control, like I was the one who decided when to start and when to stop and how far to put my tongue in, which was not very far because I know what it feels like when a boy practically pushes his tongue down your throat or bends your neck like it's made out of rubber.

Jesse was a good kisser though. If all we did was make out, it would have been cool, but we had to talk too, which was totally boring. But kissing Jesse made me hot, especially when he pressed his thing against me.

When I told Audrey about it, she said, "What do you mean, it makes you hot?"

"You know. Hot. Haven't you ever felt hot, down there, I mean?" Sometimes Audrey is like so dense. Anyway, I liked kissing Jesse, the way he made me feel, but it's like he thought he could put his hands on me just because he was my boyfriend.

Having a boyfriend is like walking a tightrope. You have to keep perfect balance between what you give and what you keep. Give too much and you're a ho; keep too much and you're a cold bitch. Lean too far either direction, you fall off the tightrope and the boy drops you.

But I don't worry about it too much. I've got it all figured out. In junior high I won't allow anything but French kissing, and if that's not enough to keep a boyfriend, then it's just too damn bad. It's not like there's a big prom or winter formal involved. Then, when I get to high school, I'll start my own five-year plan just like Mama. First year, first base. My boyfriend can touch my breasts over my shirt. Second year, second base. He can feel me up. Third year, he can feel me down. Fourth year, if we are going steady, my boyfriend can do anything but go all the way. By the fifth year, I'll be in college and dating only boys who are studying to be doctors or lawyers. I'll fall in love with one of them, and when we go all the way, he'll wear a condom until we get married, which will be the day after I graduate. I'll have a white satin and lace dress with a long train and white gloves that go above my elbows. Instead of a veil, there will be flowers in my hair, pink baby roses. My daddy will walk me down the aisle and everyone will say I'm the most beautiful bride they've ever seen.

* * *

This one time, I'm frying up some pork chops for dinner and Mama's setting the table. "Who's that boy keeps calling you on the phone?" she says.

"That's just some boy from school."

"Just some boy? He got a name?"

"Jesse Contreras. We're sort of going together."

"Those chops look done, Honey. Take them out and sprinkle a little flour over that grease. You kiss this Jesse Cardenas?"

"Contreras, Mama."

"Contreras, Cardenas, I'm just asking. No harm in asking," she says leaning over my frying pan. "He put his tongue in your mouth?"

"Mama!"

"I take that to be a yes." She's at my elbow sprinkling pepper over my hot grease and flour. "Add that milk real slow or the gravy will turn out lumpy."

"I know. I know. You act like I never made gravy before."

"So you like it when he puts his tongue in your mouth?"

"Yes, I like it if you really think it's any of your business."

"Everything that happens to you is my business. Besides, there's nothing wrong with liking to French kiss. No need to get your nose all out of joint, missy."

"My nose is not all out of joint."

"Whatever you say. No skin off my behind. You want me to put those chops in with the biscuits to keep warm while you work those lumps out of the gravy?"

I'm smashing the lumps with a fork and wondering why she always has to be so right and so nosy, and I am pissed at her and the gravy both.

She slips the chops into the oven. "Trouble with boys . . . Oh, never mind."

"What were you going to say?"

"Never mind. I can tell by the way you're mashing those lumps clean into oblivion, you won't listen anyways."

I stop mashing and add a little more milk, real slow this time. "I think it's rude not to finish a sentence."

"Rude, is it?"

"Yes it is."

"Well, la de da. Caught in the act of rudeness by Miss Manners. Okay. I don't want to be a rude on top of nosy. What I was going to say is the trouble with boys—alls they want is sex."

"Not all boys," I say, still mashing.

"All boys. Every last one of them, born-again Christian or heathen, shy or bold, only one thing on their minds and that is how they're going to get you to spread your legs and let them in. Oh, they will work you every which way. Make all kinds of promises and threats to trap you into it too."

"What about my daddy, then? Was that all he wanted?" I say, thinking that should shut her up.

"Your daddy was a man not a boy," she says. "That's why I chose him be your daddy. He was different."

"How was he different?"

"He wanted to love and take care of me, which is its own kind of trap."

"What do you mean?"

"Independence is like a muscle you have to develop and keep on exercising. When you let a man take care of you, your independence muscle gets all weak and flabby. Makes it hard on you when you've got to take care of yourself again. Don't make my mistake, Baby. Always keep that independence muscle strong in case of emergency."

"But I'm dependent on you."

"That's different. I'm your mama. You can always depend on me. Got that, little Miss Manners? I will always love you to death no matter what."

"Even if I commit some horrible crime?"

"Even if. How's that gravy coming along?"

"Can't get the lumps out."

"Well, a few lumps in the gravy never hurt," she says.

We sit down to eat and Mama acts like she can't get enough of my pork chops and gravy, even though the meat is tough from being too long in the oven and the gravy is not only lumpy, but gooey.

I guess she meant it when she says she'll love me no matter what, because that dinner was some kind of crime. Still, Mama's wrong when she says a boy only wants one thing. A boy wants at least two things I can think of: to put his penis in a girl's vagina and to bore her to death on the phone.

LESLIE

It was one of those evenings that follows rain here, the air cool, heavy, smelling of wet asphalt and, under that, some mysterious desert tang. The girls are out shooting hoops again and Eden and I are splitting a second beer. She's telling me about some five-year plan. I'm only half listening when I hear her say, ". . . of course I'll have to go back to school."

"Back to school?" That would be great," I say, remembering that school was one of the things I traded away for a life with Frank. "I was studying to be a teacher when I quit." I take a sip of beer and pass the can to Eden. "But all those years with Frank, I was just a stay-at-home mom."

"Nothing wrong with that, but I bet you wish you'd finished college."

"Only a hundred times in the last month. Frank insisted I stay home when the girls were young. Then I became, I don't know, dependent on it, I guess, until the thought of doing anything else with my life just got scarier and scarier."

"Oh right. It didn't have anything to do with your husband pounding on you and calling you stupid and ignorant every day of the week."

"Sure Frank had a hand in it, but I can't blame it all on him. I made it easy for Frank to talk me out of it. It had been so long since I'd done anything on my own, it was hard to believe I still could."

Eden hands me the beer. "Guess there's some security in the notion that change is impossible."

"That's so true, it's not funny. In fact, it makes me kind of sick to think about it, especially when I consider the effect it's had on my girls."

"You're too hard on yourself; they seem okay. They'll get over it."

"You think? I don't think I will."

"Look. You did a very brave thing. Change is scary. Believe it. You got out, and that's what's important. Plus you got a job."

"Yeah, my so-called job. Still, it was hardly even me doing all that. More like I'd invented this robot who did all the work and just dragged me and the girls along behind. What's that expression?"

"Necessity is a mother?"

"That's better than the one I was thinking of. Necessity *is* a mother. Did I tell you the other day I came home from work, Audrey had started her period, the first one, and Sammy had a couple of half-dead baby pigeons in the oven?"

Eden reaches out and pats my hand. "You told me. Things will get better, Leslie. Like I keep saying, you just got to make a plan and stick to it. The best days are yet to come."

"Right," I say, offering the can, but I am not convinced.

"Go ahead and kill it. I'm fixin' to go to work."

She groans, gets up. and is gone.

I heft the can—it's still half full—and I'm thinking about this new life of mine. Is it actually better? Not much, but at least we're safe. That's what I remember thinking at the time. At least we are safe.

* * *

The day of the pigeon fiasco I thought I'd hit bottom. Little did I know, I still had a long way to go.

Being a mother was . . . is everything to me. It's what I've pinned my worth on for nearly fourteen years. When the girls were little, I'd read to them every night, every night unless Frank needed me to do something important, like watch him eat a late supper. As they got older, especially when Frank was home, we'd squirrel ourselves away, the three of us on Audrey's bed, and read. I'd be lost in some classic, *The Great Gadsby, Anna Karenina*. Audrey would be pouring over a magazine, *Seventeen* most likely. For Sammy it would be some fantasy. Actually, it was fantasy for me too, thinking I was being the best mother, figuring if I could do nothing else,

I would always be there for my daughters. The afternoon of the pigeons I hadn't been and I felt worthless.

Sammy's crying over those pathetic baby birds—had I been there, they'd still be in the nest—and Audrey's sulking in her bedroom.

I squeeze Sammy's shoulder. "Things will be okay."

"Do you think the baby pigeons are going to die?"

For what seems like the millionth time, I tell her I don't know. "You know how it is with baby birds. At least they'll be warm. They won't suffer." Sammy nods, but tears still slide down her face. "I need to see how Audrey is feeling," I say, wiping one away with my thumb.

Audrey's lying across the bed, arm slung over her eyes. "Congratulations." I say. "I'm sorry I wasn't here, Sweetie."

"It's okay. I dealt with it."

She sounds congested and I know she's been crying too. "Sure you did. It's just that I wanted to take care of you. Your first period's kind of a big deal." I smooth her hair, feel its slightly oily weight and the heat from her scalp under my hand. "How are you feeling? Did you take some Midol?"

"It made me throw up."

"Maybe with some milk."

"It would make me puke."

"Okay. So would you like me to rub your back?" She rolls onto her stomach and I begin to massage low along her spine, happy to find something to make it better.

"Mom?"

"Sweetie?"

"You're going to be angry."

"Probably not. Want to tell me about it?" I say.

"I told Sammy about Missy and the kittens."

"Audrey, we were going to keep that a secret. You know how Sammy feels about her animals. Look how upset she is about the pigeons."

"I know. I didn't mean to. It's just that she kept whining about wanting to go back to Dad. At some point, Mother, she's going to have to deal with the whole dad thing."

"I can hardly deal with the dad thing. How do you expect her to deal with it?"

"I knew you were going to be mad."

"I'm not mad. It's just . . . Sammy's still such a baby."

"I know. I'm sorry. I didn't tell her everything, not the worst part. She didn't believe me anyway."

I lean over, kiss her ear, breathe in the nutty scent I associate more with unwashed child than young womanhood, and I'm reminded that Audrey is still a child too, despite her claimed ability to *deal with it*. "Things will be okay," I tell her.

What else could I have possibly said? Should I have shared with her my own sense of loss and failure, my uncertainty? Sometimes I can fool myself into thinking that we're all in this together, my daughters and I, like partners. But I'm supposed to be the adult, the one they can depend on to tell them everything's going to be okay. Aren't I?

* * *

Five days a week, I take the bus to and from work. I spend some ninety minutes waiting and riding. On the bus my mind easily slips into some dreamy place of childhood recollections and fantasies, not only about the future, but the past as well. Sometimes I think of nothing at all and arrive at my stop wondering how I got there.

Once I tried to determine the events that started us, my girls and me, on this course through hell. I searched through childhood memories, finding only a little girl doing what little girls do. Remembered summer afternoons under the giant sequoia tree in our back yard, sitting in the dense shade of its fringed branches, the ground cool even on the hottest days, the smell of damp earth.

Was I alone under that tree? No, Andrea, my little sister, was there, helping me dig up the ingredients for my mud pastries, patting out cookies, pies and cakes with rose petal fillings. Maybe I encouraged my baby sister to sample a doughnut of mud, sip an earthworm from between my fingers. Kid stuff.

Junior high? I was unexceptional—a chubby hard worker without special talent, I recall trying to make up for my lack of luster by being nice, helpful, a good listener. Nothing wrong with that. Those traits were the ones most valued by my father and mother.

Estrangement came later. One morning when I was sixteen I came into the kitchen for breakfast, and my mother whispered, "Your dad's gotten up on the wrong side of the bed," code for stay out of his way. In her rush to anticipate his every need, she spilled coffee on his suit, just back from the cleaners. Instantly, she was mopping at his jacket. He slapped her hand away, then twisted in his chair, fist balled so tight his knuckles went white. That's when I stepped in front of my mother, daring my father to hit me instead— a first. Usually, I just stood back and watched, then left the room.

I did not become the hero of the hour that morning, not that my father hit me. It would have been easier if he had. Instead, he stared at me as if I'd just committed some lewd act, exposed my breasts or mooned him, then turned away as if I'd ceased to exist.

Now I can imagine why he turned away, can imagine shame and guilt turned inside out and backwards until it wasn't his but mine. But back then, I was a lot like Sammy. I loved my father, needed his recognition and praise. When I resisted him, I ceased to exist. How many lessons did it take me to learn not to resist? And my mother? That morning her silence was a most eloquent statement.

So instead of openly resisting him, I began sneaking out at night to meet boys, to drink beer or vodka mixed with anything sweet, Gatorade, if necessary. These escapades, and the joint I was caught smoking in the bathroom at school, became the focus of my parent's disenchantment with me. But in my heart, I know the pivot point was that first time, the only time I humiliated my parents by acting like something might be wrong with his abuse and her passivity.

Despite my parents' predictions that I'd never even graduate from high school, I did and started college, mainly because I needed to show that my father was wrong about me. I was doing well, too, until I met Frank. But even after I got pregnant, I wanted to finish school, if only to prove that I could. So several months after Audrey was born, I told Frank about my intentions.

"What?" He had said. "You going to make a great contribution to society, be a doctor, a brain surgeon maybe? Come on, Les. Get real."

"I want to finish and get a good job. I could still be a teacher. That way I'd have . . . "

"A teacher? Who'd hire you? Look at you. Your ass is broader than the chair you're sitting in, and when was the last time you washed your hair?"

I touch my hair. I couldn't remember if I'd washed it yesterday or the day before, but the last time I'd been to the doctor, I'd weighed 118, only eight pounds more than when I first got pregnant. "My doctor says I'm doing okay with my weight."

"Well maybe your doctor can get a hard-on sticking his finger up your cunt, but all that fat on your butt turns me off."

At this point I go into the bedroom, lock the door, and start to cry. I can hear the television in the living room, imagine Frank in there drinking beer and watching a ball game. But pretty soon he's knocking on the door, then pounding. I hear Audrey crying so I open up.

"Look," he says. "I just want what's best for you and the baby. You don't need to work. Don't I make enough money?"

"I have to get the baby," I say.

He blocks the door with his arm, yells, "I said, don't I make enough fucking money?"

"Yes . . . but . . ."

"Yes but what?"

"I want to finish school. Want to prove something to my father."

"Like what?"

"Prove that I'm smart enough, good enough. I don't know."

"Forget your father. I'm here now. It's me you got to prove things to."

Audrey is screaming now. I just want to end the argument so I can go to her, but I can't think of anything to say that will make him see how much he's hurt me, make his face soften, make him move away from the door.

"Well?"

At that moment, I realize how much Frank is like my father. It occurs to me to gather up Audrey and leave. But where would I go? Not home, that's for sure. There is no place to go, and I am fat and suddenly so tired. My hair is dirty and what's the point of getting a degree. Who would hire me? Besides, Frank's taking care of everything. "You're right," I say at last.

His face relaxes then. It's almost comical how quickly those magic words work. "Look," he says. "Forget this going back to school. Instead, I'll get you a membership to a gym. A few hours a week at the gym, pretty soon you'll have your beautiful body back."

He lowers his arm so I can pass. As I do, he grabs my arm, holding me too tight as he kisses my neck. "Listen, Les. I didn't mean all those things. I love you. You know that. I just want you home with the baby. Just you, me, and the baby, that's all I want.

And that's what he got. Frank always got what he wanted.

Always plenty of time on the bus to think, pick though my life with Frank for that single moment I can point to, like a line drawn in the sand, that once crossed changed my marriage from one I could still hold out hope for, to one I must abandon. But my marriage evolved slowly, it seems, from one kind of animal into another. Picture a cat say, which might scratch, but is also capable of affection and warmth, changing cell by cell into a badger.

In the last years of our marriage, those years Frank started using cocaine, even the sex evolved from one kind of animal to another. What was once an act of love and comfort, a reward for being a good and docile wife, gradually became increasingly aggressive, until it was more hostile invasion than sex.

One particular instance stands out in my mind. The girls were watching TV in the living room. They must have been about eight and eleven at the time. Frank and I were in the kitchen. I would say we were arguing, but that's not it exactly. Frank was berating me about something, maybe the way I had ironed the crease in his pants. I was loading the dishwasher, trying my best not to listen to him, which of course, was a provocative thing to do. Frank always wanted my full attention.

So he comes up behind me. "You're not listening," he says, twisting my hair a little. And this is such a turn-on, he twists harder.

"What you're doing is so important that you can't listen? I'll give you something important to do!" His hand is on top of my head, forcing me down to my knees, and I'm momentarily confused, thinking he's trying to make me pray. You can't force somebody to pray, I'm thinking. But then I hear him popping the buttons on his Levis and I know this will not be as easy as praying.

When he finishes with his business, I feel sick and light-headed, not just because he forced me to do something I've willingly done countless times. But the girls, my babies, are watching television in the next room, and I'm thinking, what if they had wanted a glass of water or a cookie? How could he risk that?

It isn't until much later, two, three years really, that I figure out there isn't any risk involved as far as he's concerned. If the girls are in the next room or the same room and the urge comes over him to punch or kick me, or force sex on me, it makes no difference. I am an object lesson. They are in training to become me.

Yet I stayed. Fifteen years, Jesus. Years spent trying to get back to that person who could be so gentle and tender, convinced that if I just loved him enough, was a good and dutiful wife, that the angry, jealous, dangerous man would go away and the one I loved would return. He did from time to time, just often enough to keep me on the hook. And I was afraid of failure. This marriage was the only thing I'd ever done right, according to my father. If I failed, I'd be exactly what he always said I was—worthless.

I'm pretty clear about what kept me in that marriage, but I don't know what happened to make Frank the man he was. Drugs happened, yes, but they were more like accomplices after the crime. Deep down, was he just a scared little boy? I suggested this to Eden once. "Oh please, don't make me toss my cookies," was her reaction. I liked that, smile every time I think about it.

One thing I can say, they were effective teachers, Frank and my father. As I said, I was a good listener, and I learned my lessons well. I just pray it isn't too late for my girls to learn different lessons. Sammy tells me Dee writes her prayers down and drops them in a special God box. Maybe I should write my prayer down and put it in that box.

* * *

My mind does wander when I ride the bus. I think of old friends, wonder what happened to them. After I married Frank, I had only the polite, slightly prim friendships I developed with my fellow stay-at-home moms in the neighborhood—women I could keep at arm's length. Now I marvel at the friends we have here, the girls and I. At the Oasis, there's no need for pretense.

As Dee would say, you got to laugh. My sensible, plainspoken Audrey is best friends with Chablee, extravagant and flashy as a diamond. Tiny Sammy keeps company with a grown woman who towers over her like a grain silo. And I, so modest I prefer to undress in the dark, find my sanity in Eden who dances nearly naked under a spotlight. What is it we share that allows such intimate and unlikely friendships to blossom? There must be something basic we have in common besides this wreck of a motor court, but I can't say what it is. I do know that my life has gone from endangered to surreal.

One time I'm staring out the window of the bus, and there's a lot of jostling in the next seat as a woman gets settled in. I look up, and am surprised to find I know her from somewhere. But where, I'm thinking. And then it hits me. It's the woman with the Big Gulp. She's rustling though a great big bag. Takes a lipstick, applies an even coat of red. She's not talking to the Big Gulp now. In fact, her appearance is neat, her behavior sane and orderly. From her bag, she takes a big, hardbound book, looks to be a romance, and begins to read. Has she recovered her senses? Perhaps she'd never lost them, I think, and regret that ten dollars I gave her, my daughters' allowance, my hard-earned money. Still, I have to ask myself, is it more taxing to sit in a cubicle talking into a mouthpiece for a living than it is to sit at a bus stop talking into a Big Gulp? Is there a difference?

* * *

Eden and I were at the Laundromat one Saturday afternoon. All the dryers were in use and so we had to wait. When you're poor you're used to waiting. Waiting for the washer to finish so you can load the dryer, waiting for the dryer, waiting for the bus to take you home, waiting for the check so you can shop for groceries. There is no end to the waiting. It's been one of the hardest things for me to accept.

I don't share these unhappy observations with Eden. Besides I'm lucky because we're here together and the waiting is not so tedious. Eden begins to tell me how she came to live "down in the dumps," as she puts it.

"Let me guess," I say. "It all started with Chablee's father."

"You ought to get you a job as one of those psychics. Get you a little crystal ball and a bandana."

I laugh. "Right. I'm one of those women who already know how everything's going to turn out. Tell me about it anyway."

"You got all afternoon? It's one of those long boring stories."

"Boring being a code word for disaster?"

"Yeah. Right along with stupid, interesting, and. . . .

"And love?"

"No, I don't think love is necessarily a disaster. I was going to say lucky, as in lucky I didn't get killed or wind up in prison, or have my baby taken from me by Child Protective Services. Came close to all that. Was lucky to just end up unemployed and homeless with a child. Anyways, Chablee's daddy, Mukisa Abdule Muhammad, Pretty Boy, My Big Nasty for short, lordy, how I loved that man. We met at JJ's. You know the routine. What's a sweet young thing like you doing in a place like this?"

"Really?"

"Close enough. Was only nineteen. Muki wasn't like any of the other regulars. Didn't drink or smoke, no drugs—not even caffeine. At the time, it didn't occur to me to ask what a nice man like him was doing in a place like JJ's, you know? When I finally got that one figured out, I was already too far gone to do anything about it."

"What was he doing in JJ's?"

"Selling cocaine and heroin, the more lucrative drugs."

"I thought you said he didn't do drugs."

"He didn't. Just sold them. His idea of political activism."

"I don't get it."

"See, by the time we met, Muki had become a Muslim. Before that, he was a born-again, same as me; at least that's what I was raised up into. The first time he went to prison was for possession with intent. He'd been selling crack to support his own habit. While he was over at Fort Grant, he started reading a little history, a few of those Black Muslim dudes, Elijah Muhammad and I don't know who all else. Anyway, he joined the Black Muslims in prison, started calling himself Mukisa. Bought into this notion that there's a CIA conspiracy to keep black men down by flooding their neighborhoods with drugs."

"Do you believe that?" I ask.

Eden shrugs her shoulders. "Made sense to Muki. It's possible. For a fact, the FBI are bastards—all those government dudes with their three little initials are bastards, if you ask me. Anyway, when he got out of Fort Grant, he decided he'd do what he could to turn the tables on 'em. See, Muki had an exclusively white clientele. Course, I didn't know any of this at first. He told me he worked as a car salesman for Bill Breck Dodge. Gave me his cell phone number as if that was proof. He had money, that's all I knew and he was good to me. Beyond that, I didn't pay much attention. I was young and stupid, but I thought I was smart and sophisticated. Talk about code words for disaster."

"After Chablee was born, Muki bought me a house, nothing fancy, just a nice little two bedroom with a back yard and trees and a little patch of grass for Chablee to play on. Bought me a car too, brand new Jetta, bright red. Man, I loved that car. He bought me a diamond ring. Two carats. It was like an engagement ring."

"So you got married?"

"Muki marry a white woman? No way, Honey. Besides he already had a wife and three almost grown boys. Told me all about them right from the beginning. I was just like a side thing, you know? But he loved me. That I never doubted. And he'd spend the night with us maybe two, three times a week. Oh and I was quite the little homemaker. Just loved all that domestic shit, cooked his favorites. Muki loved Italian. Bought me three Italian cookbooks and a pasta machine so I could make his fettuccini from scratch. I got to be a regular what's-her-name."

"Julia Child?"

"Hell girl, I was Julia Child, Martha Stewart and what's that one with the big mouth was in *Pretty Woman*? You know, what's her name. Doesn't matter. I was all three rolled into one. Plus Muki decked Chablee out like a little princess. Me too. He liked us to look special when he visited. And that's the way he made us feel. Special. Chablee was crazy about her daddy, and he was so proud of her; thought she was so smart and beautiful. He even paid for her to take ballet lessons. Three years old, so cute in her little old tutu."

"Once you told me you had to make a choice between Chablee and her father. What was that about?"

Eden raises one perfect, slim eyebrow. "Was about somebody shooting out the living room window. Glass shattering everywhere. Muki's head was cut so bad he needed twelve stitches. Could have been Chablee's face. She'd been sleeping across our laps. After that, I asked him couldn't we go away just the three of us; start a new life someplace else, no drugs. But he wouldn't do it. I know he felt an obligation to his other family; that's how Muki was. But mostly he just couldn't leave the life; part was the money, but part was the revenge, I think. Muki hated white folks. Every one of them, except me."

Eden is pulling on a curl of hair, examining the tips where the color changes from brown to cinnamon. "After that, I told him not to come to the house anymore," she says. "Decided Chablee had to come first."

"Must have been a tough decision."

"Not so tough. It was like I'd been given this child to love and protect. Like I had this one chance to make it all up to myself for what my mama did and didn't do by being a good mama to my own child. Wasn't about to take any chances on Chablee getting hurt. She was my baby. You know? Got to have your priorities straight."

"That's how it should be," I say, wishing I'd straightened out mine years ago. But it seems a person who establishes priorities, one who makes plans, has to believe in the future. I have trouble seeing us in a better place somewhere down the line. I'm too exhausted by the present, too undone by the past. Stuck.

Eden tucks the strand of hair behind her ear and continues. "We still got together. Might sometimes meet in the park or at

McDonald's. Sometimes was just Muki and me, but it wasn't the same. Wasn't like mama and daddy and baby makes three. You know? More like a one-night stand in some motel. Didn't matter how expensive the room was, it always felt cheap after what we'd had before."

"So what happened to the nice little house?"

"Condemned by the Feds after Muki was convicted. The house, car, furniture, bank account, clothes, and my diamond ring were all provided with drug money."

"They left you homeless?"

"Told you those guys are bastards. Asked them, 'Why are you doing this to us? Me and my baby never committed any crime.' This one dude just looks from me to Chablee, and I understood that in his eyes, I had committed a crime. I'm from the South. I know that look. The other guy at least offered us a ride. Had nowheres to go, so he dropped us off at a woman's shelter. Yup. Stayed there as long as I could, then went back to JJ's. He gave me an advance. Fifty bucks, the cheap son of a bitch. On a good night, I make more for the club in ten minutes. So we moved into the Oasis. Was Dee who let that first week's rent slide."

"Anyways, that's how we came to live Down in the Dumps. Now it almost feels like home-sweet-home, Right? Oh well, could have been worse. At least we got to keep the clothes. Still got the dress Muki bought Chablee for her sixth birthday, all tucks and ribbon roses. Saved it so Chablee could one day give it to her own little girl, say it was from her granddaddy. Sold the rest."

"So how long has Muki been in prison?"

"Well, Chablee was seven. What's that? Six years. A long time. Got a long time ahead of him too. They said he killed somebody, but I never believed that."

"Do you still miss him?"

"Every damn day."

I nod, thinking how hard it is to let go of the ones who have helped ruin us. That's another thing Eden and I have in common.

* * *

Back from the Laundromat, folding clothes at my place. Just then the cooler starts to clack. The clacking is so loud and so fast, I'm afraid it's going to clack itself right off the roof. "What the hell's happening up there?" I ask, eyeing the ceiling.

"Squirrel cage," Eden says.

"What?"

"The squirrel cage in the cooler is wobbling. Got to go up on the roof and fix it or it will drive you seriously nuts."

"Get up on the roof? Can't I just ask Dee to have it fixed?"

"Can ask. She'll call the landlord who lives in Scottsdale. . . ."

"Scottsdale?"

"Up near Phoenix where the rich and the powerful live. Sort of like Oz, Scottsdale, but not quite as green. Anyways, old Dee will call him and he'll see to it the next time he comes to town, which will be sometime after you need the furnace turned on. Best fix it your own self. It's not so hard. Let me get my hammer."

It's much cooler on the roof than on the ground. The sun hanging low outlines each palm frond in a kind of golden shimmer. From the roof you can see the mountains that surround Tucson on every side. The slanting light brings out reds and a depth I've never appreciated before. Pretty, I'm thinking. Eden lifts off the side of the cooler, takes the hammer, and wacks the squirrel cage where it's knocking against the casing.

"Sometimes you got to oil the bearings on the motor, but usually all you got to do is bend this little old thingy out right here. Nothing to it," she says, with this air of competency that contrasts sharply to the acrylic fingernails, puffy hair, and hard make-up. Once again, I am amazed and envious. "Where'd you learn how to fix a cooler?"

"Jack showed me."

"You mean the wino that lives in Unit 5?"

"Well, yeah. He drinks a bit, but man, is he handy."

Back down in my apartment, the clacking in the cooler is gone, leaving just the constant croopy sigh, which is normal. When I apologize for being such a needy friend, Eden says. "Sure, friends can be a lot of trouble, but without a little trouble, life gets tedious."

I look around my apartment, dank and moldy from running the cooler twenty-four hours a day, dirty dishes in the sink, clothes piled on the back of a chair waiting to be ironed, and I think life gets tedious anyway.

Sam

People around here call the summer rains monsoons. The word makes me think of some place with banana trees and tropical flowers hanging from vines instead of a desert covered with asphalt. But everybody goes around saying, wait until the monsoons come, and oh the monsoons this and the monsoons that, and lala lala, as if it's this very big fabulous deal. I guess it is, if your idea of fabulous is a lot of thunder and lightning, yellow dust, pounding wind, and buckets of rain. Sometimes it rains so hard the streets flood and you practically need a kayak to get across. This is not exactly my idea of fun, especially if you don't even own a car, and you're walking down the street carrying two bags of groceries, and a stupid SUV whizzes by, and you get soaked right through the hefty trash bag you're wearing because nobody thought you'd ever need a raincoat in the desert so you didn't pack one when you left Santa Rosa.

One good thing about those monsoons, they cooled everything down a little, and when it wasn't threatening rain, we went back to the cemetery for our picnics. It was a relief to have someplace to go again after being cooped up by the heat. Unlike the Oasis Apartments, the cemetery wasn't paved over with asphalt or crawling with hos, winos, and drug addicts.

So this one afternoon we're just sitting under our favorite pine tree, sipping Cokes and munching chips. The breeze is making the tree tops swish like brooms. Chablee is studying the zit on her forehead in the magnifying mirror, which she keeps in her purse at all times. It is the only zit on her entire body and it is underneath her bangs where no one can see it.

"Oh yuck," Chablee says. "Zits are like so totally disgusting."

And I am thinking this is not a very sensitive comment to make in front of Audrey. Her face has been looking like a pepperoni pizza ever since she had her first period.

We've been discussing the best features of our favorite movie stars. At least Audrey and Chablee are having this discussion. Mostly I'm just lying there listening to the birds squawking and whistling in the trees, which is almost the same thing as listening to Audrey and Chablee. "Justin Eastlake's best feature is his smile," says Audrey and lala lala la. Who cares? I am thinking about Eddie, how I'd like to talk about his best feature, which is his voice. It is deep and soft and kind, and I think I just might bring it up when Chablee, who has been making goo goo eyes at her own reflection, says, "So, Audrey, what's your best feature?" It is obvious she really just wants to talk about her own great features, but Audrey joins right in, like she has already given it a lot of serious thought, and she probably has since she spends most of the day in front of the mirror picking her zits. "My hands," she says. And I admit they are looking better since she stopped biting her nails, which are currently polished in a glittery navy blue, but her cuticles are still raggedy and red.

"Yeah, you've got good hands," Chablee agrees, because Chablee and Audrey are always agreeing with each other. She takes one of Audrey's hands between her two light brown ones and examines it as if she's getting ready to read her palm. "But I really think your best feature is your hair."

Audrey is touching her hair. "Really?" she says. "My hair?"

Well, Duh! It's like Audrey picked hands, even though they are no way her best feature, just so Chablee would tell her how nice her hair is. Now it's like she gets two best features instead of one and I don't have any, since hands are my best feature because I don't bite my nails or my cuticles. But now that feature is taken, so I have to think of something else, which I have plenty of time to do, while Chablee goes on and on about her own best feature, which is her figure, or maybe it's her complexion, or is it her eyes. She can't decide.

In my head I list my features. I start with my feet, which are too big for my height. My legs are too thin. Forget my chest. My hair is limp, my eyes are just your basic pale blue nothing eyes, and the same goes for the rest of my face—not ugly particularly, just a nothing face. "I have no cavities," I say.

Audrey and Chablee look at me as if I just said pink kangaroos are falling from the sky.

"My teeth," I add. "They're my best feature." I open my mouth so they can see for themselves how nearly straight and cavity-free they are.

Chablee just goes back to the fascinating topic of Chablee, with Audrey hanging on every word. "Red is definitely your power color," she is now telling Audrey.

Audrey looks best in blue because it makes her eyes look bluer. I'm the one who looks good in red so it should be my power color. Of course, I can't say this, so I just lie back in the grass and concentrate on how the very tips of the pine trees sway as if they're waving bye-bye to each cloud as it floats past. I take a deep breath. The air smells like warm grass and the dust that's left on the rag after mom has wiped every surface with Lemon Pledge. That was back in Santa Rosa. Here we don't have enough surfaces to bother with Pledge. But I don't say any of this either. Chablee and Audrey don't care about things like how the air smells. Basically they don't care about anything or anyone that doesn't start with the letter C or the letter A.

But I have Eddie to think about, and it really doesn't bother me anymore what Chablee and Audrey do or say. Someday, when I'm fifteen and Eddie and I are allowed to date, I might tell them all about it. I smile. Won't they be surprised when they find out that Eddie the fox chose me, instead of Miss Big Boobs. Won't they be surprised that I kept it a secret from everyone for so many years.

* * *

I knock on Dee's screen door again. The swamp cooler's chugging and dripping at the window so I figure she must be home. Finally I mastered the two-deck shuffle, and I've been wanting to show her, but she hasn't been home. She opens the door, wiping sweat from her face, and the smell of butterscotch brownies hits me and I realize I'm hungry.

"Bless your heart, Samantha. Come on in; we're letting all the nice cool air out."

It's supposed to be a joke, but it isn't very funny. It's almost as hot inside as out these days. Come to find out, swamp coolers don't work when it's humid. All week the hot air's been trapped under a thick layer of grey and everybody just walks around, half-dead, sweat rolling. It's pretty gross, actually.

"Where have you been?" I ask. "I have something to show you."

"Right here, like always." she says.

"Yesterday, I came by twice. When I knocked, nobody answered."

"I was home all day. Yesterday was Tuesday, right?"

"Yesterday was Wednesday."

Dee looks up at the ceiling for about an hour, her lips moving as though she's consulting her own private secretary. Finally, she answers. "That's right, I forgot. We had an appointment with the doctor. Was that yesterday or the day before? Well, time's fun when it flies, I guess."

Dee forgets a lot, but I don't let it bother me. It's just one of those Dee things.

I check out today's refrigerator message. "Let nothing disturb or frighten you. Everything passes away except God." I have to think about that for awhile. At first, I am encouraged that everything that disturbs or frightens me will pass away. But then I think, what about all the things in the world that aren't disturbing or frightening? What about the trees and grass and animals? What about all the humanitarians? Will they just pass away? And if only God is left, what is the point? This is a disturbing and frightening thought. I take it with me to the God Box. Dee doesn't seem to mind my browsing through it. I read the latest prayers. There is one written in tight, neat print. I recognize this as the writing of the one I call Cool Dee. *Dear God, Remind Dee to buy three or four frozen peperoni pizzas.* And one written in Little Dee's messy pink crayon that says *Dear God, plese keep me form think.* A third one is written in small, scrunched-up cursive. *Dear God, Tell Michael I love him.*

I refold each prayer and pick up the gold charm, running my finger lightly over the name, Michael. Turning it over, I examine the date again, 5/14/75, and wonder, like always, what it's all about. If Dee wants God to talk to him, does this mean Michael is dead? Did he die in 1975? Who is Michael?

Dee comes in and hands me two butterscotch brownies wrapped in a paper napkin. They are still warm and I feel the butter seeping though the napkin onto my palm. I take a bite of brownie and contemplate the date on the charm. If I knew Dee's age it would help. "My mother was born in 1967," I say.

"1967?" she says.

"What were you doing in 1967." I ask.

"I have no idea," she answers.

"My Mom's thirty-four."

Dee nods. "That so?"

"She was twenty years old when Audrey was born."

"Well, I guess that's old enough to be a mother."

Dee just stares at me and finally I just ask straight out. "So how old are you, anyway? I was just wondering, though it's really none of my business."

"Is that what you were trying to get at?" Dee asks with a smile. "Well I'm forty years old."

"Forty? You look more like thirty-eight," I say. "So in 1975 you were . . . fifteen."

"That's right," she says, her smile fading as she picks up the charm.

"So who's Michael?" I ask, trying to make my voice sound casual, like it's no big deal. "Your husband?"

Dee is polishing the charm on the sleeve of her dress. "I've never been married."

"So who is he? Or maybe you don't want to talk about it," I say suddenly losing my determination to know. "I mean, if it's a painful subject. . . ."

"It is a painful subject," she says, still polishing. "Michael was my baby."

"Well, where is he? What happened to him?"

Dee just shakes her head. "Taken away."

"Taken away? Why? Where?"

"What made you ask about Michael?"

"Well, you put this prayer in the box." I pick through the folded notes; hand her the one with the prayer for Michael. Dee studies it like it's written in secret code, and I am really sorry now that I didn't mind my own business, because her eyes are filling with tears.

"Samantha, Honey, what was it you wanted to show me?" she asks.

"My shuffle. I can do both decks now."

"Well, that's just fine," she says, turning her bracelets, but I can tell she isn't that impressed.

"Listen, Samantha. I'm not feeling so good right now. Why don't you take those brownies. Come back later, tomorrow maybe, then I can see your shuffle."

"Okay. Thanks," I say, my voice sounding rusty in my ears.

Dee nods her head, but I don't think she even heard me. I want to tell her I'm sorry for being so nosy, but I'm afraid it would come out of my mouth sounding wrong, so I just take the brownies and leave, though I've lost my appetite.

I go out to the shed for the rake so I can clean the cactus garden out front, even though it's mid-morning and too hot to be picking Styrofoam and plastic bags from the spines. But I want to do this for Dee to show I care, that I'm not a just a nosy little girl.

The mama pigeon has built another nest in the shed, and I have been trying to make things up to her by feeding her bread-crumbs. When I open the door, she twists her head in my direction, and the feathers around her neck change from gray to a shiny violet-green. "I brought you something special," I say and scatter part of a brownie over the dirt floor. The pigeon, I've named her Gurt, coos and bobs her head, but doesn't leave the ledge. I sit on the bucket and wait for her to come down to eat, figuring I'll hang out with her for awhile. I think she's forgotten that I killed her babies. I don't want to think about Gurt's babies, especially now that I've just hurt Dee too. Though I didn't do it intentionally, if actions speak louder than words, they speak louder than intentions too, I guess. My eyes are burning, and I am ashamed because I'm feeling sorrier for myself than for Dee or Gurt, and that's not right because what could be worse than losing your babies? I try to focus on that, but my thoughts keep slipping back to me and the hurtful things I do, even though I don't mean to. I hate myself. I don't want to be a spoiled, selfish person, like some people whose names I won't mention. I want to be a humanitarian.

This is what I am thinking when I hear the shed door open. I turn, and Eddie is standing there as if I just rubbed Aladdin's lamp.

"Hey, Sam?" How's it going?"

"Eddie!" I say, wanting to run into his arms, like I've been dreaming about doing. Of course I don't. One, because I just can't. And two, because it would make me cry. Instead, I ask him where he's been.

"I've been around," he says. "Sometimes I see you and your friends, but you guys always look busy, so I just keep my distance. Then I saw you come in here. You were by yourself, and I'm thinking, Sam sure looks lonely; bet she could use some company. So, what are you doing?

"I came in to feed my pigeon," I say, even though this is sort of a lie. I can't tell Eddie I'm just hanging out. What kind of stupid loser would hang out in a storage shed with a pigeon? "Her name is Gurt," I add, as if that makes it all perfectly cool.

"Gurt, huh? So what do you feed her?" he says, moving closer.

"Old hot dog buns or sometimes cereal. She likes Cheerios. Today she got a brownie," I say, pointing out the crumbs on the ground and feeling stupid because who feeds a brownie to a pigeon? "Want one? It's homemade."

"You make them?"

"No. A friend gave them to me, but I'm not hungry. They're good though."

"OK, thanks," he says squatting down so we are more or less on the same level. He watches me while he eats, the corners of his mouth curling up just enough to make a dimple by each corner. His eyes are like smiling at me, dreamy eyes, grey or maybe they're green, like the Pacific Ocean on a cloudy day, whatever that color is. Those eyes, just looking at me all happy. My face turns hot, so I begin to point out all the fascinating things about Gurt, like the fact that her feet match her eyes, and the way her throat bobs and wobbles when she coos, and the pink and green on her neck when she turns her head just right. But when I look back at Eddie, he's still watching me.

"Gurt's a pretty lucky pigeon," he says, brushing crumbs off his fingers. "Would you like to get a closer look at her? See if she's sitting on any eggs? I could lift you up."

"Okay, I guess. But we'd better not touch her," I say. Of course I should not disturb Gurt at all, given that I killed her first babies, but I want Eddie to touch me. He lifts me up like I am weightless. I am eye to eye with Gurt who doesn't seem to mind. And for once, I'm glad I'm small and skinny so his arms won't get tired. "Hey Gurt." I say, feeling really happy for the first time since I can remember, and she actually stands up as if to show me what she's sitting on. "She's got three eggs."

Slowly he lowers my body, tightening his arms around me, pressing my butt against his front. There is only a slight breeze blowing through the walls. Suddenly, I am aware of how hot and close it is in the shed, and I'm getting that hollow feeling in my stomach and my ears are ringing, like crazy.

"Feel that, Sam?"

And I do feel something hard against my butt.

"That's what you do to me."

I am too embarrassed to ask him exactly what it is I do to him since it sounds like something he thinks I should already know. One thing I do know is that it's got something to do with sex, because he is kissing my neck, right where it goes into my shoulder. I know he shouldn't be kissing me like that, but I don't tell him to stop. Part of me likes it. Part of me wishes he would put me down, but I don't say this either. It's like if I don't say anything, it's not really happening.

"I know what you're thinking, Sam. You want to see what it is you do to me."

It's as if he could read my mind, though I don't say a word one way or the other. He puts me down, unzips his jeans, and there it is, right in front of my face practically.

"Have you ever seen one of these?" he asks.

I shake my head even though I have seen my dad's a couple of times by accident and Tammy Gardener's little brother's because

I helped change his diapers. But Eddie's is so different, so much bigger, the only thing that it has in common with my dad's or Tammy Gardener's little brother's, is its location.

"I know you're curious. All little girls are. If you want to touch it, it's okay with me."

My heart's beating so hard, I'm afraid Eddie can hear it banging away in my chest. "Go ahead. It won't bite you." He laughs.

I know it's wrong even as I reach out, feel it, hard, rubbery-smooth. It springs under my hand like a small, furless animal, and I jump back. Part of me is scared to death. The other part is undecided. Eddie is laughing as he puts it back into his pants and I feel stupid and ashamed, not so much because I touched it, but because I got scared, and he is laughing.

"It's okay, Sam. We're still buddies. You know I really like you. You still like me Sam?"

I nod.

"Come on. I want to hear you say it."

I can't look him in the eyes, but I manage to whisper, "I like you, Eddie."

"I thought so. You know, you didn't have to touch me. I didn't make you now, did I. You did it cause you wanted to. Right, Sam?"

I want to agree, but the words seem to crawl up my throat and get stuck there, so I just nod my head.

"Guess I better go now. Don't worry, Sam. I'm keeping my eye on you. I'll be back."

Again I just stand there, nodding like a dummy.

"Give me a little kiss good-bye." He leans down, kisses me. The sensation of his lips tugging lightly at mine slams right through me from my top to my bottom. Then he slides his tongue across my mouth. It feels like a peeled peach against my lips, and I am so surprised, I can't even think.

When he is gone, I lick my lips. They taste like butterscotch brownie, and I feel a little sick and nervous in my stomach. Though it is very hot in the shed, and I am sweating, I don't leave right away. I want to think about what has just happened; go over every detail. I'm pretty sure now I know something that Audrey, and maybe even Chablee, don't know. The fact that penises can point up is like the piece of the puzzle that's been missing. It feels a little like when you're just learning to read and you try and you try and then one day the words just start to make sense. It makes you feel smart.

I want to rush out and tell Audrey and Chablee all about it. But part of me thinks I better keep it a secret. Part of me knows I have done something against the rules. I don't know how I know this. It's not like anybody ever told me it's against the rules to touch a boy's penis. Knowing Audrey, she'd tell Mom, and that's the last person in the world I want to know about Eddie and me. Mom would definitely not be pleased. She'd tell me I'm too young for that kind of stuff. Besides, Eddie didn't make me touch him. I did it because that's what I wanted to do, right?

For the next week I find excuses to go to the shed. Every morning I rake out the cactus garden, whether it needs it or not, just because that means two trips to the shed. But Eddie doesn't come. Part of me feels disappointed, the other part relieved. And I'm confused. If Eddie is my boyfriend now, which I know deep down he isn't exactly, but if he were, then I should feel one hundred percent disappointed. I wish I could talk to somebody about all this, but there is no one. I can't talk to Audrey because she'd tell. I can't talk to Dee because she's an adult. Even if Tammy Gardener were living right next door instead of a zillion miles away, I don't think I could talk to her about it either; I don't know why. I guess I just have to figure it out myself.

* * *

Mom seems to be happier these days, at least her voice is. And she's trying to make up to me now, like finally she notices I'm alive.

One night, she comes in and sits down on my bed. Audrey is sleeping over at Chablee's like she does just about every other night, and Mom and I are alone. I put my book down and kiss her good night, but she doesn't get up to leave.

"You want to know a secret, Sammy?" she says. "When you were a baby, I used to kiss your toes."

"Kiss my toes? Oh yuck. You did not."

"Yes I did. Your toes were tiny and pink, just like the rest of you. You were such a happy baby, even though you were so little. I just loved everything about you, right down to your toes. I still do, but I wonder what's happened to my bright, happy little Sammy girl."

I look at the crud-yellow wall, shrug. "She grew up."

"Is it really that bad, Sammy?"

What am I supposed to say? Really, sometimes Mom is so clueless. I shrug again. It seems kinder than the truth.

"It's your turn, Sammy."

"My turn for what?" I ask, just wishing she'd get up and leave me alone.

"To tell a secret."

For about a second I want to tell her about Eddie; not everything, of course, just how nice he is to me, and how cute, but then I think, she doesn't deserve to know. It's like now that she's feeling better, I'm automatically supposed to feel better too. Now that she feels like telling secrets, I should too. So what, she kissed my toes when I was a baby. Well, now she can just kiss my you know what. To make sure she knows that everything is not okay with me, I say, "I miss Dad."

"I know and I'm sorry."

"Yeah, sure." I say. There is something ugly in my voice and I feel ashamed, even though I want her to know I'm mad at her. "I mean, is he really all that bad?"

"Oh, Honey. I don't know what to say."

The fingernail scar under her lip is all rosy so I have to be careful. I don't want her to go flying out the door again. "Well, I feel sorry for him," is all I say.

"Part of me feels sorry for him too."

"What about the other part?"

"The other part is scared of him."

"What's so scary? Sometimes he's mean, I know. Sometimes he hit you, I know all about that. But he's sorry afterward, isn't he. Doesn't he say he's sorry?"

"Sometimes, but sorry doesn't take back the hurt," she says, twisting her wedding ring. "This is very hard for me to talk about, Sammy."

"Why? It's like this big secret. You're not supposed to keep secrets, not from your own daughter."

"Do you know what cocaine is, Sammy?"

I think of those men in the hooded sweatshirts on Miracle Mile, and I don't want to hear anymore.

"Sammy?"

"I know what it is."

"Well, Daddy uses it."

"I don't believe you. He's not like that. Not like those guys out on the street."

"I saw it. I saw the cocaine. He uses it. I think he uses it a lot."

"So, can't he go to a hospital or something and get help?"

"He can, but he won't."

"But he's sick. Aren't drugs a sickness? You don't leave somebody you love because he's sick."

"Sometimes loving someone isn't enough. Besides, it's not just the cocaine. That's only part of why I left." Mom lets out a great big sigh then, like this is just too much to bear, but if it's too much to bear for her, what about Dad? What about me? It's too much for me to bear too.

"So why did you then?"

"Your father and I had lots of problems. Lots. Even before he started doing drugs."

"Like what?"

"Sammy . . . you must know . . . you must understand. . . ."

"No, I don't know, and I don't understand," I say. Though I do sort of know, I don't want to admit it, not to my mother, not even to myself, because to understand means we can never go home again. But I won't tell her that either.

Then she says, "Sammy, I just can't talk about it. Not right now, anyway."

It's like I've won some weird little prize and I almost smile. "You think I'm too young to understand," I yell. "Well I'm not. I'm not a baby any more, Mother."

"I know, Honey. It would be a lot easier if you were. But some things are just better left unsaid. You'll just have to trust me on this one. Do you trust me, Sammy?"

I tell her yes, but I don't. Not really. And that's okay, I'm thinking. She's got her secrets; I've got mine.

* * *

It seemed like a long time before Eddie came back to the court, but the whole summer was like that, like it lasted about a hundred years. It was just a normal, quiet morning. Mom was already at work. It had rained during the night. The sun was covered by a cool curtain of cloud and Audrey was still asleep.

As usual, I'd gone to the shed to get the rake so I could clean around the cactus garden. All kinds of little weeds had sprouted. Dee had told me the best time to pull weeds was after a rain, not that she ever asked me to weed the garden or rake out the trash. I just did it because there was nothing better to do. Besides, a funny thing had happened on those blue-gray mornings after a rain, I had begun to like that cactus garden, with its smell of dirt and greasewood.

Inside the shed, the ground is damp where the rain had blown in through the cracks in the walls. It feels cool on my bare feet. The baby pigeons hatched awhile back, and are already so big they just about push old Gurt off the shelf when she feeds them. I scatter some breadcrumbs. The babies are fluttering and squawking for food, but Gurt's calm as can be, cooing and pecking up the crumbs, taking her time.

I jump when Eddie comes through the door, startled, I guess, because I'd stopped believing he ever would. He just stands there for a minute, smiling, then says, "How's my girl?"

It's the first time he's called me that, and I figure I must really be his girl, just like I've been dreaming. The idea makes me so nervous my hands start to sweat. My stomach gets all weird again and I'm wondering, is this what love feels like, because it's not such a great feeling.

He leans down, kisses my mouth, puts his tongue on my lips. I'm supposed to open them. Right now I don't want to, even though all the times I imagined kissing him, I opened my mouth like they do on the soaps. Part of me just wants to leave.

"What's wrong, Sam? Don't you trust me?" He asks, face suddenly all sad and gloomy.

The part of me that wants to leave doesn't trust him, but the part of me that wants to stay does, so I say nothing.

"I've got something for you. Hope you like it." He takes a ring out of his pocket and slides it on my finger. "It's real turquoise and silver," he says

A butterfly is outlined in silver and filled in with turquoise. The ring is too big for every finger but my thumb and I'm holding my hand up in the air to keep it from falling off. "It's really cool," I say, wondering if this means we're going steady now.

"Dang!" He says, his face getting cloudy again. "It's too big."

"I could wear it around my neck."

"No, I want you to wear it on the ring finger of your left hand," he says.

The significance of this hits me and I feel like a bird, not a big old pigeon like Gurt, but the little bluebird of happiness is fluttering around my ribcage.

"Well, I guess I'll have to get you another one that fits." He smiles as he takes the ring off my thumb and puts it in his pocket. "So how's Gurt?" He asks.

But I'm still thinking about the ring. Even though it doesn't fit, I want it as proof that he's real, that he loves me. "Her babies are almost full-grown," I finally answer because the ring is already back in his pocket and that's that. "You want to feed her?"

I give him a crust of bread, my hand shaking. He notices and starts to laugh. "Why are you so nervous?" he asks, pulling me to him. My face is against his flat stomach. His arms around me feel good, like floating and I breathe in his smell, which is Right Guard and cotton that's been dried on a clothesline. He kisses the top of my head. "You're so beautiful," he says. "So little, so perfect."

When he unzips his pants, the sound rips down the center of me. I don't want to touch his penis again, but how can I say no now, when I didn't say no before?

"Don't worry, Sam. Nobody's going to make you do anything you don't want to. Remember that, okay? Relax." His voice is kind and quiet. "I'm not going to hurt you. I would never, ever hurt you.

I love you, Sam." he says and I want so very much to believe him, because when I'm with him I am this one very special person and that's what love must be.

He pulls down my shorts, my underpants. Kisses me there, puts his tongue there. It turns me to stone. I can't move. Can't speak. Can't run away, because I am made of stone now.

* * *

It's Dee who finds us. She picks up the shovel and hits him with it—I don't know how many times. She hits him long after he's stopped moving, then shoves him aside and pulls me to my feet. Uses my underpants to wipe my legs. There is blood. Lots of it. Dee helps me on with my shorts. There is mud on my hands and under my fingernails. She tries to wipe it off. With the tips of her fingers, she brushes my cheeks. She brushes and brushes though I'm certain I'm not crying. Dee doesn't say a word. Not one word, and she is sweating, her face red, red, red, so red I'm think she will boil over.

I'm not walking so good, so she half-carries me, half-drags me home. There are sirens and police and an ambulance, but I don't even turn my head to look out the window.

Then Dee is gone, but Mom is here, and she is crying. I am not crying. I am thinking if he dies, it will be my fault. I am quiet, but inside my chest, there is a terrible echo, like I've been hollowed out. I think of all the blood, and I am thinking and thinking, and thinking this is like vampires.

DEE

Now Samantha is just a tiny thing. Don't judge by appearances, though, because you'd judge wrong. She's got something big inside her, something the Lord put there to give her strength. Nobody sees this but me.

Awhile back she comes over, acts normal, just like before. Sits down without a word and starts shuffling the cards. So we start to play canasta, best two out of three like always, only halfway through the second game she says, "I wonder how Gurt's doing?" Those wide blue eyes are hard on her cards, and her little mouth is one straight line.

Gurt's a pigeon Samantha's been trying to make into a pet. She lives in the shed, is why she hasn't been out to see her lately. "I bet she misses you," I say.

"You think? I haven't been feeding her."

"Well, she can probably fend for herself, but I think she misses you. I got some old bread in the fridge." I say this, but I know that it's not pigeon food Samantha needs from me.

"Want to come with me?"

"Sure," I say, though it's September, still hot as the dickens, and that stuffy old shed is the last place I want to go, what with my breathing problems and all. But with the help of the Lord, I haul myself out there. After all, He has placed this child in my path. "Hope I don't scare that pigeon to death with my wheezing," is all I say.

By the time we reach the door to the shed, I am huffing, sweating. My joints, knees, and hips, the places we store our pain, are aching, but Samantha is gripping my hand hard, so I have to be the brave one this time; have to stick it out. Stick it out.

Inside, the dust swirls in the sunlight slipping through the cracks. There's this kind of light in there, I can't put my finger on it, but the light, gold and dusty, is familiar in a way that I know, not in my head, but in my chest. It grips me there; makes it even harder for me to get a good breath.

Everything is the way it was before. The shovel's gone, of course, but everything is just the same as it was that morning. I don't know if Samantha notices, but we don't need to point this out, and I make that clear to everyone.

"Looks like she's not home." I'm whispering because it feels like we're trespassing, and I'm afraid of getting caught. I'm trembling. I know this doesn't surprise anybody. But don't you worry. I'm going to stick.

"Gone for good," Samantha whispers.

"Maybe she's gone out to get her some more babies."

"She won't come back. Gurt's too scared."

"Could be. It was awful scary," I say, waiting for Samantha to let loose what she's got tied up inside, but she never does. I put one hand on her shoulder. It's as tight as a guy wire on a revival tent. "Ready to go?"

She nods but does not move. Her little hand is like a steel band around my fingers. Doesn't let loose. Just holding it all in. She's remembering. So am I.

That man—I have to keep reminding myself, was a full-grown man, not a boy, I nearly killed—Samantha's thinking about him, blaming herself. I know the way guilt works on a girl's mind, turning things inside out and backwards.

But who is the guilty one? Certainly not Samantha. It was me that hurt him bad, but how do I explain that it wasn't me either, not exactly, anyway. Can't explain how I walked into the shed that terrible morning after the rain. Needed the shovel to tidy up my aloes. Opened the door. This boy was on top of her. She wasn't yelling or struggling. Just laid beneath him, eyes wide open, arms and legs stretched out stiff like a starfish on the beach, white little-girl panties down around one ankle. It was all right there before my eyes, but I couldn't quite piece it together. Can't explain, except it was like I was dazed by the heat, by the dusty-gold, swirly light.

Or maybe confused was it, like tuning into the middle of a movie with the sound turned down. For the life of me, I couldn't figure out what was going on.

The shovel was in my hand. Something about the handle, brown and rough against my palm, turned a switch in my head. The picture flickered and I was so filled with rage; sick to my stomach with it.

Little Girl was the first to see it for what it was. She just took hold the shovel, started smashing the boy on the head. Hit him again and again until the back of his head was slick, and nobody could stop her. That's just how it was. Later when it came clear to us, the power of Little Girl's rage, some of us praised her to the sky. But not me. I fear for her soul.

So now Samantha and I are standing there in the hot shed, dust swirls and there's buzzing, maybe it's bees buzzing, and Samantha says, "Will you tell me about Michael?" Sudden like that, her voice small and tight like the rest of her.

"God bless you, Honey," I say, but I am thinking, Lord, you want this of me too? I know in my heart the pain I'm feeling is just the Lord's mighty hand on my shoulder directing my path, but sometimes I wonder why His hand needs to press down so hard.

"Let's go back to my place where I can sit," I say, guiding her towards the door when her feet still don't move on their own. "Can't hardly breathe in here, let alone think."

All the way to my place, I'm trying to clear my head. It's like some of that dust and buzzing has gotten inside and is making me tired. Got to pick and choose what needs to be said and what can be left alone. There's so much dust and noise no single thought can cut through it. I would just like to move over, but it's Samantha that's asking, and she is asking me, understand? ME! SO SHUT UP. DO YOU UNDERSTAND?

Once inside, I get us each a glass of Kool-Aid, but neither of us seems to be able to swallow, so the glasses sit untouched, sweating on the table. I watch the water drip and pool on the oilcloth. Samantha is drawing on the table with the glass sweat. Looks like a flower she's drawing. And I am trying to choose a place to start. My heart is pounding. Tuck my hand into my wet armpit, and I can feel my breast slam against it with each beat, I'm so upset. LeRoy is raking his paw over my shin, not hard enough to hurt, just hard enough to remind me that he is there. I pick him up and kiss the top of his head. "Sweet boy."

There is no good place to begin, so I start in the middle. "I think I told you when I was fifteen, I had a baby. They took it away and I never saw it. Don't really know if it was a boy or a girl. For a long time, I didn't think about it. Then a few years back . . . it's hard to explain, but a few years ago, I got to thinking about my baby. I got to thinking and thinking. Well, I decided I had to give that baby a name. I don't know exactly why, it was just something I needed to do. I bought a little book of names. You ever see one of those? It's got every name you can think of and some you never would in a million years. The book tells what each name means. Out of all the names, I chose Michael. It's Hebrew from the Old Testament. One who is like God, it means. Michael is an archangel, a guardian and warrior. He's got a sword and he conquers Satan. Michael was the strongest name in the book, so that is the name I gave my baby."

"What if the baby was a girl?"

"Then the baby'd be Michelle. It doesn't matter. I just wanted to remember I had a baby once. That's all. Bought that gold charm and had it engraved with his name. Had to make up the date of birth—I just can't remember it—but I'm sure of the year. I was fifteen."

"But Dee, how come they took your baby?"

"Well, I guess they thought I was too young to care for it," I say, but that is not the exact true answer, and I can see Samantha understands this. It is the exact true answer she wants and needs. To tell it is more than my heart can bear, I think. But that isn't true either, because God never makes you do something your heart can't bear.

"Did you love Michael's daddy?"

"Oh my, Samantha. It's more complicated than that."

"What do you mean?"

"I mean, Michael's daddy was not just some boy I thought was cute, some boy I was in love with. Michael's daddy was a grown-up man."

"Like Eddie?"

"Yes," I say and watch the wheels start to turn behind those big eyes of hers. "But there are worse things that can happen," I say, trying to make the wheels stop turning, but those eyes just get bigger.

"Worse things! What could be worse?" she says and I see I'm going to have to tell more than I intended.

"A worse thing for me, I guess, was when my mother left me— left us, my sister and my baby brother and me. We were all so little. I was five or six: I just can't say for sure, but I could recite my alphabet, had already learned to say it backwards. Anyways, I don't know why she left. I don't remember her ever being angry or sad. Just one day she was there and then she wasn't. Maybe she was unhappy; what does a little child know? My dad, he tried to raise us up for awhile, but there were three of us, me being the oldest. Then there was Lollie, she must have been about three at the time. Frankie, he was barely walking."

"Like I said, Dad tried to raise us up, but we were all so little and he started to drink some and it got to be too much, I guess. The three of us went with his sister, my Aunt LeeAnn. Years later, when I got pregnant, it was her who sent me to a kind of a foster home. Had my baby there and they took it away because I was so young. That was a hard time."

"Did you ever see your father?"

"When we were little? Oh sure. He came by now and again if it suited him, but my mother never came back."

"Your mother shouldn't have left you."

"Well I pray about it, to understand and forgive."

"What about your sister and brother?"

"Lolly's married, got two kids in high school already. She lives up near Phoenix. Now let's see, what is it Frankie does? Something to do with computers out in California, San Jose. He's been married, divorced, married, divorced, married. Currently, he's divorced. I think I got that right," I say, laughing, because what else can you do? "No kids, thank the Lord. He sends me a Christmas card just about every year. If I can ever get away from this place for a few days, I'm going to go out to California and visit him. I've been invited."

"What about your dad?"

"Dad passed away."

"Oh. That must be sad. Did he ever say he was sorry for giving you away?"

"Not that I recall."

"Do you forgive him?"

Samantha is asking all the hard questions—ones I still haven't sorted out for myself yet. Fact is, some of us do, some of us don't. Right? Doc says, we all need to communicate so we can work together as one whole person. That's okay for her to say, since she doesn't have to listen to the noise when we all communicate. Some things, I think we just have to agree to disagree about. Our father is one of them. "I don't have one good answer for that one, Honey," I say and want to leave it at that.

"Did he know about Michael?"

"He knew because I told him."

"What did he say?"

"Said it didn't happen. I think one reason he never said he was sorry was because saying so was admitting that it happened to begin with. But he did cry, so that means something. He felt bad enough about it, I guess, bad enough about his whole life to drink himself to death. Doesn't change a single fact about my life, though. God rest his soul."

"So you forgive him?"

"He never asked for it, at least never asked me. Maybe he prayed to God about it. I do hope so. Anyways, it was a long time ago. None of us talk about it anymore. Maybe I'm the only one remembers."

Well, I guess that satisfies her for now, because she starts shuffling the cards and we finish up best two out of three, but the whole time I got to listen to the committee.

You are a big fat liar. Liar liar pants on fire.

Stuffed full of lies; that's why you're so fat.

And on and on until I just want to lay my head down and go to sleep; makes me so tired. Well, I didn't lie. I never lie. None of you are any help nine out of ten times anyway, so you can just keep your opinions. You want to criticize, start with yourselves.

Must forgive and forget.

Bullshit!

He will punish all who offend him.

Not all. Please not all.

I can't think with so much buzzing going on and Samantha wins all three games.

After she leaves, I find myself standing in front of the open fridge, partly because it's the coolest spot in the place, partly because there is something inside me I just got to fill up. Seems everything we feel—anger, guilt, fear, shame, doesn't matter what—we can reduce to the one feeling we can do something about, and that's hunger.

Lately, I've been losing time again. Doc says it's just the stress—Samantha and all. I understand it, but that doesn't make it any easier. Each time I close my eyes, the ground starts slipping out underneath me. I get scared and sick. There's a click and the video flashes on for a second. I never know what somebody's got picked out for me, but there are these holes in my life that some folks seem bound and determined to fill in. Sometimes, bits and pieces flash to the surface. Each one is like a bar of wet soap. If I try to hold on to it too tight, it just slips away.

But some things I remember crystal clear, like my mama's beautiful long red hair falling over my face. And my daddy. He was a handsome, hard-bodied man. Just the opposite of Mama, he was dark, with the bluest eyes. Mama's eyes were a soft, golden brown, amber, I'd guess you'd call them. I remember Aunt LeAnn. Looked like my daddy, lean and dark, but where Daddy was easy in his body, Aunt LeAnn was stiff as if her very own skin were an irritation.

Of course, I could never forget Uncle Buddy . . . well, he was nothing like my daddy. Uncle Buddy was soft as a girl, and gray—hair, eyes, even his skin was sort of gray. And he never touched liquor, wine, nor beer either.

One of my earliest, true memories was my head resting on his soft belly, belly hairs tickling my ear and his hand on the back of my head, gently easing me down, down, down into that wiry, gray nest. I was six, maybe seven. Me curled there, his soft hand tucked in the back of my panties and up between my legs, rocking, rocking me. Uncle Buddy was not a forceful man. Gentle he was, just coaxing and rocking, one hand steady on my head, the other between my legs, all the while rocking. So easy and gentle I never even cried. "That's it, little girl," he'd purr when I got it right.

Doc says Uncle Buddy and Aunt LeAnn were like good cop/bad cop. I asked her, what are you talking about? And she explained it all to me. But I wasn't a criminal, just a little child. Why would they want to work me that way? Something to consider, is all she said.

I didn't argue with Doc, but if they were in cahoots, that means Uncle Buddy didn't really love me and that just isn't so. I do have to say, whatever way you look at it, they were mighty fucked up.

You said the F-word.

Didn't say it. Thought it, is all.

Same thing.

Is not.

What the hell difference does it make. They were fucked up, we're all fucked up. Don't be such a candy ass.

That's right. No candy asses allowed. I must say, sometimes I do amuse myself. My life, I can accept the buttinskies. Can accept that others have lived parts of it. Should be grateful, I suppose. But sometimes I hate it. Hate it even though it's what the Lord hath prepared before me. Though I know I must embrace them all to be whole, sometimes I hate them, even Brad who I've always tried to shield. And Sister Sunshine. I get so sick and tired of Sister Sunshine with her eternal goody-goody isn't-life-just- sweet-as-pie love for all creatures in the world NO MATTER WHAT attitude. Think, what a phony. Who I'm hating, of course, is just me. Just Dee is all.

So I am looking around in the fridge. There's Little Girl's applesauce already mixed with cream. Brad's still got half a pizza in there, some cold fries, and a liter bottle of root beer. The twins bought us a bag of bran muffins, I see. I look inside. There are two and a half left. Sister Sunshine must have her bananas; I take out one of those. Big Dee's cottage cheese needs to be eaten, and there is a pound of ground round; Lord knows where that came from.

There is a Sara Lee cheesecake in the freezer. Bought it myself yesterday. Was going to bring it out on some special occasion, but with all the food lined up on the counter, it looks like somebody's having a potluck and we're all invited. I guess that's special enough, so I put Sara out on the counter with the rest.

While I heat up the frying pan for the hamburger, I eat the pizza. Pizza is good cold. LeRoy is dancing around my legs. I toss him a slice of pepperoni. "That's my little precious."

* * *

Of course the police wanted to know all about what happened in the shed. They kept coming back, the same two officers—a man, I forget his name, and a lady. Officer Liz Escobar is her name.

The third time they come to question me, I begin to get worried. Do I need a lawyer, I wonder. Somehow I just never imagined that they might charge me with a crime, though I guess they could. They keep calling him the suspect, this Eddie Shear. Suspect means they don't know for sure he did what he did. Well, I know for sure.

Officer Escobar and the other one always ask the same questions: How long have I lived in the court? Why was I in the shed? Did I know the suspect, Eddie Shear? What is my relationship to Samantha?

These are the easy questions.

"Why did you hit the suspect with the shovel?" says Officer Escobar. She's young and carefully made up—eyebrows, thin black arches and short dark hair, which she rakes back off her forehead just about every two minutes. Some kind of nervous habit, I guess. She wears a thick belt, weighed down by her gun, her nightstick, and radio. It bites into her waist. Hard to look at anything else but that hand in her hair and her belt, the mean way it bites into her when she sits down.

Officer Escobar has to repeat the question. "Why did you hit the suspect with the shovel?"

"Do you think I should get a lawyer?"

"You haven't been charged with anything, Ma'am."

"Please call me Dee, Honey. Everybody does."

"If you want to get a lawyer, Dee, it's your right to do so, but we're just trying to figure out what happened in the shed that day. Can you tell us why you hit the suspect with the shovel?"

"Didn't I already say?"

"Yes, but we want to make sure we got it right. You hit the suspect with a shovel because . . . ?"

"It was the only thing handy."

"But why did you hit him?"

"He was hurting her."

"In what way was he hurting her?"

I open my mouth, but nothing comes out. For what's seems like a long time I can think of nothing to say. The committee is quiet too. They're putting it all on me, as usual.

"Dee?" Officer Escobar says, reaching out to touch my hand. I place my own over hers. I'm beginning to sweat and the bottom is dropping out of my stomach, but I'm finally able to say it. "He was holding her down, hurting her. She was a tiny child and he was holding her down."

"Was he having sex with her?

I nod.

"Would you say that Samantha was struggling?" Was she screaming? Is that why you went into the shed?"

"Yes," I say. "Yes, she was struggling; trying to scream, but he had his hand over her mouth. She couldn't scream. Couldn't breathe. Couldn't move and he was pounding into her, grunting like an animal, like a pig, a filthy pig. And she was under him, so small, I could hardly see her. So small she disappeared."

I am breathing hard, now, wheezing.

Officer Escobar pats my knee. "You all right, Dee?"

I nod my head yes, but I am not all right, not at all. Though I am not crying, there are hot tears streaming from my eyes.

"Just breathe. Try to relax and breathe. I know this is hard for you. Can I get you a glass of water?"

I shake my head. The other officer is checking his notebook, waiting for me to catch my breath. After awhile he asks, "Did you hit the suspect more than once?"

"I hit him more than once."

"More than twice?"

"I hit him more than twice."

"Did you hit him three times?"

"I don't know. I hit him until there was blood."

"Why did you keep hitting him?"

"I don't know."

"Were you afraid that he might attack you?" Officer Escobar asks. "Is that why you hit him so many times?"

The other officer shoots a look at her and she says, "At any time did you feel threatened by the suspect?"

I think of the shovel handle, its hard, splintery surface against the palm of my hand. Something about that shovel, the light in the shed, but I can't remember what it was, exactly, just the rage flooding over me. "I don't know." I finally answer. "I'm sorry. I can't say, exactly. Can't say why I kept on hitting him, except that he was still moving. When he stopped moving, I stopped hitting. Stopped when I was sure he couldn't hurt us any more."

"What do you mean by us?"

"Did I say us?"

Officer Escobar nods.

"Well, I guess I meant Samantha and me."

"Then you were afraid he would attack you too?"

"I must have been to do what I did. Just can't get it all that clear in my mind; it was all so sudden. But that's the truth, what I remember of it. I'd say more if I could. I hope you believe me. I never lie."

Officer Escobar doesn't say if she believes me or not. She does pat me on the shoulder. Who can say what this means? The other officer closes his notebook, matter of fact, like he'd just written me up a parking ticket.

After they leave, I write out a prayer. My hand is shaking, and I am afraid, not for me, but for Samantha. That man, that Eddie, is going to try to put it all on her.

Dear God,

Please hold Samantha in the palm of your hand

Let your sword of justice fall on the truly guilty.

I fold the prayer once, fold it again. "Let go let God. Let go let God. Let go let God," I whisper, and slip it in the God Box under the picture of Jesus.

Why don't you just flush it down the toilet?

Shut up!

Stupid. Everything you say is stupid. They didn't believe a word of it.

Shut up! Goddamn you!

* * *

Samantha's rummaging through the God Box like always. I suppose she just wants to make sure nobody has tampered with her prayer, or maybe she's just curious about who and what I pray for.

There's a message on the refrigerator: Don't criticize the Bible. Let the Bible criticize you. It's been there since yesterday. About twenty-four hours too long, I think, and push the words back into letter limbo.

I take out the Cheese Whiz I'm going to spread on some Hi Hos for Samantha. Notice it's empty. Notice, in fact, that there is precious little fit to eat in the refrigerator even though I just spent nearly fifty dollars on groceries the day before. Suddenly I am very tired of being me, but Samantha's out in the living room, holding up a prayer and asking, "Who's Jack?"

I put the plate of plain crackers in front of her. "A friend," I say. "He lives in unit 5."

"That's The Sidewinder. You pray for him?"

"Sidewinder? My friend's name is Jack, and yes, I pray for him, just like I pray for you. Why do you call him a sidewinder?"

"We call him The Sidewinder—actually it's Audrey and Chablee who call him that—because he walks kind of sideways."

"He can't help that."

"He can't? I thought it was because, you know . . . He's a drunk, isn't he?"

"He's got his problems just like the rest of us, if that's what you mean. Alcohol is certainly one of them, but that's not why he walks the way he does."

"So why does he?"

"It's some sort of problem with his balance. Got it during the Gulf War."

"Oh, then I guess we shouldn't call him The Sidewinder anymore."

"That's right, Honey, but not so much because Jack was disabled in the war. Shouldn't call people names because it's hurtful. Hurts them, but it hurts you too in the long run," I say, wondering what they call me when I'm not around. I'm about to ask her about it when I remember Samantha is one child who doesn't need to be sent on any guilt trips. I know she's doing a good job of that for herself.

"I saw you two the other day out by the mailbox," Samantha says, refolding the prayer and dropping it back in the God Box. "Is he like your boyfriend, or something?"

"He's like my friend."

"Oh, I was just wondering," she says. "Not that it's any of my business."

"God bless your heart, Samantha. It is your business. It's your business 'cause we're friends. That's what it means to be friends, right? You take an interest in my life. I take an interest in yours."

She chews that up with a Hi Ho. "So if Jack were your boyfriend, you'd tell me, and not say he was just a friend."

"Right," I say, not knowing exactly what it is Samantha is getting around to, but knowing she always has something going on in that little head of hers. Wheels always turning, always looking for some reason or answer, some kind of recipe for how to best proceed through this life in order to avoid pain. I've been following the wrong recipe most of my life, and have no idea why Samantha seems to think I've got the answers she's looking for.

She is making a flower out of the Hi Hos, each cracker a petal, and she has suddenly become very quiet, very pale, small. "Something bothering you, Honey?" I ask, knowing it's a stupid question.

"What do you think is going to happen at his trial?"

"Well, I don't know exactly. I figure, I'll testify, and the police and doctors you saw will testify, and that will be enough. You already made that video. Maybe they won't need you in court, maybe they will. I hope not."

"But Eddie will testify, right?"

"I think. Does that scare you?" Samantha is taking the cracker flower apart, stacking the petals in twos. "Does that scare you?" I ask again.

"Can I tell you something and you won't get mad?"

I take her little face in my hands, look right in those blue eyes of hers. They are wide open and seem to be swimming in the middle of troubled waters. "You can tell me anything in the world, and I won't get mad."

"I'm afraid he'll tell. . . ."

"Tell what, Honey?"

"Tell that I let him."

"Is that it? You let him?" Samantha doesn't answer, but it's finally clear what she's asking. It makes me light-headed and scared. I'd like to move over, but I've got to stick because what I say is important to this child, important to me, to us. I nod my head, smile, try to give myself a little more time, but Samantha is already beginning to pull back; I can feel it. Jesus, guide my words, I pray and begin—I don't know how.

"Samantha, do you remember when I told you about Michael? About how I was fifteen when he was born, but his daddy was a grown man?"

Samantha nods her head, but she's not looking at me.

"What did you think when I told you that?"

She just shrugs her shoulders, and I can't think what to say next. It's like my head has gone empty. This is almost funny because there have been so many times when I crave just such emptiness, but now, all the buttinskies who normally can't keep their mouths shut seem to be waiting on me.

"Did you think I was bad?" I ask. Samantha shrugs again, and I figure I need to start over; figure the only way to say it is direct— no pretty words or leaving Samantha to fill in the blanks. I take a deep breath. "When I was about your age, maybe a little older, my uncle, Uncle Birdie, was his name, made me have sex with him, just like that Eddie did you. I didn't really want to, but see, I loved my Uncle Birdie. He was the only one since my mother went away who was ever kind to me. I was afraid to turn him away."

"So you let him?"

"I let him in the sense that I didn't stop him, and I didn't tell a single soul about it, even though there were people who maybe could have helped me. But I was afraid to tell. I don't know. I guess I was afraid of losing the only love and comfort I had. If that's letting him, I let him."

"Sort of like I let Eddie."

"Exactly."

"Your uncle is Michael's father."

"Yes."

Samantha is opening and closing the lid to the God Box, pushing things around inside with her finger. "There's more," she says.

"I'm listening."

"I touched him. This was before . . . you know. He didn't make me. I . . . I just wanted to know what it felt like, you know . . . his . . ." Samantha swallows hard, her face changing suddenly from white to red.

"His penis," I say.

Samantha nods, picks up the bottle with the sliver of the true cross, studies it hard, as if this is the first, not the hundredth, time she's seen it.

I swallow hard too. "The thing is, Samantha, and I want you to really hear what I'm saying. Are you listening?" I say and touch her hand to be sure. Make sure every one is listening. Samantha puts the bottle back in the box, but doesn't look at me. "When you're little, like you are, like I was, and a man takes advantage of your love and your trust that way, the sin is his. It's Eddie's sin, Honey, not yours. You are not the guilty one, no matter how curious you were. The law says so, but more important, Jesus says so."

"How do you know Jesus says so? Is it in the Bible?"

"Maybe not in so many words; not everything that Jesus says is in the Bible."

"Then how do you know?"

"Because he whispered it to my heart."

"When?"

"Just now."

"Oh," she says and closes the lid on the God Box. "So do you still love him?"

"Uncle Birdie? I suppose part of me still does."

"Which part?"

"The little girl part. The part of me that is still so sad and lonely," I say and am suddenly struck by the awful truth of it.

"Do you think it's okay to still love him even after all the bad things he did to you?"

"Yes," I say. "But you've got to understand that it's like Jesus-love, freely given, no strings attached. You don't owe that man anything. Jesus-love, like forgiveness, takes away any power that Eddie person ever had over you and brings peace to your heart."

I can't tell whether Samantha's still listening or not. She picks up the double deck of cards and starts shuffling; shuffles about ten times.

"Going to wear the spots off," I say. She shuffles once more, then pushes the stack towards me so I can cut.

* * *

This happened sometime back. I'd been standing out at the bus stop. To tell the truth, I don't even know what I'd been doing there. It was hot, I know that much, and who should pull up but Eden, the woman in unit three.

She rolls down the window and I can feel the air conditioning against my face as I lean in. "Hey, Dee," she says. "You want a ride to the ABCO? I'm on my way."

Since I don't know where I was intending to go when I started out, I say, "Well, bless your heart, I certainly do." I can always use something at the grocery store.

"So Miss Dee, what have you all been doing?" she says, in that sweet voice of hers. I wish I had something to tell her, but as usual we've been doing nothing that a woman like Eden would find in the least bit interesting.

"A little of this and a little of that," I tell her, just to make conversation. "I'm working on a new recipe for a contest."

"What kind of a contest?"

"Oh you know the kind they got in Family Circle. I found this one while I was waiting to see my doctor. Its main ingredient has to be one of the Hormel potted meats. I'm considering basing mine on Spam or maybe Vienna sausages. How's that pretty little daughter of yours?"

Eden's smile stretches a little wider. "Chablee's just fine and full of herself, as usual."

It's always been clear to me that Eden's crazy about that girl and proud to be her mother. "Well, it's good for a girl to hold a high opinion of herself," I say.

"You got that right. I've read, it's the ones with poor self-esteem who get themselves in trouble."

I think about that for awhile. Something about the *get themselves in trouble* part makes my jaws tight, but I don't think she means it like it sounds. I figure somebody who does what she does for a living has her own story to tell. It's probably not a very pretty one either, so I don't fault her. Besides, Eden has always been friendly to me, something women who look like she does rarely are.

"Everybody's saying you're a hero. You know that?"

"Hero?"

"For what you did to that man, that pervert. Did you know he'd told the girls he was only sixteen years old? Planned to do what he did right from the first time he laid eyes on that child. If you ask me, what you did was a service to the community."

I don't know what to say. It's something I don't want to take credit for, shouldn't take credit for. I mumble something about how what I did had nothing to do with being anybody's hero.

"You're too modest," she says. I'll tell you one thing though, if that had been my little girl, my Chablee, that creep would weigh six ounces less, give or take two ounces," she says, making little scissors motions with her index and middle fingers. "Cut those suckers right off. No anesthetic, either."

When I don't say anything she adds, "You think I wouldn't?"

"Not at all," I say. I think you would."

"Damn straight. A woman in this world's got to be tough to survive—got to be tough on the outside and keep the inside soft;

don't I know. I would do anything in the world to protect my baby. Chablee's the soft part of me, by damn, and I'm a survivor."

"I am a survivor too," I say, almost believing it. Eden looks at me.

"I can tell," she says, and smiles right into my face. "Anybody who ends up living at the Oasis has got to be some sort of tough, I'd say. Otherwise you'd flat-out die. The heat and the roaches alone are enough to kill you."

Tough on the outside and soft on the inside, I'm thinking. Like Eden says, that's what we survivors got to be. What good does it do to live through the nightmare if you lose the softness inside. I think of Big Dee, tough inside and out and so unforgiving. I guess she can afford to be. She doesn't give a damn whether anybody loves her or not. But I'm a survivor. Eden and I are both survivors. We've got that in common.

"You spend a lot of time with Sammy, right?" Eden says. "How do you think she's doing?"

"Samantha's hanging in there, I guess."

"Well, I worry about her. My Chablee says she hasn't made any friends yet at school. Of course, Chablee's her friend, but she can't spend every minute with poor, little Sammy."

"Give it time. Something tells me Samantha will come out all right. She's pretty tough on the outside too."

"Well, Chablee is encouraging her to go out for soccer."

"That should help." This is what I say, but what I'm wondering is, how *poor little Sammy* ever managed to survive without Chablee nearly the whole summer when she was practically dying of loneliness. And what kind of a world is this anyway, where you got to get raped to find yourself a friend or beat the hell out of somebody with a shovel to make a good impression. The thought makes me see red. Makes me want to scream and yell. I would too, except Eden would think I was crazy for sure. Besides, like us, Eden is just trying her darnedest.

When we get to the ABCO, we go our separate ways. "Meet you by the car," Eden says with a wave of her hot pink fingertips. I grab a cart. As I push it around, I get to thinking about Eden, about us both being survivors.

That's where the similarity ends.

But she's got her child. Where's mine, I wonder. Still, I've got Jesus. Got to keep that in mind.

Haven't always taken Jesus as my savior, that's for sure. I wonder whatever happened to Mrs. Berry? It was her tried to bring me to the Lord. Every Sunday we'd go to the Full Immersion Baptist Church. Mr. and Mrs. Berry and all those kids, seven kids besides me, filled up one entire pew. Two were hers, two were his, the rest, like me, just odds and ends. I was the oldest and pregnant. Don't remember much, but I do remember Mrs. Berry and that church. Miss Sunshine got baptized, full immersion. I remember that. She did it for Mrs. Berry. We'd already been baptized once when we were little, but I guess the only one it took on was Big Dee.

You can lead a sinner besides cool waters, but you can't make her drink.

I didn't participate in that baptism. Wasn't participating in much. My head was turned away from the Lord back then. Didn't think there was any help for me.

Now we know from where our help cometh.

Amen.

Mrs. Berry was right there holding my hand as I went under when they took Michael from me by cesarean. I know he went to some good family, one who would love him and give him everything he'd ever need in life. Probably in some university right now, studying to be a doctor or a lawyer. Maybe he's studying to be a preacher. That would be all right, but I'd rather a doctor. I'd like to try to find him. One day I just might.

Who'd want a fat, old whore for a mother?

Best to leave it alone, maybe. All those wild years. Wild is the way some people would describe it. To me I just went numb. All I seemed to want back then was to fill up the great big hole that was Dee.

Filled your hole with dirt.

That's all there was. Never felt a thing. All those men. Did it because they wanted me to. All they had to do was ask. Some didn't even have to do that. Who was that woman, I wonder, who laughed when they whispered ugly, lay still when they passed their hands over this body, looked at the ceiling as they poked it hard and fast, moaning crying like it was really something, like I was really something. Who was the woman who walked away without so much as a backward glance. When it was over, all that meant less than nothing. Left me more empty than before.

Back when I was in group therapy, some women complained the abuse robbed them of their sexuality. They were real bitter about it, but I don't feel that way. Saying I was robbed of my sexuality is like saying somebody stole my garbage. Doc says that's the point. Maybe it is, but I just don't give a damn about it.

I pass the canned meat section. This recipe contest I've been thinking about has a cash prize of $100, inclusion in Hormel's Best Recipe Collection, and a case of selected canned Hormel products, which is a good deal because we all like those, except, of course, Little Girl, who won't eat a thing that's not piled with sugar. I put four cans of Spam in my basket, which is already almost full.

When I get back home from the ABCO, LeRoy is tippy-tapping around. I pick him up, we snuggle, then I put the groceries away. There is a sixty-four ounce jar of Skippy extra crunchy, three frozen pepperoni pizzas, a jar of jalapeños, bran muffin mix, a giant jar of grape jelly to go with the peanut butter, I suppose, some marshmallow fluff, fourteen little cans of gourmet dog food, because nothing is too good for my little boy—Big Dee's disgusted because we forgot her Lean Cuisines—and those four cans of Spam.

All I remember putting in the cart is the Spam and the dog food. Still, Spam plus jalapeños, puts me in mind of something with a Mexican twist. Could call it Spam Fiesta or maybe if I add cheese, could call it Nachos de Spam. Spamish rice, sounds kind of cute. I'll have to give this some thought.

In the meantime, I take one of the pepperoni pizzas and pop it into the oven. While I'm waiting for the timer to ding, it starts up like a tape I wish I could erase.

You know she sold him.

I'm not listening this time.

Sold him for parts.

Not listening. NOT LISTENING.

Cuts you open. Takes the baby. Uses him for spare parts.

Liar!

It's a boy. You heard them say it. A boy. Cut him up in parts just like a chicken.

Liar! No such thing ever happened.

You're the liar. Deny and lie, lie and deny.

I don't know who this is but you better shutup, I am thinking. Thinking until I'm dizzy and sick. I shut my eyes tight, recite ZYX WVU TSR QP OMN KLJ IHG EFD CBA, over and over until it's quiet.

Doc says it's possible. I say it's not possible. My boy is alive and well, probably living in Phoenix. Tell her it's the work of Bones, trying to drag me down, down, down to the bad place. Doc says that's possible too.

I write out a prayer.

Dear God,

Keep Michael safe from harm.
Keep us all safe from Bones.

I fold the note, drop it in the God Box, still too sick and exhausted to do much more than that. LeRoy is hiding in the bathroom, poor little guy. It's still light out, but I call to LeRoy. Never mind the pizza. We both go to bed.

This is your life, Dee.

You don't have to keep reminding me.

I climb in, so cold, despite the heat, and so weary. Have to close my eyes even though I'm afraid to. The bed begins to fall out from under me. My stomach takes a loop, but it doesn't do any good to turn away. I have to look. The girl is wearing a skirt with box pleats and a white blouse with a round collar. The blouse is untucked and she is hot and sweaty.

Sweaty because I played tetherball with William after school today. He sits behind me in Mrs. Alden's class and sometimes he tickles the back of my neck with the point of his pencil. I think he's my boyfriend, but I'm not sure.

I open the front door and Aunt LeAnn is sweeping the kitchen. "Why are you late?" She says.

"I was playing tetherball."

"Look at you. You're all sweaty and what happened to your shirt?"

I shrug and tuck my shirt back into my skirt.

"I asked you what happened to your shirt?"

I shrug again and she grabs my shoulder. Shakes it. "You've been with a boy," she says. "I can smell his spit."

"I don't have spit on me," I say, but Aunt LeAnn's getting bigger and bigger, and I'm scared.

"Liar! You were slobbering with a boy."

Her lips are pressed flat and blue over her dog-teeth, so I keep quiet.

"You know what boys want? What all boys want?" She grabs me there, under my dress. "Do you know what boys like to do to dummies like you?"

Where is everybody? Uncle Birdie, Lollie and Frankie? But it is just Aunt LeeAnn, and she's so big now, she's bigger than a house.

"Well, if you think you can come into my home with spit on you, it's time to learn," she says. Taking up the broom, she shoves me towards the bathroom.

"Take off your clothes," she says, running hot, hot water into the tub.

I'm not going to do it, but she pinches my chest, pinches it and twists.

Then I'm on the bathroom floor. She pushes me down, down, down on the cold tile is cold. Smells like pee. She takes the broom handle and tries to poke it inside me. I push it away. The handle is old and rough. Splinters poke my hand.

"Lie still," she yells in her quiet voice, then pushes and pushes in and out. I lie still as can be, very very still.

"This is how I learned. Now it's your turn. It's just like what boys will do to you if you keep on acting nasty."

She pulls the broom handle out, wipes it on my white blouse. "Get in the tub and wash off the spit." She stands there and watches until I lower myself into the hot water. "Clean the floor when you're done," she says, closing the door behind her.

In the tub, I watch red feathers float from between my legs. The light through the shade is yellow, like Aunt LeAnn's big yellow dog-teeth. When the water is cold and pink I can get out of the tub if I don't make any noise.

Later, when the house is dark and quiet, Uncle Birdie comes in my room with the medicine.

* * *

Wasn't long after I found Samantha under that boy, her mother came over to see me. We'd been expecting her, so we weren't so surprised

"Well Leslie, I say. Bless your heart, come on in. Can I get you some ice tea?"

"No thanks. I've only got a minute," she says, looking around. "Your apartment's so cheery. I can see why Sammy likes to visit."

For some reason, that hits me wrong. Samantha comes over to see me, not my cheery apartment. But I try not to harbor bad thoughts; jealousy is all it is. "Sit down," I say and she does.

"I meant to come sooner. It's just that I couldn't . . . talk about it. I still can't, but I wanted to thank you for . . . you know."

"I do know, and I don't want you to thank me. I don't want anybody to thank me. That boy almost got killed."

"He's a grown man. You gave him what he deserved."

"Yes," I say, not knowing how to explain to her how it wasn't me that made his blue-black hair turn red. Wasn't me; I would never. "Came close to killing him."

"I wish you had," she says, her face so white and calm I know that's what she would have done.

"Two wrongs wouldn't make it right."

"Wouldn't begin to make it even. Sammy might have to testify."

"I know. It just tears me up. We've told the police over and over just how it was. Maybe Samantha won't need to."

"How was it? No, don't tell me. I don't want to know. Don't want to ever think how it was."

"Well, it's over now."

"No it's not. Certainly not for Sammy. Not for me. Not for any of us."

She's right, of course. I look into her eyes, then. Only God can heal the pain I see there. "The Lord will help her. Will help us all if we allow it."

"That's giving the Lord a lot of credit. If we give Him all the credit, does that mean we can give Him all the blame? I'd like to blame God, but I don't have your faith."

That's the devil speaking.

That's pain speaking.

"You got to offer it up to the Lord," I say. "He sees your pain." She's nods, gets up, her face weary. "You know, it's not your fault. You're doing everything you can. God's always watching. He sees how hard you try."

"Does he? That sounds all well and good, but I've got a daughter, still just a baby, and he wasn't watching her, was he?"

"That's what it seems like," I say, wishing I had something smarter, more reassuring to offer her, to offer myself. I reach out to her then. Put my arms around her and she leans into me for a moment, one single golden moment. When God cannot comfort, we can only turn to each other. What else is there?

* * *

Now that Samantha's in school, we don't get together so much. But not so long ago, she was over and I'm just happy to see her. It's raining out, fine and cool. I'm sitting in my big chair, LeRoy snoring on my lap. Samantha's standing by the window, letting the rain that's sifting through the screen spatter her arm. For a long time she just stands there real still, not moving or talking. I can't say if she's deep in thought or having no thoughts at all, just feeling the wet on her arm. It's peaceful being there with water dripping off the roof, just the three of us. I inhale deep. "Umm. Smell that air."

She sniffs the air. "What is that smell?"

"Just wet desert. Greasewood, mostly."

"Greasewood?"

"That scraggly little old bush growing in with the cactus out front. Smells good doesn't it?"

"I guess," she says, turning away from the window. "Who's Bones?"

The question doesn't surprise me. Nothing Samantha says surprises me anymore. "That's a good question. Wish I had a good
answer."

"Is he like . . . you know, a real person?"

"Seems real."

"Like a vampire?"

"Scary like a vampire, except Bones is part of me. Samantha,
honey, this is just real hard for me to explain. All I know is that
Bones is with me; I don't know why or for how long."

"Why do you need to pray for protection from him?"

"Why indeed. I guess the best way to explain about Bones is to
say he's the part of me that's hopeless. That part that wants to roll
over and let life go on without me. The part of me that Jesus hasn't
touched yet."

"Is that possible?"

"Must be."

"Is he like the devil in you?"

"You can call him that. But I just call him Bones."

"I don't know if I believe in the devil anyway."

"I don't know if I believe in the devil either," I say, even though
that's the first time I've thought about the possibility. That's the
thing about having Samantha around; her questions always get
me to thinking. "Seems if the devil were just one fallen angel, God
could get rid of him easily enough."

"Maybe She doesn't want to."

"Who? God?" I have to smile. "Now that one's a deep thought;
kind of scary. Why do you suppose God wouldn't want to get rid of
the devil?"

"Maybe She thinks it's not Her job. Or maybe She thinks if She
got rid of the devil she'd put herself out of business . . . or

"Maybe because the only devil there is, is inside us. Lord knows
there's enough hell on earth."

"Maybe. So did you read my prayer?" she says, plucking it out
of the God Box.

"You asked me not to."

"So you didn't?"

"Right."

"Anybody else read it?"

"Not that I know of," I say.

"Oh," she says and tosses it into the trash. "That's what you do when prayers are finished, right?"

"You mean when God answers a prayer? That's what I do."

"Do you want to know what my prayer was?"

"If you want to tell me."

"I prayed for Mom and Audrey and me to go back to Santa Rosa with my dad."

"So when are you leaving?"

"We're not," she says with that little poker face of hers. "God's answer was no, at least for now."

"Sometimes that happens. So what do you think about it?"

"I think it sucks, but there's not much I can do about it, is there. God's the boss, right?"

"Right," I say. From the smirky look on Samantha'a face, I think she only half-believes this, and I'm still wondering what is really going on behind the wide eyes and tight line of her mouth. "I'm being selfish here, Samantha, but I'm glad She said no."

"Who?"

"Weren't we just talking about God? Anyways, LeRoy and I would miss you something awful."

She smiles now, not a big smile. Shrugs. "You want to play Canasta?"

"You deal them out, I say. I need to go out back for a minute."

The rain has let up. The marigolds have given up the ghost, cosmos too. Even the Zinnias are tired and worn out. But the aloes are plump. Some are still in bloom, red and yellow heads dipping under the weight of rain. One tiny hummingbird hovers, poking his beak in and out of each flower. There is a crack in the clouds and when the sun catches his feathers, he glitters purple and green.

As I kneel at the edge of the garden, my hips start aching, but under my knees, the ground is damp and cool, soft. Gently, I ease an aloe out of the ground. It's a baby, just two leaves, chubby and folded in on each other like a child's hands in prayer. I wipe the soil from its white roots. They'll reach down as deep as they need to stay alive. I want to give Samantha something beautiful from me.

This is the best I can to do. It doesn't look like much now, all by itself, but love doesn't need to be big and splashy.

There's so much I might say to her. I know how hurt she is, understand, maybe even better than she does right now, the nature of that hurt. I know she thinks it's her fault and wonders how anyone can love her now. That's what they do, you know. They make you think nobody can love you. Make you think you brought it on yourself; make you feel stupid and bad, ugly. That's how they keep you quiet. If you feel bad enough, stupid enough, ugly enough, nobody needs to put a hand over your mouth.

Wasn't your fault either, Hon. The Lord knows it; wants you to know it too.

Not my fault either. It's taking my heart a long time to learn that.

Thank the Lord.

Can't forget the Lord.

Little Girl came to me last night, glow-in-the-dark-cross tight in her little fist. Took me by the hand, took us all, and led us to the open window.

"Look," she said, so I draw back the shade, surprised to see it isn't the court, with its palm trees and circle of cactus and quartz glowing under the moon, but another yard, this one just dirt and a swing set beneath the Chinaberry tree.

I heard the back door slam, and there was Daddy, my mother limp in his arms, her long red hair catching the moonlight. I'd forgotten how her hair caught the least light, contained it like fire in a lantern. And suddenly, I felt such a need, such a painful need to bury my face in that hair, wrap it around my little fist and breathe in the smell of her hair, her skin. Was like the rain itself, the smell of her.

I started towards the door, but Little Girl held me back, whispered, "Don't make him get his belt."

So we stood there, all of us like stones, as he laid her inside the trunk. Watched him slam the lid down hard, our mommy inside.

"Daddy's driving Mommy over to Jesus' house," Little Girl said, and started to cry. "I'm scared to be alone." I wrapped my arms around her then, held her tight so she wouldn't be scared anymore, while my own tears and everybody else's just streamed and streamed.

Pretty soon everybody was back to sleep but me. For a long time, I lay there, not surprised or even sad anymore, willing at last to believe what Little Girl has been trying to tell us all along. Mother didn't run away, didn't leave us behind. She loved us after all.

If there is a purpose to my life, to my pain, I can't say. Maybe it's all just God's wicked-cruel sense of humor. Surely God had the power to protect one small child, but like Samantha says, maybe He, She, or It just didn't want to. If that's the case, who do I need to forgive and for what purpose? Seems that to truly forgive those who hurt me—Aunt LeeAnn, Uncle Birdie, my father—maybe I need to forgive God first. Have to pray on that one. That one will take a lot of prayer. But Mother doesn't need anybody's forgiveness. She's with Jesus, just like Little Girl's always said.

Knees creaking, I rise slowly. Pull one last clod of dirt from the aloe root, thinking, it's like Samantha, this little aloe. And like me—tough on the outside so the inside can stay soft. Through the bad times, it may shrink, may curl up, get ugly and dry. But all along it's holding on tight, digging its roots in deep to keep the secret, inside self soft while it waits for a little rain. Sometimes it has to wait a long time.

* * *

Samantha's birthday was last week—twelve years old—and we were all invited for a picnic at the park. I let Brad and Little Girl pick out Samantha's present, since I'd already given her mine.

It was one of those dazzler kind of days, fall here in the desert, so clear the air seemed to shimmer in the breeze. After lunch, Eden, Leslie, and me were just sitting at the picnic table watching the girls run around with the soccer ball. Somebody else might think that isn't much of a party, but for me, it was the best afternoon I can remember.

So the girls are jogging, skipping, galloping up and down. Samantha's been letting her hair grow. Got it pulled back into

French braids. They've come loose at the sides and she keeps tucking strands of hair behind her ears while she dribbles and passes the ball back and forth to Audrey and Chablee. There is something so beautiful about this scene, just because it seems so blessedly normal. It's like a moment of grace and my eyes tear up as I watch.

Eden says, "Look at the three of us. Just like soccer moms. What do y'all think of that? Before you know it we'll all be moving up to the foothills."

Leslie must think it's fine that Eden's just made me an honorary mom. She pats me on the knee just then and it feels like we, Sister Sunshine, Big Dee, Little Girl, Brad, and the others, are a part of something bigger than ourselves for once, which has got to be pretty big given our size. The notion makes us smile inside. It's a good feeling, kind of like taking the letters of the alphabet, which don't mean a thing by themselves, and spelling out words, then putting the words into sentences and the sentences into a story. It feels whole.

I don't know where this life of mine is headed. But I don't need to know what I'll be doing ten years from now. Just need to know what I have to do next. Right now the next thing to do is to give Samantha as much love as she'll allow and pray God will do the rest. Given what all I've witnessed in my life, maybe it's foolish to count so hard on God, but deep in my heart I feel such a need to. Should tell Samantha this. She won't believe me, probably, but with the Lord's help, in time she'll see it's true. Dee doesn't lie.

CHABLEE

When Mama first told me what happened to Sammy I about freaked. I just couldn't get it out of my mind how somebody, somebody I knew, somebody I even thought was a fox could do that to somebody like Sammy, somebody so little and well . . . Sammy's still practically a child, no chest, no nothing. You know what I'm saying?

So I'm sitting on the floor. Mama's combing through my hair with her fingers, first braiding it and then unbraiding it, and I'm not saying a word. I just can't. And Mama's like all worried so she goes, "What is my baby thinking about so hard?"

I want to explain how scary my life is all of a sudden. Guys like Eddie, and all those sick dudes who drive up and down Miracle Mile looking for pussy—same men I used to laugh at—well I can't laugh at them anymore because of what happened to Sammy. It's like these men, these nasty, dirty men have some kind of power over me and I'm not safe anymore. None of us is safe because women and girls have what they want deep between our legs where they can dig in with their grimy fingers and stinky pricks whether we say so or not. I try to explain how everything has changed, how I can't sit on the stoop in my nightie any more, or sleep with the windows open, how I can't walk to the store or shoot hoops in the alley without being afraid somebody is watching and waiting for their chance. I feel so mad and pissed and scared, like somebody has stolen something from me, something important that I loved, and shit all over it. I want to explain all this, but alls I say is, "Wish my Daddy was here." Then I start to cry a little.

Mama just keeps braiding and unbraiding my hair, her long fingernails raking against my scalp. "I'm sorry Baby; I wish I could make it better," is all she says and I know it's true, but it doesn't help.

"I hate feeling like this, all scared and weak inside. Nothing's the same since Sammy . . . you know."

"Since Sammy got raped, Baby."

"Since Sammy got raped." I say, wiping snot away from my nose.

Mama hands me a Kleenex, says, "It's an ugly, hard word to have to say. But we got to face reality and reality can be sure enough ugly."

"Do you think things will ever be the same again?"

"The same? I don't think things will be the same ever again, but they'll get better. I promise. Maybe you'll never be your old self anymore, but you'll be your new self, a beautiful, grown-up self."

"I gonna take one of those karate classes or maybe kick-boxing," I say.

"Maybe we can take one together," she says, and I like that idea because I don't want to have to go anywhere by myself ever again.

Then she says, "You know, don't you, if anybody ever messed with my baby, I'd tear him a new asshole."

She could do it too, with those fingernails of hers, and I think maybe I'll ask her if I can get me a set, paint them bright red. Thinking about tearing some nasty man a new asshole makes me feel better and I stop crying.

* * *

I remember the first time I saw that Eddie, remember thinking, I'd like to get me some of that. Audrey too, she thought he was fine. Right after we met him, we're over my house, Audrey has her leg up on a chair because her knee is all swollen where she fell on it, and I'm touching up her pedicure. "Would you give up your celibacy for Eddie?" I ask her.

"Right," she says with a snort. "Somebody like Eddie is going to be hot for somebody like me. He must be at least sixteen."

"Just pretend he wanted you. Would you?"

"Would you?"

"He is one hellafine dude."

"He's hellafine, but he's too old."

"That's just it. You want somebody old your first time. Somebody with experience so he won't hurt you. First time you go all the way, it hurts like hell if the guy doesn't have experience."

"If it hurts like hell, why would you want to do it?"

"Don't be stupid. It only hurts the first time; after that it feels good."

"I know that and don't call me stupid, stupid," she says and punches me in the arm, not hard though.

Anyway, we both thought he was fine, but when I think about it, there was something definitely creepy about him, the way he picked Sammy up to make that basket. It was like he was coming on to her. I see that now. Any normal dude would have come on to me, or at least Audrey.

I should have known there was something wrong with him from the start. But back then, Audrey and I would spend hours getting our make-up and hair perfect just to go sit on the stoop or shoot baskets until it was too dark to see the hoop, hoping Eddie might walk by. It makes me feel sick at my stomach now to think we went through all that, so some pervert might stop and say hi, might hang around a few minutes and flirt. If he had asked, I would have stepped back in the alley with him and made out like mad and then what? Would he have dragged me into that shed and done to me what he did to Sammy? That and maybe worse, is what I think, remembering that thirteen-year-old girl in the cemetery. There hadn't been anyone to save her, like there was Sammy. I think of this almost every day, even though I try not to.

I used to like being alone at night while Mama was at work, nobody to tell me what to do or when, no one to hog the remote, but since Sammy got raped, I hate it. Going to bed is too creepy, so I sit up on the couch, all my clothes on plus my Nikes. I can't watch TV unless the volume is turned off, or play my Walkman, can't run the cooler even because I have to listen for footsteps in the gravel by the door or a rustle in the weeds under the window. With all my clothes on, the windows shut tight, and the cooler off, all I can do is lie on the couch and sweat. I sweat and listen. Every time a bug hits the window it's like a bolt of electricity rips straight through me. My skin gets prickly and my heart is practically crawling up my throat.

Mama has an ax handle, used to keep it under her bed. Now I keep it tucked behind the couch cushions. But still I can't sleep, not until Mama gets home, which sometimes isn't until JJ's closes at one AM. Instead of sleeping, I lie there thinking of ways to defend myself from a rapist. Besides beating his brains to mush with the ax handle, I think about biting his arm through to bone, or jabbing my thumbs under his eyes and pushing until they pop out and roll on the floor like gumballs.

I can't talk about this to anybody, not even Mama or Audrey. Even though I think they'd understand, Mama can't stay home from work every night, and Audrey's on her own trip. There's nothing Audrey could do to help anyways, except maybe hold my sweaty hand. I hate the way I feel, all scared and jumpy. I'm ashamed of the things it makes me do.

After school one day, Mama and I are watching the news. Some dude, who had raped a bunch of women on the East Side, shot himself right under his chin when the police tried to arrest him. "There's one less rapist to worry about," she says. "But I do feel sorry for his mama."

It doesn't make me feel any better that this one rapist is dead because I know there are others. It doesn't make me feel better to think about his mama either. To think that dude and Eddie have mamas who probably love them no matter what, like my mama loves me, to think these rapists were little boys once, makes me feel worse. Makes me think that any boy on the street, maybe even Jesse, could turn out like them.

Or Jesse could turn out to be like Audrey's daddy, a man who beats his wife and kids. That's almost as bad, maybe worse, because your daddy's supposed to protect you. Or a boy could turn out like my daddy. No matter that he's a good daddy who would never hit me or Mama, what good is he to us now? Can't protect us locked up in prison. It's like Mama says, better not to depend on anybody but your own self. But how can I depend on myself when I'm so scared all the time?

Just before school started last August, I was over Audrey's giving Sammy a pedicure. I guess I wanted things to be like normal. At the same time, I wanted to be kind to her, as if putting polish on her toes could help make up for what's happened to her. I wanted her to feel that nothing had really changed, which was stupid. Of course everything had changed, or I wouldn't have been giving her a pedicure. Right? I know that too, but I just needed to do something to make things feel less weird.

So I have Sammy's lotioned-up foot in my lap, rubbing a pumice stone over her heel, and I'm trying to act all normal, so I say something like, "When I get married, I'm going to have three kids. I'm going to have a boy first and then twin girls. That way, my girls will have a big brother to watch over them."

Audrey says, "I'm not getting married."

"Don't you want any kids?" I say.

"I'm going to adopt a baby. That's the only way you can be sure."

"Be sure of what?"

"Be sure . . . This is stupid," Audrey says. "No way you can ever be sure of anything."

"I know that," I say, sticking cotton between Sammy's toes. "It's just a game. What about you, Sammy?"

She smiles like she's given this a lot of thought. "I'm going to marry a veterinarian and live in the country, because he's going to be the kind of vet that works on horses. We're going to have horses and maybe some chickens, and I'm going to be his assistant, so I'll have to go to vet school too. That's where we'll meet. We're going to have six kids, three of our own, and three orphans from China, maybe, or India."

Audrey and I just look at each other. It's like all of a sudden, Sammy is just this nice, normal little kid, one who's never had a fear or a worry in her life, one who's never been smacked around by her daddy or raped in a shed. "That's cool," is all I say. I don't want to burst her bubble.

* * *

It seems that my life has been twisted right out of my hands. Like I watch myself say and do things, and have no power to stop myself even if it hurts people I care most about, which mostly winds up hurting myself.

My mid-term report card was two C's, three D's and one F in PE. I tore it up in little pieces and flushed it down the toilet so Mama wouldn't see it and ground me for the rest of my life like she always promised she'd do if I brought home anything less than a B on my report card.

It's not like I couldn't be getting A's and B's. Last year I brought home a bumper sticker that said, "Proud parent of a straight-A student at Prickly Pear Elementary." Mama didn't put it on her car because she didn't want anybody from JJ's to know where I was going to school because she says you never can tell what is going on with some dudes who hang out at JJ's. Anyways, she stuck it on the refrigerator door. It's still there, and every time I want something to eat, I look at that bumper sticker and lose my appetite.

I can bring up those grades easy. All I have to do is start turning in my work, which isn't even that hard. Every day I tell myself, just finish it and get it over with, but somehow I never do.

One day Audrey is over just chewing on her cuticles. I know what's wrong, but she isn't talking and I'm not asking. Problem is I sat with this girl, Kirsten, and some of her friends at lunch. They are all cheerleaders with designer everything, and the most popular. When Sammy passes by our table, I start to search though my backpack like there is something important in there that I just have to find right this minute, instead of moving over so she can sit next to me like always. She finds an empty table to sit at. Nobody else sits with her and after a while she gets up, throws her lunch in the trash, and disappears. On the bus, she sits apart from Audrey and me.

I wonder if I'd be sitting with Audrey if Kirsten took the same bus as us. But she lives in the foothills with all the other rich kids. Audrey's probably wondering the same thing and that's why she's chewing her cuticles. It's not even that I like Kirsten all that much, but if you're not for Kirsten, you're against her. And it's Kirsten and her friends who have all the cool parties with swimming pools and DJs.

"Want me to style your hair," I say, trying to make it up to Audrey even though it shouldn't matter who I sit with at lunch. She tells me she doesn't feel like it.

Then I tell her we should go to the mall on Saturday. She says, "With who?"

"With Sammy."

She nibbles a little more skin off around her thumbnail. "How come you want to go to the mall with Sammy when at lunch you wouldn't even sit with her?"

"I didn't even see her come in," I say. "Besides I can't be baby-sitting Sammy every minute."

"Nobody's asking you to."

"No, but everybody expects me to. I can sit with anyone I damn well please."

"You hurt Sammy's feelings."

"She tell you that?"

"Like I've only lived with her all her life. She didn't have to. I should know how she feels by now. Besides Kirsten Baldwell is a snob and a back stabber. She will use you like a piece of Kleenex and throw you away."

Even though I know Audrey is right, certainly about Sammy and probably about Kirsten, I hear myself saying, "Like hell. You're just jealous."

Right then, Audrey gets up and goes home, and she and Sammy don't stop by the next morning so we can walk to the bus stop together.

Next day, I'm sitting with Kirsten. Sammy comes in and sits at a table by herself again. I know I should get up and sit by her, or at least invite her to sit with me, but instead, it's like my butt is stuck to the chair with Super Glue and my lips are sewn tight shut. Meanwhile Kirsten is talking about which girls are losers. She doesn't mention Sammy or Audrey. Maybe if she had called Sammy or Audrey a loser, I would have gotten unstuck from that chair. The fact that she says nothing about them means they are so far down the list of losers, she doesn't even know they exist.

As I sit there pretending to agree with everything she says, I'm thinking there is not one thing about me that I can trust her to know. She's all talking, talking, talking about this girl who gets her underwear at K-Mart and how she only buys her underwear at Victoria's Secret, while I'm thinking of all the lies I will have to tell so Kirsten and I can be best friends.

The day after that, I'm getting some stuff out of my locker and George Balderon comes up and says he's glad I dumped Audrey, says she's nothing but a ho. I guess he thinks Kirsten and I are all tight now so he can say anything he wants about Audrey. "That's a damn lie." I say.

"Who you calling a liar, bitch?" he says to me.

"Who you calling a bitch, punk?" I say and shove him in the chest. He shoves me back and I sock him in the eye and pretty soon we're mixing it up, four arms spinning like helicopter blades. Girls are screaming and boys are yelling fight, fight, fight. Everybody is crowding around, all blood-thirsty, until the assistant principal, Mr. Warrick, comes and breaks us up, hauls our asses to the office. I have a bloody nose, but George's eye is puffy and already turning a nice shade of purple.

Forget who started it and the fact that this is my first fight ever at this school; I get three days of in-house suspension, which is so totally boring I'm almost sorry I beat George's sorry ass. George who's always mixing it up with somebody, I guess cause he's so short he's got to prove something, gets sent home for three days which is no way as boring as in-house. One good thing, I get caught up on some of my classwork while I'm in there, because if you say one word the in-house dude, Mr. Fargo, makes you pick up all the shit off the floor. No way I'm picking up somebody else's mess. I'm nobody's slave, so I just keep quiet and do my work for once.

Then the first day I'm out of in-house, I'm getting ready for school. I put on these black Lycra shorts and matching tank top, which my mama does not even know I own, because Kirsten is going to wear the same outfit to school and we have agreed to dress like twins. Kirsten has long blond hair that goes down to her shoulders where it curls up in a perfect flip like on the cover of *Seventeen* magazine, and part of me knows she wants me for a friend because no way we look anything like twins. No matter how we dress, standing next to me, she will look, blonder, thinner, prettier, better in every way. Even so, or maybe just because, I'm spending a lot of time that morning putting on all kinds of make-up I'm not allowed to wear to school. Mama comes in to see what's taking me so long.

She goes, "Why aren't you getting ready for school?"

"What do you think I'm doing?"

"Beats me all to hell, since you certainly can't go to school wearing that white trash outfit with your butt and your titties hanging out, not to mention all the shit on your face."

"They're called breasts, Mama."

"Breasts? When you dress like that all anyone sees is tits and ass. That's what you become, no mind, no soul, just tits and ass."

"You should know."

"You bet your little brown bottom I should know! But I get paid to look like that. You like being nothing more than a piece of ass, when you turn twenty-one you can get paid for it too. In the meantime, get ready for school."

"Whatever."

"Whatever?" What the hell's that supposed to mean?"

"I don't know," I say, selecting a lipstick, Red Fire, from the tubes in the Lucite holder on my vanity.

"You don't know. You don't know? Well I know. It means that what I say is shit. What I say means nothing. First, you get into a fight at school with some idiot because he tells a lie that everybody knows is a lie so why bother. Now you got some other bee up your butt. You need to straighten up, Little Missy."

"If you say so," I answer, spreading a thick layer of Red Fire over my lips.

"What?" Mama says and slaps the lipstick right out of my hand. "Who do you think you're talking to?"

That's when all this stuff comes flying out of my mouth, just like that girl in the movie, what's it called, *The Exorcist*? Just like that, I'm throwing up all these ugly words and at that moment, I mean every one of them. I start off with, "You don't know what it's like," and I end up with, "I wish I were dead." In between is filled with stuff about living in a dump I can't bring my friends to, stuff about my lying to everybody about what Mama does for a living, how's she's practically a whore because don't men get off on her dancing almost naked in their faces and how's that's different from selling her body, stuff about where my daddy's at, and how I have to lie about that too, what a mess my life is and how it's all her fault.

"What?" She says again.

"You heard me," I say, "I wish I were dead." I'm like wiping fistfuls of snot off my face, but Mama's face is dry and white as a sheet of paper. "I'm out of here," I say and sweep the make-up off my vanity and into my purse. That's when I knock Daddy's angel to the floor. For a second, I look at the pieces, then I'm gone. Mama doesn't try to stop me, doesn't say good-by, kiss my butt, nothing; just watches me walk out the door.

It isn't until I hit the sidewalk I realize that probably for the first time in my life I've stepped over some kind of a line that will forever divide my life into before and after. I take out my magnifying mirror. My face is looking like some kindergartener art project. No way can I go to school, which is the only place I've got. So I just start walking. I can feel somebody watching as I turn down Miracle Mile, could be some whore, could be a crackhead, a pimp, or just some crazy bum. I don't turn my head to see who it is; I don't dare. A car slows up beside me. From the corner of my eye I see a man lean toward the open window, feel his hot eyes try to pull me in, but I keep staring straight ahead, my heart pumping, pumping so hard. Finally, he gives up and drives away.

Without intending to, I end up standing at the feet of Miss Lily Crabb, like I'm waiting for her to rise right out of the ground and say something to me that might change how things are.

Should have kept your mouth shut, is all I hear.

Too late now, Grandma.

A little sun filters through the trees and I sit down in it, needing that bit of warm on my skin. I want to be hating my mama and my daddy too, but mostly, I am hating myself. And I am ashamed, not so much about who I am, but how I am. I can't blame that on my daddy's being locked up at Fort Grant or my mama's dancing at JJ's. I'm ashamed how I think Kirsten Baldwell and all her fancy little friends are more important than Audrey and Sammy Wallace, ashamed how I need someone like that so much I am willing to lie about everything that's me, ashamed how I hurt everybody's feelings, and I am ashamed how I don't have the guts to change or make it better.

I wish I could go back to summer, before Eddie ever was. Even better, I wish I had gone up to him that first afternoon and laughed in his face, run him off like my mama had that old drunk, or hit him with my fist like I did George Balderon. I wish I'd told Kirsten to go to hell. Who gives a damn where she buys her underwear, anyways? I wish we could all go away some place and start over. All of us, Audrey, Sammy, me and our mamas could go off some place different where there's ocean or maybe some snow. Last summer it seemed things were going fine. I wish I understood how my life got to be so messed up. Sometimes it almost feels like I'm the one got raped.

The sun's making leafy patterns on my arms and legs and I'm trying to figure out where I'm going to go. Can't stay here with Grandma the rest of my life. Mama was almost fifteen when she ran away from home, but I won't even be thirteen until December. And what about Mama? What is she thinking right this moment? Is she sorry? Is she crying? Thinking I might never see her again makes my own eyes sting, and I'm beginning to miss her bad already. A shadow comes between me and the sun. I look up and Audrey tosses a bag of chips on my lap. "Your mother is out looking for you."

"My mama can kiss my ass."

Audrey just shrugs. "She's like totally hysterical. Came looking for you at school. When she found out you weren't there, she had me pulled out of class."

"No way."

"Yes way."

"So what did you tell her?"

"The truth. I haven't talked to you in a week. I hear you beat up George Balderon. What's up with that?"

"George is a punk."

"I heard you fought him because he called me a ho."

"Same thing."

"That was pretty stupid of you."

"You're welcome."

"Oh, like I'm supposed to be all grateful. Is that what you expect?"

"I don't expect anything."

"What about Jesse? He and George are tight."

"Jesse and I broke up, I guess. He hasn't called me since the fight."

"That's too bad."

"Not really."

"So what does Kirsten think about all this?"

"Kirsten can go to hell," I say, not sure whether this is just another lie.

Audrey sits down on the other side of Grandma, opens her own bag of chips, and starts munching. "I thought you were like in love with Kirsten and all her cheerleader friends."

I shake my head. Even though I fight against it, I feel the corners of my mouth pull down. I study the sun leaf on the back of my hand real hard, because if I look at Audrey's face I will start to blubber for sure.

"Aren't you going to eat your chips?"

I tear open the package, but I can't put anything into my mouth because it hurts just to swallow my own spit.

"Your mother might call the cops if you don't let her know you're okay."

"Let her. You're going to get in trouble for ditching."

"Mom will probably write me a note."

"I'm like in so much trouble."

"Your mother will get over it."

"It's not just my mother. My grades suck, I've been mean to Sammy and I . . . You were my only real friend. Kirsten is just Kirsten. She'll probably drop me now that I'm not going with Jesse anymore, not that I give a shit," I say, and this is a lie for sure because I do. I just wish I didn't.

"We can still be friends if you want to."

I do want to, but that means lunch with Sammy and being seen around school with Audrey instead of Kirsten. It means no parties with swimming pools and DJs. It means being just me instead of being somebody like Kirsten who everybody wants to get next to, everybody except Audrey and Sammy, I guess. That's what it comes down to. But Audrey is sitting right here with me now so what else can I say, but that I want to be tight like we used to be before all this shit came down? It feels like my world is spinning, and I'm afraid I might just spin right off. So I reach over and for awhile I hang on to Audrey, hang on tight, which seems a lot easier than trying to explain how I feel.

* * *

By the time I get home, the sky's smoky-purple. I feel kind of let down because the house is dark. Looks like Mama has already gone to work. I start to reach for the light switch.

"Don't turn on the light."

"I thought you were at work."

"Work? How could I go to work not knowing whether you're dead or alive? My skull is splitting in two and my eyes are just about swollen shut from crying. Where the hell have you been?"

"Just walking around the mall," I say, which is the truth, at least part of it, because after we left the cemetery, it seemed like the place to go. And since we were both already in trouble, I figured we might as well make the best of it.

"The mall? I've been sitting here for hours, hours, Chablee, while you have been trotting your ass around the mall?"

"Sorry, Mama."

"You're sorry? Sorry doesn't begin to touch it."

"Want me to get you an aspirin or something?"

"I don't want aspirin. I want to slap your face. Wish I could make myself do it.

Come here. Sit right here beside me. That's all I really want right now, my baby to come sit beside me."

I sit next to her on the couch. "I'm sorry about your angel. Do you hate me?"

"I don't give a damn about the angel."

"But Daddy gave you that angel to watch over you. Now who's going to protect you? Don't you hate me? You must hate me."

"Hate you? Chablee, baby, don't you ever listen to a single thing I say? I love you so much, sometimes I make myself sick. I love you too much," she says, then snaps on the light. Her face looks ruined and blurry like it's been left out in the rain—much older than it had this morning—and I can see she's telling me the truth. Right then I realize Mama doesn't have to ground me, or slap me, or punish me in any way for what I did, because I'm hating myself bad and that's worse than anything she could think of to do to me.

"One of these days," she says. "If there is a God in heaven, you will have a little girl of your own."

"But Mama, see? I'm not a little girl anymore," I say, even though I feel tiny sitting next to her.

"Don't interrupt me. One of these days you'll have a daughter of your own, and you'll understand what you have put me though today." She puts her arms around me then, hugs me to her. For a long time, we sit like that, Mama hugging me tight to her chest like she might never let me go, and all I can think is, I don't want to ever love anybody as much as my mama loves me.

* * *

I'm sitting on my bed, trying to glue the angel's head back on, wishing I didn't have to go to school tomorrow. Jesse and George have turned everybody against me, including Kirsten. Big surprise. But that's cool, Jesse and Kirsten were definitely not my type anyways. But who is my type and what type am I? That's what I want to know.

Audrey, Sammy, and I have joined the Pink Panthers. That's the same soccer team I played with last year, but Mama probably won't allow me to play once she finds out I'm still flunking PE. I'm going to flunk math too, unless I pass three make-up tests with a B or better. Getting B's on the tests is not the problem, math being not all that hard for me to get. The problem is that I have to take the tests after school, which means I miss my bus, which means asking

Mama to pick me up, which means telling her I'm flunking, which means she'll be asking why didn't she get a progress report. She's going to be so pissed when I tell her I flushed it down the toilet, she will ground me for life, not that it matters, grounded or not, my life sucks, except I do want to play soccer. Of course, I could just lie about it, like always, but I'm trying not to do that anymore.

Sammy's twelfth birthday was last week. Her mama gave her a surprise party, with hot dogs and cake at Randolph Park, big whoop. When I was twelve, Mama took me to see *Phantom of the Opera*. Went to a fancy restaurant first for dinner. We wore our best clothes and acted like we were all rich.

I felt sorry for Sammy. The only people there, besides her own family, were just Mama and me and Dee from across the court. It was kind of cool, though. We all acted like we forgot about it being Sammy's birthday and had other plans. Then everybody but Sammy and her mama went to the park to get things ready. When Sammy got there, we all jumped out of the bushes and yelled surprise. Sammy was like in shock, even though it was impossible for Dee to hide her big ass behind a bush.

But Dee's cool. I used to think that fat was all she was. But she bashed Eddie's head in, which is the least he deserved for what he did to Sammy, and that takes guts, especially if you're so fat you can hardly breathe. I guess there are worse things in the world than being fat, though I'm glad I'm not. It's hard enough to be me as it is.

I got Sammy a diary for her birthday. It's covered in blue velvet and has a lock and key. If I'd had a diary like that when I was her age, maybe I wouldn't be in such a mess now. Maybe if I had written down all the stuff that bothers me in my own private diary, it wouldn't come out my mouth as lies. Maybe I wouldn't say things to Mama I can't take back. Sometimes it's better to keep your thoughts under lock and key. Anyway, I hope Sammy liked it. She said she did.

One good thing, Mama's signed up for real-estate school. She's still going to dance for awhile, but when she gets her license, she'll quit. And soon as she starts making big bucks we'll move. It's her new one-year plan, so I know it will happen.

I tell Audrey and Sam all about it. "I wish we could move," Audrey says. "I hate this place."

"Maybe we could all move into one of those townhouses together. We could share a bedroom."

Then Sammy goes, "Where will I sleep? On a couch in the living room?"

"We'll get one of those bunk beds, you know, a single on the top and a double on the bottom. Audrey and me will be on the bottom and you can have the top bunk. That's the best spot. It will be so cool; we'll be like sisters," I say and we spend the next hour talking about how there will be a pool and a rec room where we can have parties and hire a DJ. We'll have our own stereo in the bedroom, and of course, a TV and a telephone with a private line, and one of those big stand-up mirrors. Each of us will have our own wall for posters or whatever we want.

Sammy's all excited. "I'm going to have the Dixie Chicks on my wall."

"I'm going to put N'Sync on mine," I say.

When Audrey doesn't say anything, I ask her what she is going to put up on her wall. She doesn't answer right away, and I'm thinking she's going to spoil things. Finally, she says she wants Mariah Carey, but I can tell, to her it's just let's pretend. Maybe it is, but it doesn't hurt to pretend that someday things will be different, that we'll be happy and together in some nice, safe place. Pretending is not the same as lying.

Anyway, even if we don't move to a nicer apartment, at least now, when somebody asks what my mama does, I can say she's studying to be a real estate agent. Besides, I'm not so sure I want to move unless Audrey can come too.

* * *

I'm getting weird. I keep having these dreams about Eddie. Sometimes we're out by the shed, like we're playing basketball, but we're not. Sometimes he is standing by my locker at school, or in my bedroom, just sitting at my vanity. But always, he is smiling, laughing at me like I'm some sort of joke. And even though I'm scared as hell, I'm like wanting him to notice how soft and crisp my hair is, how my skin is all *café au lait*. Wanting him to put his hands on me, to kiss me. I want to run away but I can't, even though he's not touching me, or even blocking the door. Sometimes the shoes I'm wearing are so big and heavy I can hardly lift my feet off the floor, sometimes it's my own legs that weigh a ton, but always, for some reason, I can't move. Then wham, I wake up, and it's like I have been shot through with dozens of icy-hot needles. If Eddie was a ghost, I'd say he was haunting me.

I haven't told anybody about these dreams, not Mama, not even Audrey. What would they think if they knew I was wanting to kiss the dude who raped Sammy? I don't know what to think myself, but after I dream of Eddie, it takes a long time to go back to sleep. When I'm awake, it's like I hate him, which is what I'm supposed to do, but when I'm asleep, I can't do what I'm supposed to do. It's making me freak.

And I'm wondering about Audrey. We haven't practiced kissing lately, but I think about it. Wonder if kissing her makes me a lesbian. Wonder if she's been thinking about it or if she's just put it all out of her mind. Hard to tell with Audrey. But I can't deal with that right now. If kissing her means I'm a lesbian, then that's what I am. Who cares? Mama will love me either way.

Lately, Mama's been acting a little weird too. Been looking at me crosswise, as if at any moment she expects me to reveal some deep, dark secret. Like she just can't wait for me to tell her all about it so she can give me some of her good old cracker advice.

"You're not letting your little light shine," she says. Says, "Don't hide it under a bushel." I just ignore her. Mama says all sorts of shit like that. Most of it makes no sense. Besides, I don't want to be some little light. I want to be a big light, like one of those searchlights that beam across the sky when there's a new Wal-Mart opening or something. And what the hell is a bushel anyways?

I know she's only trying to help, but there's no way I can explain to her or anybody else how hard my life sucks. It's like my feet are glued to the floor. I can't go forward and I can't go backward. Stuck where I am, and hating that too. How long do I have to wait for something to happen so I can get to the next part of my life, which has got to be better than this part?

When I was in third grade, my teacher brought a caterpillar to class in a jelly jar. Seemed like we fed that caterpillar parsley for weeks. One day when we got to school, instead of a caterpillar there was this ugly thing stuck to a leaf. Looked just like a glob of bird shit. We thought the caterpillar was dead, but the teacher said not to worry, it had just become a pupa.

I think that's my problem. One day I'm this cute little caterpillar, having a fine time walking around and munching on parsley, the next I'm a pupa. The thing about pupas is that they can't move, can't change the leaf they're sitting on, can't get up and walk away, can't do anything but wait to be eaten alive or changed into a moth or if they're lucky, into a butterfly. So in my pupa heart I'm waiting to become something else. Someday, my true self will bust out. In my heart, I know I will be some kind of butterfly—not a moth, but a big beautiful butterfly and I will float safe, just beyond everybody's reach. It's just a matter of time. Still, the waiting is scary.

LESLIE

There are days when I'm just plain mad. It's a painful sensation, like a small fire burning in my chest, and things that I'd normally blow off become intolerable.

Just the other day I came home from the Laundromat. I go into the girls' bedroom and there's a pile of dirty clothes on the closet floor, soccer shorts, tees, socks, underwear. Just then Audrey gets home from practice.

"Where's Samantha?" I demand.

"Dee's, I guess," she says, dropping her gym bag on the bed.

Somehow this small, too casual act is more than I can stand and I start in. "You guess? You're supposed to keep an eye on her. And why can't you do one single thing I ask?" I pull her by the arm over to the closet and point to the pile of dirty clothes. "Why the hell weren't they put in the laundry bag?"

"Jesus," she says, wrenching her arm out of my grasp. "I had practice. Sammy said she'd do it. She was supposed to do the dishes too. How come you never yell at her?"

"She's over at Dee's?" I say, chastened, but not satisfied. "I didn't realize it was her turn."

I rely on Audrey too much, but somehow, I want her to share my burden, need her to understand how my life feels, how it seems I can't make any headway. Want her to understand how I feel stuck and frustrated, and sometimes angry, teetery, always on the verge of losing my balance. I reach out for Audrey then, putting my hands on her shoulders, maybe just to steady my insides. She shrugs, and my hands slip off as if those shoulders are dipped in ice.

"This isn't easy for you," I say. "But it's no picnic for any of us."

"Sometimes you act like a crazy woman."

"Sometimes I feel like a crazy woman," I say, wanting her pity as much as her understanding. "Since Sammy was hurt, I just seem to. . . ."

"Sammy was raped, Mother. Raped. You got to say the word out loud. How do you expect Sammy to deal with it, how can any of us deal with it, if you can't even say the word?"

So now I practice saying the word. My little daughter was raped. A man raped my little daughter. My life has fallen into two pieces: the piece before Sammy was raped and the piece after she was raped. The word rape still gets caught in my throat like a chunk of raw meat.

* * *

The hardest moments are the quiet ones. When it's quiet, questions and accusations flood my mind until I want to tear at my skull and howl like a banshee. It all comes back to the notion that if I had left Frank when the girls were little all the outcomes would have been changed. There would be no Oasis Apartments and my daughter would still be a little girl, safe with her little girl things in some nice home I, not Frank, had provided.

Living with Frank was like walking around in a straitjacket, but I was the one who slipped my arms into it and held still while he laced up the back. Why did I stay? Was I crazy? I ask myself this daily, but it only leads to the other questions. Why did my mother? Why do I still care what my father thinks about me, wonder what will become of Frank now that he's alone? Why do I care about what happens to these men who did me such harm?

For years I longed to hate Frank, thinking that would make it easy for me to walk away. But now I realize both hate and love are fed by passion, and it was passion that kept us bound together. If love has an opposite, it's not hate. It's indifference. So now I long for indifference.

Whatever insights I gain in the quiet moments quickly dissolve like sugar in boiling water. Instead of feeling lucky to have gotten out of Santa Rosa alive, I feel guilty because there are women, like Eden, who would not have stood still for any of it. I'm envious of her strength and resolve, her optimism. Where does it come from? Her mother and stepfather make my parents look wise and kind by comparison.

One warm evening, I asked her about it. We were at our usual station on the stoop trying to cool off with tall glasses of iced tea.

"Came from my real daddy and his mama, God rest her sweet soul. Poor white trash, is what my mother always called them. See. Daddy, being a handsome devil, was good enough to fuck, but not good enough to marry."

"Even when she got pregnant?"

"Even then. I'll have to give it to my mama, in her own ugly way, she was sort of a liberated woman. Was way before her time, my mama. Anyways, she had ambition, and Daddy was just a cracker. Back then in the South, there was no question where a baby belonged—belonged with its mama, which was just my poor luck. Still, as long as she was single, when it suited her, I got to spend time with Grandma. Suited her pretty often."

"So your grandmother raised you?" I say.

"And my daddy, for awhile. My mama was right, though. Daddy was a cracker, and Grandma and all my kin right down to the snuff and the bad dental hygiene. But they knew how to love a child. There was a safety net with all that family—aunts, uncles, cousins, that a girl like me couldn't fall through."

"When Mama married, I was maybe ten at the time, Daddy Elder wouldn't allow me to even visit my grandma because she and all them were just white trash. Used to think it was because he was jealous of my daddy, but he just wanted to corner me all along and didn't want me to have anyone to run to. Old goat was just biding his time."

"When you left home, why didn't you go to your father's family?"

"Well, that's because they were just poor white trash. It's true. I didn't want to grow up to be like that, poor, ignorant, and worked to death by people who were kind enough to throw a few dollars their way—picking fruit and itinerate roofing was the family line of work—but wouldn't say hey if they passed them on the street. Bottom line, I didn't want to get my finger nails dirty. Besides, by then, Grandma'd had a stroke, or something. I should have gone to live with my daddy, but I had it in my mind to leave. Never did like that hole anyways. Like I said before, I was young and stupid, but I thought I was smart and sophisticated. Ever know anybody like that?"

I smile. What else can I do?

"When you smile, that little scar under your lip looks just like a bitty crescent moon. How'd you get it?"

"It was my fifth anniversary present to my husband," I say, patting the scar with my finger.

"Mean you just walked up to your sweet ever-lovin' and said, 'Happy anniversary, Darlin', why don't you bust me in the lip'?"

"Might as well have. I gave him a diamond studded horseshoe ring for good luck. By then I should have figured sooner or later, he'd hit me in the mouth with it."

"Well, never mind. It's a pretty little scar. Listen girlfriend, someday some nice man's going to run his tongue along that scar like it was chocolate syrup and you're going to be happy as a clam it's there."

"I don't know . . . I don't think I could even consider. . . ."

"Well I do know. And I know about scars, the kind you can see and the kind you can't. Man who can love your scars is one you want to seriously consider."

"Was Muki that kind of man?"

"Muki was that kind. Sometimes I hold out a hope for us when he gets out of prison, but mostly I've given up on the idea we'll ever have any kind of life together. Still, a woman's got to dream, because I sure haven't come across anything worth my ass during waking hours."

Got to have a dream, I'm thinking. A woman has to make a plan and a dream, with herself in the center of some happy ending.

* * *

Except for the brief summer monsoon, there's very little rain here. That, of course, is why it's a desert. But we've all cried and sweated so much in the last six months, I'm surprised it hasn't burst forth—

flowers and green replacing spines and thorns. Would I find relief in that?

We are becoming soccer moms, Dee and Eden and I, if you can imagine anything so unlikely. They cover the weekday games while I'm at work, but every Saturday all three of us are in attendance. We bring folding lawn chairs. Sometimes we even sit in them and try to behave ourselves. It isn't always easy.

Last Saturday, Eden and I are leaning against the hurricane fence that surrounds the field. Dee arrives late, huffing and sweating even though it's a fine afternoon with a light breeze. The grass is a miracle of cool green and the sky, blown clean of dust and exhaust, is flawless. We each wear a visor with the team's name, Pink Panthers, embroidered across it.

"So what are our chances?" Dee asks, pulling the bill of her hot pink visor from front to back.

"Slim to none," Eden says, pointing her chin toward the field.

Those odds suit me. Even though the season's just begun, I don't want the Panthers in any playoffs. Every time I see one of our girls take a spill, my stomach lurches and I get light-headed. Dee pulls a box of Chips Ahoy from her bag and passes it around. I take one to keep my stomach from going sour.

"Look, look. Sammy's got the ball. Yee haw," Eden shouts. "You go girl."

I'm holding my breath, watching her as she maneuvers the ball towards the goal, almost fawn-like. She is easily the smallest on the field, the most vulnerable. Then glancing towards a teammate, Sammy fakes a pass to the right, then slips the ball past the goalie, into the box. It's the play the girls have practiced over and over again.

Chanting, "Samm-y, Samm-y, Samm-y," the three of us do a rather pathetic, but enthusiastic, wave.

Amazingly, Sammy gains control of the ball again. As she picks her way around the opposing players, I watch with horror as a guard from the other team, a big girl, runs up from behind and slips a leg between Sammy's, watch as she goes down hard. Eden and Dee grip my arm to keep me from running onto the field, but I break free, my saliva turning coppery in my mouth. The coach and I reach Sammy at the same time. Her eyes flutter open.

"Sweetie?" I say, taking her hand. "Are you all right?"

"I think she just got the wind knocked out of her," Coach says to me.

"You think? Sammy honey, just the air?" She nods her head, and suddenly my own feels light. I lower it between my knees. Eden's hand is on my elbow and she guides me off the field.

"Jesus, girl," Eden says. You got to get a grip."

I nod, knowing I have just mortified my daughter, and there will be words to that effect when we get home. But it's like I have somehow determined that Sammy will never be hurt again, that I will protect her from all harm, that my love will form an invisible shield around both my girls, and they will never have to experience pain again. That this is impossible only heightens my sense of inadequacy and frustration.

To my relief, the coach makes Sammy sit on the bench. I care not one bit that this is not how Sammy wants to spend the rest of the game.

Once we get home from the soccer game, Sammy surprises me. She doesn't criticize my behavior; seems to have forgotten all about it. Her only urgent need is to learn how to French-braid her own hair. "Can you teach me, Audrey?" she asks. I hold my breath, but Audrey is feeling generous. Sammy, who has been growing her hair out since we left Santa Rosa, sits down and Audrey quickly pulls her hair into a tight braid.

"It's like the back of my head's been zipped together," Sammy says from the bathroom, where she is examining it with a hand mirror. The look seems to satisfy her.

After dinner, Audrey and Sammy take turns French-braiding my hair. Their hands on my head, gently weaving the strands, feel like absolution.

We change positions. My fingers comb through Sammy's fine, silver ash, hers through Audrey's dense brown waves. "We're like the three wise monkeys," I say.

"Hear no evil, speak no evil, see no evil?" Audrey says.

"No, not those three," I say. "We're the three really wise monkeys."

"Oh yeah? Which ones are those?" Sammy asks, but I am at a loss for names. Instead I ask my own question.

"Do you girls still miss Santa Rosa?"

"Yes and no," says Sammy, but Audrey holds her own thoughts.

"Did I ever tell you how I met your father?"

Both girls are silent, waiting, almost fearing, it seems, what I might have to say. I begin to tell them all about it anyway so they can hear from me how it was—ask whatever questions come to mind. It's my intention to tell them anything they want to know, even if it's not pretty. The truly wise monkey sees evil and calls it by its name.

* * *

So what does my life amount to after thirty-four years? It scares me how hard it's been and how little I have to show for it. But I've got friends, first Eden and now Dee. More important, I've got my girls. In spite of me, in spite of everything, they are changing in ways that feel almost like progress.

The other day I come home from work and Sammy flings the door open. She's jumping up and down, her normally pale cheeks bright pink.

"Look," she says, raising her arms above her head. "Hair!"

And sure enough, there are at least a half-dozen strands, light brown and fine, under each arm. Is puberty progress? Sammy seems to think so, but to me this simple declaration is more than progress, it's a miracle.

If we were were still living in Santa Rosa, would she have shared this event with me? I doubt it. Secrets provided protection against Frank's ridicule, I guess, and I suppose I couldn't be trusted either. Somewhere along the line, I had become like my own mother: silent, passive, untrustworthy.

But now she makes me a gift of this little milestone. It is such gifts that keep me from relenting in the face of the unrelenting sameness of my days, of my nights.

Each night I crawl into bed, find the impress of my body on the thin mattress, and roll into it. How many heads, shoulders, hips have been cradled in those shallow basins? Too many. I lie there, sometimes to dream another life unencumbered by love and all its tailings. Perhaps I am alone on an island surrounded by a warm and azure sea. I walk into the placid surf, dolphins greet me, caress my legs with their slick, dark bodies as I swim forward towards a point where the sun boils the ocean. Some nights I masturbate. I do this without hope or fantasy. If I come, the effort exhausts me and I sleep.

* * *

There are people—my younger sister is one—who expect you to spill your guts and then get over it. But some things are so wrong you should never get over them. Dee seems to understand this. I honor her for this understanding.

By some miracle, profane or divine, I can't decide which, that man, how I hate to say his name, survived Dee's beating. Some people would be repelled by the degree of Dee's violence that morning, want to distance themselves from her. Not me. I am in awe of Dee, would like to think myself capable of the same outrage and force. And I am grateful. She acted in my stead.

Sometimes I think I need a car to pull us out of our static marginality. Sometimes I think, with a car I could finish college, get a better job. But then I think about the registration, the license plate, the insurance, all a potential paper trail leading right through my daughters' bedroom window, and I think, why risk it? I am in limbo which is neither a rock nor a hard place, but someplace I have come to by omission or commission. Either way, let it rest.

The prosecuting attorney told me that man claims the sex was consensual. Claims he had a relationship with my Sammy. A relationship? It makes me sick, but with what I can piece together from the little Audrey and Sammy have told me, they did know each other. Maybe it's true, inasmuch as an eleven-year-old child can have a consensual relationship with a twenty-eight year old man. But it makes no difference to me if she said yes, or even pretty please, I still want to see him burn in hell.

There are many things I would do differently if I could. But if there were only one thing I could do over again, I'd relive the day

Sammy and I argued about going back to Santa Rosa. Instead of trying to protect her from the truth, I'd tell all the reasons we had to leave, outline every punch, each rape, and trust her to somehow get beyond it. If I had, maybe she would have trusted me, confided in me. Now more than ever, we need to trust each other with the scariest facts of our lives, because ignorance and secrecy are more dangerous than the truth, no matter how ugly.

* * *

Shortly before we left California, Sammy brought home a little tabby cat, a stray. The cat was very pregnant, so I made a box for her in Sammy's closet and she had her kittens there. She was a sweet animal, a good mother.

But it isn't long before Frank hears the kittens mewing and comes in to investigate. "What's Sammy been hiding in her closet?" he says. Sammy's at a swim party, so Audrey answers for her. "Just some kittens," she says.

"She wasn't really hiding them," I say, hoping to head off Frank's anger. "It's just that they're so young they need to be kept somewhere dark and quiet."

"How come nobody shared this development with me?" he says coolly, and though there is no menace in his voice, I set my jaws and wait, my stomach filling with lead.

Gently he picks up each kitten, their eyes barely open, examines one after the other with care. He pulls a pillow off Sammy's bed and removes its case, then takes mama cat and her female kittens, there were three, and drops them in.

"No more mamas, no more babies. He smiles, says, "Sammy can keep the males."

I don't say a word. Don't even ask what he intends to do with the kittens. From the bedroom window Audrey and I watch him swing the pillowcase against the big oak tree in our front yard. Three times he swings the pillowcase against the oak and then throws it into the garbage can where Sammy might find it. He means for her to find it.

"Damn him. Damn him," Audrey whispers, tears choking. "They weren't hurting anything. He's a maniac. Why didn't you stop him?"

Audrey doesn't really expect an explanation from me. She already knows I can't protect myself, my daughters, much less four little cats, from this man. "Promise not to tell Sammy about this," is all I say.

"What am I supposed to tell her when she sees Missy and three kittens are gone?"

"Just tell her he took them down to the office. Tell her he knows someone who wants to give them a good home." She promises, and at thirteen enters into her first adult conspiracy.

After he has left for the office, I take the pillowcase out of the garbage. I have to wrap it in a beach towel and then a plastic bag before putting it into the trunk of the car. Hope no one sees me throw the bundle into the dumpster behind the strip mall a few blocks from home. When I return, I feel strangely calm, and my choice, there is only one, becomes clear.

I imagine the scene: my mother, standing at the sink, can of Comet Cleanser suspended, while she listens to my father's end of the telephone conversation. Frank explains that I have deserted him, stolen the children. "Did she run off with another man?" It's the only thing my father would want to know. Both my father and Frank would assume there was a man involved, or how else could I have managed? What might my mother be thinking at that moment? Inside her head, might there be a small voice cheering me on?

I compose a note telling him why I'm taking the kids and leaving. *Dear Frank,* I write. *If I don't leave you, one of us will end up dead and the other in prison. If I don't go now, there won't be anyone to take care of Sammy and Audrey. Believe me. You don't want to come looking for us.*

For days I read that note over and over again until I start to believe that I'm capable of taking the gun and shooting him. When I'm absolutely convinced, I pack up the girls, leaving the note on the kitchen table.

I brought one of Frank's guns with me, the one from the top of his closet. Mostly, I just wanted him to know I had it. I keep it hidden under the hide-a-bed. Knowing it's there gives me some peace. If Frank shows up, I'll point it at his chest, the chest I once laid my head against, thinking that here at last was the man who will love and care for me the rest of my life. I'll pull the trigger.

Another thing I brought along was a photo album Sammy gave me for Mother's Day when she was six. On the plastic cover is a picture of Pocahontas the way Disney envisioned her, a buxom, wasp-waisted beauty. I often study the pictures inside the little album. My favorite is of the girls. Audrey has her arm slung, almost protectively, around Sammy's shoulder. Her smile is reserved but pretty, just the merest upturn at the corners of her mouth. Sammy's smile is too broad and gap-toothed to be pretty, but there is a certain winning enthusiasm that I love. She is a happy child in that picture. I like to be reminded of that child.

Though Audrey, with her brown waves and hazel eyes, looks like me, inside she is nothing like me. She's cautious, a little stand-offish, or maybe self-sufficient is a better word. She knows what she wants, goes along easy-does-it until she gets it. Goal-oriented is how her sixth-grade teacher put it. I'm grateful she's not like me.

It's Sammy, all edges and longing, I have to worry about. I see so much of myself in her. Needy. I recognize it. Understand that it makes her a danger to herself. How do I protect her from neediness? How do I protect her from a need for her father's love and acceptance? Like me, she won't find it, but she'll probably keep on looking.

I've got the gun, but it won't protect Sammy from herself.

* * *

My daughters are learning to speak a few words of Spanish from their friends on the soccer team. Soccer's big down here and the girls are becoming little jocks, braiding each other's hair now before each game. When they get knocked down, they are instantly back in motion. Audrey even wears her athletic bras to school. "To ward off the gropers," she says. Laughs when she sees my expression, and I am supposed to be reassured.

Against all odds, it's Sammy who's becoming the team's most fearless player. It terrifies me, but she's tough and resilient.

Audrey, who's getting tall and talking basketball now, is proud of her little sister, encouraging. When they're not playing soccer, the girls spend a lot of time shooting hoops. Women's sports at the university get good press; maybe there's a scholarship in the future. Scholarship or no, each month, I follow Eden's example and put a small chunk of my paycheck into a savings account for my daughters' education. That's my plan and my dream, the girls in college. It's enough for now.

Sammy seems to be making her own mysterious way. There's not much I can do except wait for her to reveal to me how I can help—if I can help. The girls seem to be growing closer, and that can only be good. Sure, they have their moments. They rage at each other and at me. Sometimes they do sneaky, dangerous things. There are still times I just want to run away and hide from them; they can be so ugly. But they can also be loving and funny and brave.

* * *

When things seem to be going along pretty well I have a terrible urge to call my mother. Does she suffer because we're gone? She must. And she must blame herself, at least in part, for it. I want to tell her not to. I want badly to tell her I love her. Tell her I forgive her for those years of silence. Does she crave forgiveness as I do? She must. Is a phone call really such a risk? Knowing what I know, I don't think I can wait until both girls are legally adults. In six years, my mother will have given up hope.

Eden has been trying to convince me that we can afford to go to San Diego with them over Thanksgiving. Says she'll even loan me the money. From a phone booth in San Diego, I might risk a call to my mother. Would she tell my father? Would they keep it a secret from Frank? Would telling my mother I love her be worth such a risk? I need to talk it over with my daughters.

* * *

The other day Dee, Eden, and I were standing around the mail-boxes, sharing our observations, like three mother hens.

Eden's saying, "Oh the make-up and the clothes. Chablee's just cranking her neck like a mud turtle, way on out there."

"I know what you mean," I say. "The girls are in such a hurry to grow up."

"Yes and no. Seems one minute those necks are out to here," Eden says, stretching her own neck out. "Can't wait another minute to be on their own. Next minute, they get scared, want to pull them back in. Trouble is they won't fit in the shell anymore. So there they are, necks stuck out. . . ."

"Unprotected," says Dee.

"You know it. Hell, we all do. My Chablee, she thought she was hot shit, now she's wanting to be mama's little girl again, but she's way beyond that. There's things she's already learned, things she's already done, not that she's told me about any of them—but a mother knows, doesn't she—and she can never be a little girl again, never go back into that nice cozy little shell. Can't ignore her breasts, can she, or the blood that spoils at least one pair of panties every month. Isn't easy being a woman in this world and it starts way too early, before you're really done with being a little girl."

"Amen to that," says Dee. "So how's it going for you, Leslie?" She pats my arm, gentle, like she's afraid I might shatter.

I shake my head. "It's going. The other day I burned dinner. That doesn't sound like such a big deal, but it's not like the girls and I can just hop in the car and go to McDonald's." Eden and Dee nod encouragement.

"Anyway it was one of those last straw kind of things, and I started to cry and the more I cried, the more I wanted to cry until I couldn't stop. But then the girls came in from shooting hoops. Sammy started in right away, rubbing my neck. Audrey began cleaning up the mess and nobody was saying a word."

Dee pipes up. "Those girls really love you. Must be doing something right." That's all, no praise the Lord or thank you Jesus; Dee is giving me all the credit.

So I've been thinking, yeah, I must be doing something right. This realization presses lightly against me, urges me forward, like a hand at the small of my back.

Once in awhile you read about people who, through a force of will, can move small objects, open drawers, for instance, lift a pencil. Some nights I lie within my own imprint and try to concentrate all my negative energy, send it down through my limbs and out into space. I think the release of this pent-up enmity, self-loathing, and guilt might nudge me forward. This is the only thing left that I need to do. Just the barest nudge would set me in motion.

SAM

Ever since what happened with Eddie, everybody has started being nice to me, and that's scary, like I have some life-threatening illness, leukemia, or a hole in my heart. Even Chablee is being nice. She gave me a manicure and a pedicure, two coats of professional base and topcoat, two coats of Key Lime Pie in between.

I was assigned a counselor. She's nice in a way, but I think it may be a trick to make me lose concentration, because as long as I concentrate, I am not afraid. This has nothing to do with backwards alphabets or glow-in-the-dark crosses. It's about not being afraid in the first place, which takes concentration and no crying. When I cry, Mom cries. She touches my face, her hand cold like a marble hand and not like her hand at all, and she cries, telling me it's all her fault. When she cries, my irrational fear, which is a lot like sadness, comes back. So first and foremost, I must never cry about anything, and that takes concentration.

Every night, late, Mom comes into our room, just stands there. Audrey is humming in her sleep, but I'm almost always awake. When she comes into our room at night, I shut my eyes. Don't move a single muscle.

I lie to my counselor. At least I lie about the things that really matter. But sometimes I forget what really matters until it's already out of my mouth, which is why concentration is so important. It makes me invisible, sort of, which is peaceful in the same way sleep is peaceful if you are not having a bad dream, or freedom. I don't mean freedom like in democracy, but freedom to do anything, anything at all because no one will notice. This sounds crazy, lots crazier than it feels. To me it feels like normal.

Mom told me he is twenty-eight, not in high school at all. When she first said that, I hated her, but now I don't. So Eddie was not my boyfriend at all, not that I ever really believed it deep down, but the possibility that he did love me made everything less weird. The worst thing is that I might have to see him in court. They video taped my testimony, but couldn't promise I wouldn't have to go into the courtroom to tell what happened. He would be there, look me straight in the eye. What would he say? Would he call me a damn liar, tell everybody that I touched him first? Say that he only did it because I wanted him to?

They say I'm a victim. Not to my face, but behind my back they say things like "not her fault." But I know the truth and the word victim is not part of it. That's what scares me the most, and this is not an irrational fear. What will happen when people find out the truth about me? They won't be all nice and friendly anymore, that's what.

"Let Jesus be your voice" has been on Dee's refrigerator for days now. Jesus is her solution to everything. But Jesus was a man so he didn't have to worry about it, did he? And really, what would Jesus say if he were me?

* * *

When school started last fall, we all went down to register together—me, Audrey, Chablee, Mom, and Eden, who kept telling me how pretty I was getting, which I knew was a stinking lie. Anyway, Chablee and I are in the same class. She's changed a lot since the beginning of the summer. I've moved her up to fifth place on my advantages of Tucson list, right behind Mom, Audrey, Dee, and Fido—that's the cat we got from the humane society. We chose her because she's got personality. Mom calls it spunk.

It helps to have a cat. At night, she wraps around my head like a turban. It's hot but it's good, because cats can see in the dark and are extra-sensitive about things that shouldn't be there, like cockroaches and more importantly, vampires. In fact, since we got Fido, I haven't had any problems with vampires. This is both good and bad. One thing I've learned is that you can't always name the thing you're most afraid of, and that just makes it all the more scarier. In some ways, it was easier when I could just call it vampires. Now what do I call it? Still, I keep the glow-in-the-dark cross handy just in case. The backwards alphabet helps too. I say it over and over when it's hard to concentrate, when I get to thinking and can't stop.

Audrey's mostly being extra nice. That's good, I guess. At least she's stopped yelling at me and pinching me, and she says I can sleep with her any time I want, though lately, I haven't needed to. If I wake up in the middle of the night, all I have to do is reach out and run my hand over Fido's belly and she starts purring real loud and I know she's awake and keeping an eye on things.

Right after it happened, Audrey put her arms around me, asked me if it hurt, and there were tears in her eyes as if she really cared whether I lived or died. So I told her the truth. "Yes, it hurt."

She kissed my cheek like she hardly ever does, whispered, "I'm sorry." And I could hear the sorry in her voice, but like Mom said, sorry doesn't take the hurt away. So I told her, "It hurt really, really bad, Audrey." But I didn't tell her how many different ways it hurt, still hurts. The kind of hurt Audrey wanted to know about is over. But it still goes on hurting because I knew it was wrong, but somehow, not on purpose, I let it happen. It hurts because I thought he'd liked me, loved me even. It hurts to find out he chose me not because I was special, but because I was the loneliest, smallest one.

Now I think I understand how Mom could leave Dad even though she still loves him. Love hurts. It's scary and it hurts in ways I'd never ever thought about.

Awhile back, I wrote a prayer asking God to send us back to Santa Rosa. I put it in Dee's God Box and waited. Well, I know now it's not going to happen. Either that means God said no or God just doesn't give a damn. Either way, part of me doesn't give a damn any more either. So I wrote this letter to Dad.

Dear Dad,

    I think Mom still loves you, even though she can't live with you anymore. Audrey's mad at you, but I think deep down she loves you too. I know deep down, I always will, even though you have done things that are very wrong. I'm not sure what all those things are, but Mom decided it was best for all of us to leave. Sometimes it is better to run away than stick around hoping that your dreams will come true. I found that out the hard way. Part of me blames you for that, but part of me knows I have to take responsibility for myself now that I am no longer a child.

> Your daughter forever
> Sam

Of course, I didn't send that letter either. I wrote it for myself and sometimes I like to read it. Even though it's not exactly true, it's not false either. Someday I hope to believe every word of it. If I can still love Dad after all the mean and bad things he has done, not blame him for the things I do, then maybe people will still love me after all the things I've done.

My counselor says I'm very wise for my age. But I don't always feel in my heart what I say with my mouth.

When I'm eighteen and on my own, I'll go back to Santa Rosa to see my father. When he opens the door, Willy and Nilly will be rubbing up against his legs. At first he probably won't recognize me, but I'll recognize him even though his hair will be gray and his face wrinkled because his grief and guilt will have prematurely aged him.

He'll say, *Leslie, is that you,* because by the time I'm eighteen, I'll look just like Mom did when she was that age.

"No, Dad," I'll say. "I'm your daughter, Samantha."

"Samantha? But you're so tall and grown-up."

Then I'll tell him I forgive him for ruining my life. Dad will start crying from happiness because he's been waiting all these years to hear those three little word: *I forgive you.* He'll thank me again and again for being so understanding and kind.

"It's all right, Dad." I'll say. "I just thought you should know." Then I'll kiss his cheek and get back in my . . . some kind of red convertible, and drive away to college, probably Stanford or at least Berkeley.

Part of me actually believes all this could happen. Part of me says, "Yeah, right."

* * *

Dee gave me one of her aloes. "It will grow and flower," she says. "Just like you." I know how special they are to her so I tried to act all thrilled and delighted, but to me it's just something that will probably end up dead since I'm not particularly gifted when it comes to plants. Still it's the thought that counts, and I'm sure Jesus would say, "Thank you very much. This plant is perfectly delightful." Even Jesus would lie, under the circumstances.

Though I thought it would die right away instead of turning our piece of dirt into an aloe paradise, I went ahead and planted it because it couldn't hurt. It's still out back all by its lonely little self. But Dee says, "Just trust the Lord to make it grow and mulitply." That's Dee. She's always saying stuff like that and I wonder why she thinks so. Didn't the Lord take Michael away from her? This is something I want to know.

It rained the other night. I went outside first thing in the morning to see if the aloe has grown and multiplied yet. So far not, but it's still alive and I guess that's a good sign.

* * *

Like I said, Chablee has changed a lot, so mostly I'm glad we're in the same class. That way, there's one person I can usually eat with at lunch, that is, if she's not eating with some of her other so-called friends. For awhile she was hanging around this one girl, Kirsten, who's like a total snot. I happen to know that the only reason Kirsten wanted to be her friend was because Chablee was going steady at the time with this eighth-grade guy named Jesse Contreras who's a total fox.

What happened was Chablee tried to fix Audrey up with his best friend, George Balderon. The plan was that the three of us,

Audrey, Chablee, and I would go to the mall this one Saturday and accidentally on purpose run into Jesse and George, and Jesse's little brother, Carlos, who was supposed to be my age. The plan was that I would hang out with him while the others went off to do whatever.

When I said I would do it, I thought Jesse's little brother would be a fox like Jesse. But as it turns out, Carlos just turned eleven and is only in the sixth grade, and when he looks up, which he does all the time because he's even shorter than me, I can see the boogers in his nose.

"Why don't you guys play some arcade games," Chablee says to us in this voice she saves for those special occasions when she's trying to get you do to something she knows you really don't want to do, like spend the afternoon with some little booger nose.

"No money," I say, figuring that would put an end to their plans. But then Jesse gives us each a five-dollar bill. Five dollars! Like it's nothing but a piece of paper. Now I know this is just to get rid of us, but I don't care so much anymore. Mom never allows us to play the arcade games, so this is like my only chance. But five dollars doesn't last very long if you're not particularly gifted at blasting drooling aliens. I run out of money long before Booger Nose who's surprisingly good at blasting drooling aliens. I watch him play for about eight hours, which is better than trying to talk to him. At least I don't have to look up his nose.

Eventually, Carlos runs out of money too. So then he pulls out a pack of cigarettes and asks me if I want a smoke. I figure why not, and reach out for one.

"Not here," he says, glancing quickly around. "We'll get kicked out."

"So where?" I say, and he tells me to follow him. We end up outside. All along the wall facing the parking lot are these humungous red oleander bushes, which seem to be the best thing to plant if you want to cover up something ugly. In Tucson, they're all over the place. We crawl behind one. It reminds me a little of the mock orange hedge I used to crawl behind when I was little. There's plenty of room back there and it's cool and shady. We can't see anybody and nobody can see us.

Carlos lights his cigarette, then lights mine. I watch to see how he's doing it. He blows the smoke out of his nose like he was practically born with a cigarette in his mouth. I try it, gag, try it again.

"Just breathe in a little," he suggests.

What's the big deal about smoking, anyway? I mean, why do people do it even though they know it gives you bad breath and cancer? I figure it must feel good, right? This time I don't choke, but my head begins spinning and so does my stomach. I crush out what's left of the cigarette in the dirt.

"It's okay," he says. "It takes practice. I didn't like it at first either."

"Then why did you keep on doing it?"

Carlos just shrugs and I figure that's as good an answer as any. How can anybody explain why they do stuff they know isn't good for them, doesn't even feel good, is what I'm thinking, when I feel his arm snake around my shoulder, like he thinks I won't notice. If it's his arm on me, or the smoking, I don't know, but I have to fight to keep from puking. When my head and my stomach stop swimming, I get this crazy idea from out of nowhere. I scrunch my shoulders and his arm falls away. "You want to play a game?"

"What kind of game?"

"It's called 'Touch me' but there are rules."

"So what are the rules?"

"You can touch me," I tell him. "But it has to be where I say. And when I say stop, you've got to stop."

"Touch you where?" he asks.

"Places—I don't know—the ones I tell you. But first you have to swear you'll follow the rules. You got to stop the exact minute I tell you to. Swear to God."

"I swear."

"Okay, you can touch me on the knee," I say, and feel his hand, which is warm and damp, cover my knee. "Stop!" I say, and he pulls his hand away.

"Now you can touch my back." He does until I tell him to stop. "Now you can touch my back under my shirt." His hand slides under my shirt. When I feel it inching around to my front, I say, "Stop." He obeys.

"Now you can touch me down there." I spread my knees.

He hesitates for a moment, then touches me between my legs with his finger.

"Stop," I say. He does and I unbutton my shorts. "Now you can touch me inside my underpants.

"His hand reaches down, his finger worming along my crack. I close my eyes and hold my breath. "Stop!" I say, clamping my knees shut.

When the breeze blows through the oleanders, the light flickers and it's like standing underwater. For a long time, neither of us says a word. Finally, he asks, "Do you want to touch me?"

"No," I say. "We're done."

"Can I kiss you, at least? I did like I promised."

"I said we're done." Then I face him square on, and for the first time look into his eyes, which are dark and shiny like little coffee spills. Nice eyes. I close my own eyes then, lean to whisper in his ear, "My Dad has two guns. He keeps them loaded at all times. If you tell anybody what we did, I'll get one of his guns and shoot you."

"You're crazy," he says, backing away. But I grab his wrist, not tight, and stare right into his face until I know he won't tell.

When we finally find the others, they're making out behind some potted plants beneath the escalators. I guess they think nobody can see them, but everybody who passes by takes a good long look, shakes their heads, or just plain laughs. Carlos is looking at me like maybe we should join them, but I'm like no way.

I clear my throat, the way they do in movies when somebody catches somebody else doing something totally stupid, like making-out like mad behind a potted palm. So then Jesse and George treat us all to Eggees, and Audrey, Chablee, and I go to out to catch our bus.

When we get home, Audrey asks me if I had fun. I tell her the arcade games were pretty cool.

"It was kind of gross the way you guys were making out where everybody could see you," I say.

"What?"

"Every person in the entire mall could see you guys slobbering all over each other."

"You are such a little liar," she says, her face getting red. "Besides, we weren't slobbering."

"You were tongue kissing."

"Shut up!" she says.

"You shut up," I yell, suddenly so furious that I want to pound her face in. "You leave me alone with some booger-nose sex maniac all afternoon so you can make out with stupid George, who's not even one bit cute, behind a potted plant and I'm supposed to shut up. I could have been raped for all you cared!" That got her attention.

"He didn't try anything, did he?"

"No. And it's a good thing too," I say. "I would have kicked him you know where."

"I'm sorry, Sammy. We shouldn't have left you alone."

"Sorry doesn't take away the hurt."

"Now you sound like Mom."

Well that just makes me madder. "I sound like Mom? You're the one who's just like Mom."

"I thought I was supposed to be just like Dad."

"You're just like both of them," I scream. "Only worse, because you don't give a damn about anybody but yourself."

"So what do you want me to do? Bend over and kiss your royal ass?"

"I just want you to take responsibility for what you did."

"Well, I said I'm sorry. Next time we go to the mall, you won't be invited. And when you're twenty years old, you'll still want to crawl in bed with me, but I won't let you. You big baby." she yells.

That's when I go for her throat. Since Audrey's nearly twice as big as me, in no time she's sitting on my chest, knees pinning my arms down, and I'm twisting underneath her, trying to butt her in the head or kick at anything I can reach with my legs, which is mostly thin air. But she just holds on tighter, riding up and down on top of me like some cowboy, her face red and sweaty.

"Don't call me a baby," I yell, spit flying. "I hate you. I hate you so much. You were supposed to watch out for me! None of this would have happened if you'd been watching out for me!" Audrey lets go of my wrists then, rolls off and into a ball, knees practically touching her chin. This turn of events is so sudden, so startling, I stop crying.

"I'm sorry," she whispers. "I'm sorry. How many times do I have to say it. Look, Sammy, what that pervert did to you out there in the shed was not my fault."

That's not true, I want to scream. I want to blame her. Blame Mom. Blame Dad. Blame Eddie. Blame anybody but the person I blame the most, and I'm crying again. Audrey puts her arms around me then, holds me tight, and I let myself cry against her.

"Sammy, please tell me it wasn't my fault," she says, and starts crying too.

And I should just tell her that, but my throat is too achy and tight, so I just wrap my arms around her and we hold on to each other. Hold on for dear life.

* * *

Things didn't work out for my sister and George Balderon because Audrey's about two feet taller and a year older than him. In addition, George kisses like a gorilla. At least that's what Audrey says, and she should know since she kisses herself in the mirror so much. Ha, ha, ha.

Anyway, I'm not sure what all happened, but the very next week, Chablee beat the you-know-what out of George Balderon because he said something nasty about Audrey; I don't know what. Then Jesse broke up with Chablee, so Kirsten dumped her too. Big surprise.

Since then, Chablee and Audrey have let me hang out more with them. Every day, I've been eating lunch with Chablee and her friends, since Audrey has second lunch and we have first. I've asked Chablee not to tell anybody that I'm no longer a celibate, and she promised.

"If anyone wants to mess with you, they'll have to go through me first," she says. And I know that's probably true, because look what she did to George Balderon. Part of me feels good about that, but part of me wishes people would stop treating me like a child, which I can never be again. All of me wishes we never came to Tucson in the first place despite the five advantages, but all of me, one hundred percent, knows that this is what happened, and that's that. So I ripped the Advantages and Disadvantages of Santa Rosa list out of my notebook. I can't go back there, at least not for a long time, so what's the point?

I took the list and my unsent letters out to the shed. It was the first time I'd been out there by myself since I lost my celibacy. One by one, I took a match to the list and the unsent letters to my dad and watched them go up in smoke. When they were burnt to a crisp, I mixed the ashes with the dirt and spread them around my aloe.

* * *

Life's not quite so boring in hell as it used to be. For one thing, the temperature has finally dropped down to 149 degrees in the shade. It's nearly Thanksgiving, so I'd say it's about time. We've started playing league soccer with the Pink Panthers. This was Chablee's idea. She did it last year and said it was cool, and so far so good. I didn't think I'd be able to do it at all, but I'm good at it, sort of. Chablee says that's because small girls are usually faster and can dribble better.

Mom can only go to the Saturday games because of work, but Dee and Eden come to every game. I thought it would be like so embarrassing to have them all out there, three women instead of one mom and one dad. But it's pretty cool, actually, like having your own personal cheerleading squad, all of them in their Pink Panther baseball caps.

And if I fall, Mom's right there. It's not like she can keep me from getting hurt, but it's nice to know she's out at the end of the field watching and cheering me on.

Lately she's been telling us the story of her life, how she met Dad and how things were when she was a little girl with grandma and Grandpa and lala lala lala. She's suddenly become this new mom who wants to tell us all this stuff. I guess that's good in a way, even though sometimes it gets pretty boring. My old mom wouldn't even try to communicate, not really, so I suppose I'll just have to deal with it, like Audrey says. There are worse things than being bored.

Mom's said she's sorry about a million times. It wasn't her fault in the first place. I know this and I've told her so, told Audrey too, but sometimes I still want to yell at somebody, blame somebody.

My counselor tells me to put blame where blame belongs. Says what Eddie did was not only wrong, it was a crime. She calls him a sexual predator, a child molester. Says he belongs behind bars. When somebody else says that, like my counselor or Dee, I can believe it, but when I say it, I'm not so sure. What I know in my head, I don't always feel deep down wherever it is that I keep my feelings.

* * *

Last week was my twelfth birthday. Mom gave me a surprise party at Randolph Park. It was kind of nice in a way. The park's right in the middle of town and it's got a zoo and picnic tables. The only people were Audrey, Chablee, Eden, Dee and Mom, which was okay, I guess. I had to pretend that I was like all surprised and delighted, but I got some pretty cool stuff. Mom made her so-called famous potato salad again, even though it wasn't Fourth of July. She also made my two most favorite cakes, chocolate pudding and lemon. Two cakes for just six people! After we ate, we dribbled the soccer ball around, Audrey, Chablee, and me. Randolph Park has lots of grass. It's not as green as in Santa Rosa, but it's humongous so there's room to practice our moves.

Chablee gave me a diary for my birthday. It's got a lock and key and a special pocket to keep a pen. Anne Frank named her diary Kitty, but I'm just going to write to myself, since I'm the only one who's ever going to read it, unless someday somebody finds it and wants to make a movie. I've already written pages and pages. This is my latest entry:

Dear Sam,

My chest is sore. You know what that means. It means my breasts are getting ready to start growing. It's only a matter of time. Already I have hair under my arms. It's funny, like one day I looked at my armpits and it wasn't there; the next day it was.

Mom bought me a razor so I could shave. She also gave me a flowered plastic make-up bag filled with all my supplies for when I start my period. I guess I should be all thrilled and delighted about these developments. Part of me is, but the other part thinks NO BIG DEAL. After all, it's not like I'm just some kid anymore who gets all excited over every little thing. I mean, it will be nice to have breasts and all, but I'm not sure I ever want to start my period, because that means technically, I can start having sex. Well, technically, I already did and it wasn't at all what I thought it would be like. The word gruesome, disgusting and painful describes what I think about sex. Even though it's only supposed to hurt the first time, that still leaves gruesome and disgusting.

That's all the news for now. Remember, just put one foot in front of the other and hold your nose, because sometimes you step in a pile of dog doo. Ha, ha, ha. That's supposed to be funny.

Love ya,
The Voice of Wisdom

* * *

This one afternoon, I'm just rummaging through Dee's God Box while she's making me a peanut butter and mayo sandwich. "How was school?" she yells from the kitchen, though the kitchen is so close I could be in it in two steps.

I pick up the bottle with the sliver of the true cross in it, give it a little shake. "Sucks," I say. I know I shouldn't say *sucks* while

I'm holding something sacred, but it's also a sin to lie. The truth is school sucks.

Then she asks did I make any new friends. No is the answer and Dee hands me the sandwich. "Don't want any either," I add, tossing the bottle back into the God Box. Then just to change the subject, I ask her a question. "Do you think God's a man or a woman?"

"Well there is certainly a lot of talk about that," Dee says. "To my way of thinking, God is not one or the other."

"That makes God an it," I say, holding a bit of my sandwich under the table where LeRoy is waiting.

"Seems to me, you call animals it."

"Humans are animals," I say.

"Sure," she says. "But God's not human. God is something else. You can call God *She,* I guess, but that wouldn't be any righter that *He.* Lots of people call God different names, but if you got God in you heart *He* or *She* or *It* will answer when you do. Every day I call on God to relieve the pain in my heart."

"You mean the Michael pain?"

"Among others," she says."

"So why do you think *It* does what *it* does?" There is an ugly tone creeping into my voice, but I don't care. I want answers here and Dee's the only one I know to ask.

She pretends not to notice my tone. "You mean God?"

"Yes. Like why did *It* let them take Michael away from you?"

"Because I was only sixteen when he was born."

"But lots of girls younger than that get to keep their babies."

"True, Samantha," she says. Dee looks up at the ceiling for a long time and I think maybe she's praying. Finally, she says, her voice tired and flat, "Samantha, Michael was my uncle's baby."

That shuts me up for a minute. I always knew Dee had some deep dark secret, but now that I know what it is, nothing changes. She's still my friend, and in a way I love her, not just like a friend and not like a mother or a sister either. Dee's in her own special category of love.

"So why do you think God makes people suffer?" I ask, softer to show that I'm sorry, and because I need to know now more than ever.

She strokes my hair with her big, gentle hand. "There's lots of people smarter than me who've tried to answer that question. It's like asking what's the meaning of life?"

"What is the meaning of life?" I ask, because I guess that's what I've been trying to find out for a long time.

Dee sighs, adjusts her copper bracelets. "Where to begin," she says, lowering herself into a chair. "Sometimes when things are bad in my life, I think this is not my real life. My best, real life hasn't started yet. But that's not true. We're living our real lives, right now, Samantha, every day." She reaches out for my hand, and adds. "I think . . . life's made up of bests and worsts. All we can do is put one foot in front of the other."

"And sometimes we step in a big pile of dog poop."

She laughs. "Bless your heart, Samantha. It's true. And when that happens all we can do is keep walking until the stink wears off. That's what God intends us to do. Keep walking from beginning to end, enjoy what you can along the way, learn from it, and leave the really worst things behind you like a bad stink."

* * *

Dee always says you got to look for the bright side. And I try to, but if you think about it too much, what does that mean? Not a whole lot. I don't say that to Dee, of course. It would only hurt her feelings. Besides, it seems like looking for the bright side is sort of like backwards alphabets, glow-in-the-dark crosses, unsent letters, or even planting an aloe. Who knows? These things might help. At least they don't hurt. Right now, it's important to look for the things that don't hurt, because no matter how sorry you are afterwards, sorry doesn't help. What does help is knowing that things change and sometimes for the good. Look at Mom. She's changing, and though sometimes it's hard to tell, I'd say the changes are for the better. Audrey's changed. She's a lot nicer to me, and we're getting along better. And I've changed. Mostly, I'm all grown-up now.